ABANDONED

AN ANNE WILSON THRILLER
BOOK 2

BY

MHR GEER

ISBN: 979-8-9871159-4-7

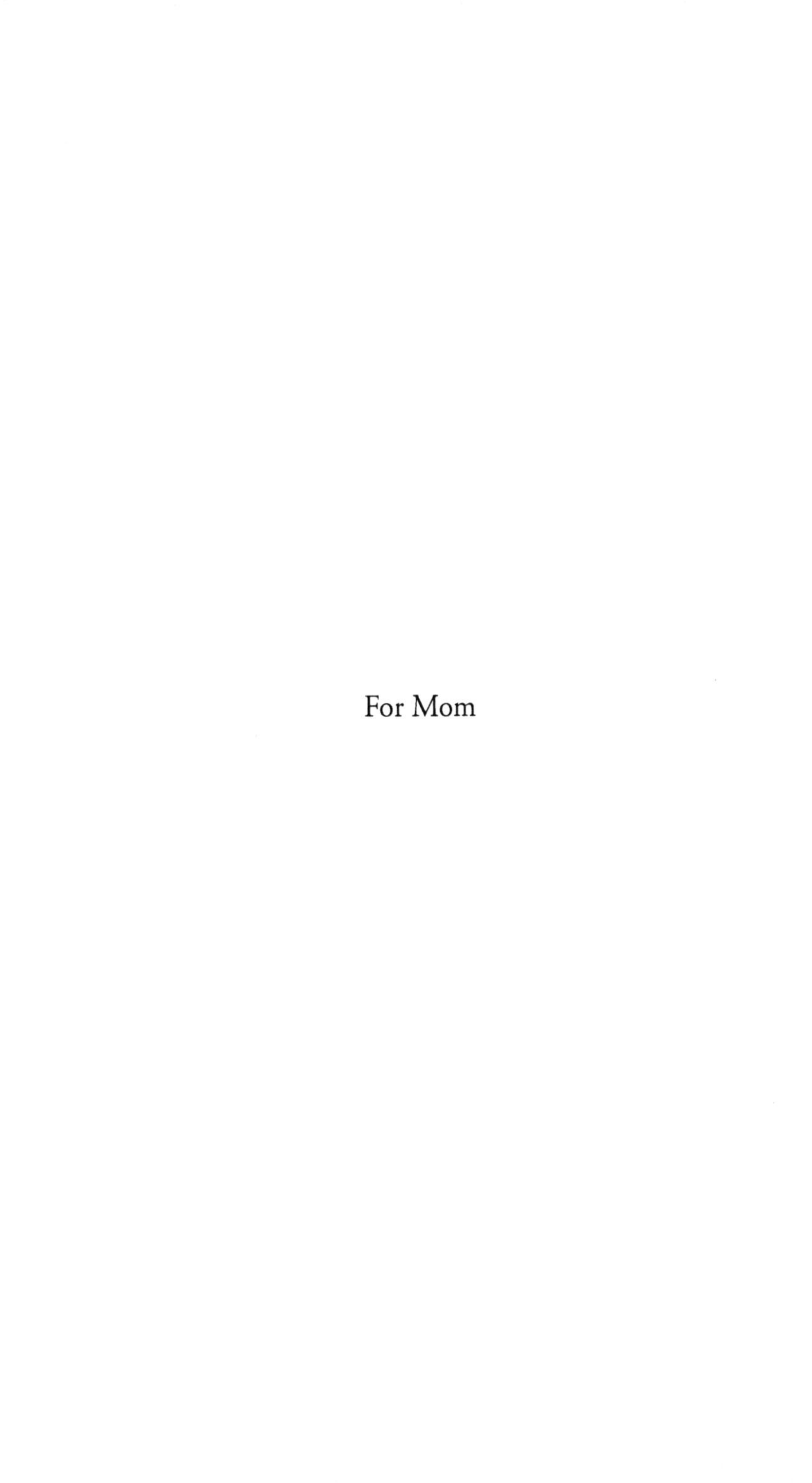

For Mom

CHAPTER 1

I read Sandy's text with a mixture of relief and dread. *Trouble. Can you come?* For seven months, I'd put my life on hold, waiting for her inevitable bad news. I was ready for a challenge—a chance to *do* something, but my stomach tightened as I texted her back.

Where are you?

Guadeloupe. Find Goti. Bring your keys. She's in 316, she answered.

The last time I'd heard from her, she'd been much farther south on Bequia—a tiny island I'd never heard of. Guadeloupe was larger and closer; I could catch a direct flight. The number 316 referred to the slip number for her boat: *The Second Chance.* I had no idea who or what Goti was.

I opened my laptop and searched for a flight, but my finger hovered over the purchase button. Trouble meant something serious. I'd almost died the last time she'd asked for help. I shouldn't have even stayed friends with her after what she'd done. But part of me missed the adrenaline and excitement of Sandy's adventures. Part of me even missed Sandy. I wanted to go—not for her. I wanted to run away.

I booked the last flight of the day and went to find Luke. He was in the kitchen, chopping onions.

I kept my voice casual. "Sandy needs me. I have to fly to Guadeloupe today."

He paused mid-slice and looked up. The kitchen shutters were closed against the late afternoon sun except the one behind him—left open for the breeze. His messy curls cast a shadow across his face. His eyes glistened—moist from the onion, but his expression was too dark to read.

"What is it? What's happened?" he asked. He set down the knife and wiped his hands on a dishtowel. "Do you want me to come?" It was barely a question.

"No," I answered too quickly. "I'll go. I'll figure out what her problem is."

"Is that a good idea?"

I walked into the bedroom, dragged my suitcase from the closet, and tossed it on the bed. He kept talking, but his words were lost in the wall between us. I pulled T-shirts and tank tops from hangers and tossed them into the open bag without folding anything. Seven shirts, seven pairs of shorts. One dress.

When he appeared in the bedroom doorway, I avoided his glare and moved to the bathroom.

"What's so urgent?" he asked.

The woman in the mirror frowned. Her dull, blue eyes were edged with dark circles. I ran a brush through shoulder-length hair and packed toiletries into a travel kit: sunscreen, mascara I rarely wore, and a new jar of moisturizer I'd bought a few days after my thirty-third birthday when tiny lines appeared at the corners of both eyes.

As I reached for my deodorant, I bumped the plain white mug on the counter, and my toothbrush tumbled into the sink. Finding a cup that matched the slate tile of the backsplash had been on my to-do list, but the only time I remembered the errand was when the toothbrushes spilled out of the too-small mug.

"You want to go," Luke said.

I sighed and walked back into the bedroom. This had become our argument. He'd tell me what I wanted. I'd tell him he was wrong without being able to explain why.

"There were things I never told you about Sandy. About the money," I began.

"I know—"

I cut him off. "But you don't know. I promised Sandy I wouldn't tell you." I raised my hands as he approached. I needed distance. If he touched me, I'd hesitate. I'd stay.

"Anne," he said softly.

"No! Don't do that. Don't use that voice. I know it's a bad idea. And I know you don't want me to go, but I was *always* going to leave when she called, and you knew that. I don't have time for this right now. I have a flight to catch. Can we skip past this—"

I stared at the gray, faux-woodgrain floor tile I'd selected when he'd asked me to choose a pattern—his transparent attempt to make the house *ours* instead of his. I'd tried, but my additions were out of place in the oversized, modern house. I nudged a tuft of orange in the rug at the foot of the bed. The bright colors had complemented the breakfast nook in my Homestead house, but they were garish in Luke's house. The rug didn't fit.

Neither did I. Luke designed and built the house. Nothing I did would make it anything other than his.

He was quiet, watching me stare at the floor. The tension grew until I looked up at him. He raised his head in a quick nod and walked out of the room. I called a taxi.

#

On the plane, the tension in my shoulders eased. I regretted my hasty exit, but one more night wouldn't have changed anything. It wasn't Luke's fault. He'd tried to help me adjust to life in Saint Martin. My unhappiness was unreasonable. How could anyone be depressed in a custom-built villa on a Caribbean Island? At first, the white sand beaches and the warm, aquamarine water had been enough for me, but it was an *island*, and in the last six months, it shrunk until it became my prison.

I'd applied for several jobs, but there weren't any openings for a mid-level corporate accountant. Luke offered to help me find a job, but I declined all his suggestions. I lived in Luke's house. I ate Luke's food. I needed to find my own job.

For the first month, I stayed busy. Luke involved me with every decision in the final stages of the construction of the house. Paint chips. Plumbing fixtures. Pillows. And then we moved in. We spent two weeks arranging and rearranging the furniture. I returned to Florida when my house closed escrow and packed my life into a shipping container.

Luke returned to work. He started a remodel on the north end of the island, and the silence in the house became unbearable. I tried shopping, but the options were limited; we already had too many throw pillows. I drove my new, sporty white Mazda CX, but on an island only twelve miles long in any direction, I went in circles. And I always ended up at the police station.

Inspector Moreau was kind during my first three unscheduled visits. We drank coffee in brand-new chairs in his expansive office—he'd secured a promotion for the arrest of Dominik Cerna. Cerna was already serving a three-year sentence for money laundering. Few people knew the true reason for the promotion: Moreau was selected to form a task force to review the data I'd delivered on a USB drive. In addition to the evidence of Cerna's money laundering network, the drive contained details about the activities of several criminal organizations.

Each time I visited, Moreau introduced me to new team members and told them I'd taken down the entire network of money launderers. The story was exaggerated—I'd done little more than stumble onto the information, but I enjoyed the confidence boost.

The police station buzzed with energy. Moreau's team was a collaboration of government agencies from various countries—a grab-bag of acronyms. Moreau told me it would take them years to follow up on all the leads.

On my fourth visit, Moreau introduced the latest member to join the team: Special Agent Otis Fox—on loan from the Financial Crimes division of the Secret Service. Fox was tasked with the investigation of the wires originating from the US.

"You're a bit of a legend here," Fox said as he shook my hand. "I could use your expertise."

My eyes widened. "With what?"

"Moreau has built a good team, but we're missing a forensic accountant." He leaned closer and spoke in a low, conspiratorial tone. "A lot of these guys are field agents. They forget the importance of the numbers-guys. You know the saying, 'Follow the money?' We won't have a money trail to follow without an accountant."

"I'm not an accountant," I said.

He smiled. "Moreau said you worked in a corporate accounting office. You have specialized knowledge." He gave Moreau a questioning look. "She obviously has the skill set and understands what we're doing here." Moreau frowned, but Fox continued, "She'll stay in the office— no field work." Fox turned to me. "What do you say?"

"I'd love to help," I said in a forced-casual voice. I stared at Moreau and held my breath.

He sighed. "You keep showing up here. We might as well put you to work."

I beamed.

The following morning, I filled out paperwork and tried not to fidget while waiting for the background check results. In two days, I was approved for a work permit, and then I was parked at a small desk in a windowless corner with a towering stack of bank ledgers.

For a few weeks, I enjoyed the tedious work. I had a reason to leave the house. But the stack of bank ledgers thinned, and they weren't replaced. Agent Fox told me he'd call when he had another project. Alone in Luke's house, the days seemed longer and impossible to fill. After a few weeks, I stopped checking my phone and eventually stopped driving past the station. I settled into a mundane routine.

Many days, I did nothing but sit at the edge of the patio, legs dangled above the sandstone rocks that descended to the narrow beach. I stared at the horizon. The reflected sunlight that danced just above the waves was mesmerizing. My eyes blurred, and dazzling, gold water sprites flitted in the frothy space between water and air. On cloudy days, the sprites were absent, and the horizon was lost in an infinite grayness. And on the days when the sea became angry and the air got heavy, I watched dark clouds cross the sky and break open with torrential rain. On those days, my head hurt with the strain of peering through sheets of water, trying to see through the storm.

Months ago, Luke caught me in a good mood and asked, "What do you think about all day?"

"I don't think," I lied. "That's the point."

He'd wrapped his arms around me and kissed me—the way he used to kiss me as if he could take away the pain and replace it with something better. But that wasn't how grief worked. His love couldn't supplant the pain of losing my family. The two things— his love and my pain fought to coexist.

The plane banked, and Guadeloupe appeared below—verdant mountains rising like a mirage from the endless sea. I pressed my forehead against the window. Waves approached the island as harmless cobalt ribbons and disappeared into frothy, aquamarine shallows, but miles offshore, deep, ink-black waters spawned storms capable of swallowing the insignificant landforms.

My stomach tightened again as the plane continued a steady descent. Sandy's one word: *Trouble* was foreboding. Someone knew something—not the police. If the police knew, I would have been hauled into the station for questioning. *Trouble* meant something worse.

Sandy and I hadn't discussed scenarios—as if we could prevent anything bad from happening by never speaking about it. But I'd imagined things.

I gripped the armrests as the plane landed and shuddered to a stop. I checked my phone. No new texts. No calls. There was no point in calling or texting Sandy for details. Her paranoia—caution, she called it, prevented her from using the phone. I had to find her.

#

At the taxi stand, a stout, black woman shouted at each group, "Where ya headin'?" The two sides of her orange safety vest were tucked beneath her arms. She grinned at me and repeated her question.

"The marina," I answered.

"Ya jus' got on the ground, and yer aching to get back off and onto the sea?" Her sing-song accent was more Jamaican than French. She bustled me into a taxi and shouted my destination through the window. The driver nodded, and we sped away.

I texted Sandy, *Just arrived. On my way to the marina.*

The taxi dropped me at a complex web of boat slips that stretched out of sight, and I headed toward a building marked *Office.* The door closed behind me, muffling the sounds of the harbor.

"*Bonjour,*" a woman called out. She looked younger than me—late twenties at most. Her dark eyebrows didn't match the blonde hair that swung from a perky ponytail.

"Bonjour," I mumbled. My French had improved since moving to Saint Martin, but I was still self-conscious about my accent. "I'm here to visit a friend in slip three-one-six. Can you tell me how to find that?"

"Of course," she answered, setting a paper map on the counter between us. With a red marker, she drew arrows along the map. "There's another parking lot closer to that area. Do you have a car?" I shook my head. "If you want to rent one, you can take a taxi to this area." She flipped the paper over and revealed a second map of the surrounding town. She studied the image for a moment, tilting her head until she found what she was looking for. "You can rent a scooter here." She drew a circle on the map with her red marker and flashed a bright smile. "Can I help with anything else?"

"No. Thank you."

"Well, don't hesitate to ask."

I left the office and followed her directions—back the way I'd come along the wide sidewalk, a right turn onto a dock, and a left to find Sandy's slip. I flinched as a gull screeched overhead. I didn't share Sandy's fondness for the noisy chaos of harbors. A passing dinghy created a wake that squeezed rubber bumpers between docks and fiberglass hulls. The squeaking clashed with the metallic clang of halyards swinging high above, jarring my nerves. I quickened my step.

Sandy's boat, *The Second Chance,* was a fifty-foot power boat moored between two similarly sized sailboats. I slowed as I approached, peering inside. The door was open. I shaded my eyes from the glare of the setting sun, but I could only make out dark shapes within. I almost called out, but the greeting caught in my throat as a man in a suit emerged. He was followed by a second man—neither of them familiar. Sandy didn't appear behind them.

I turned to leave, but my suitcase wheel caught on a cleat.

"*Aidez-vous?*" the first man asked. I panicked and yanked the bag too hard. It slipped from my hand and fell onto the dock. "Hello? Can I help you?" he repeated.

"I'm looking for Sandy," I said as I reached down for the suitcase handle.

"Who are you?"

"A friend. Who are you?" I demanded.

He reached into his pocket, pulled out a leather case, and flipped it open to reveal identification. A cop.

"I am Detective Ari Fournier. Who are you?" He was less polite this time.

"Anne Wilson. I'm a friend of Sandy's."

"And you're here because…" His words trailed off. He expected me to fill in the blanks, but I had no answers.

"She asked me to come. Is she here?"

"Miss Brown was arrested this morning. She is being detained at the Guadeloupe Police Station. I am executing a search of her boat."

Arrested. I let out a long breath—one I'd held for seven months. She'd finally gotten caught. But if they knew, why wasn't I arrested, too? Is that why the cops were on Sandy's boat? Waiting for me? I glanced behind me, but I couldn't run.

"Arrested for what?" I asked.

"She is being charged with murder."

I gasped and covered my mouth with my hand. I'd expected to hear extortion or blackmail. Not murder.

"Murder?" I echoed. "Who?"

"I would like to ask you some questions. Do you mind stepping aboard for a moment?"

I ignored his offered hand and stepped onto the deck.

CHAPTER 2

Inside the cabin, the breeze through the open windows made the heat barely tolerable. The other man stepped off the boat. He stood beside my discarded suitcase and turned his back to us, swiveling left and right—guarding us? Or discouraging me from leaving?

I sat and wiped the sweat from my face. The detective took his time settling into the leather seat across from me. He seemed young to be a detective—in his thirties. He leaned back and crossed his legs, removing a notepad and a pen from his jacket pocket and smoothing his dark slacks. His olive-brown skin wasn't even damp.

"Where do you live?" he asked. His English had only a slight accent—like he'd spent time in the States.

"Saint Martin," I answered. He scowled at my American pronunciation.

"When did you arrive here?"

"About an hour ago. I came directly from the airport."

"You said your friend asked you to visit. Do you know why?" I shook my head. "Does Miss Brown visit Guadeloupe often?"

I hesitated. Sandy wandered from island to island. When she got bored, she moved on. I'd visited her three months ago when she landed in St. Bart's—it was only a ferry ride from Saint Martin, but I had no idea how often she'd visited each island.

"I'm not sure," I answered.

"What do you do for a living?"

"Nothing at the moment." One of his eyebrows rose, and I quickly continued, "I only moved to Saint Martin a few months ago."

He nodded slowly. "And before?"

"I worked for a company in Miami. In accounting."

"And that's what you will do in Saint Martin?"

I shrugged. Was this a job interview? Why did he care? "Can I stay here? On Sandy's boat?"

"No," he answered.

"Is this where the…you know…happened?"

"Did Miss Brown own any property in the Caribbean?"

I shook my head. "This boat was her home."

"Did she have any family here? Any close friends other than you?"

"She's from Florida but doesn't speak to her family. I don't know her other friends."

"When was the last time you spoke to her?"

"A week ago, maybe. I can check. She wasn't here yet. She was in Bequia." I remembered because I had to look at the map. "She told me she was headed north to visit me."

"If you were expecting her back in Saint Martin, were you surprised when she asked you to come here?"

Nothing about Sandy surprised me, but I didn't tell him that. "She didn't put a timeline on it."

"So, coming here wasn't planned."

"For me or her? I certainly didn't plan this trip. She texted me a few hours ago. I barely caught the last flight out. Speaking of which, I need to find a hotel if I can't stay here. Can I go?"

He ignored my question. "Did she mention that she was coming to Guadeloupe?"

"No. But it's on the way. She never traveled very far in a day. Sometimes, she stayed on one side of an island and then moored for a night on the other side before heading into open water. She was cautious about that because she was usually alone on the boat."

"Was she always alone?" he asked.

"I don't know. Probably."

"Does she have a boyfriend? Or a girlfriend?"

I shook my head. "Not that I know of, but she's outgoing. She probably knew half the people here at the dock after only a day. She likes people. It was why she enjoyed traveling so much. She likes new things."

"And you don't?" My eyebrows shot up, and the detective uncrossed his legs and recrossed them the other way as if the question also surprised him. "I will need your contact details, and I would appreciate knowing where you're staying."

"I would also appreciate knowing," I muttered.

I gave him my cell phone number. He studied me while I tried not to fan myself with my hand. After a long moment, his face softened.

"I can recommend the hotel here in the marina. It's not fancy, but it's affordable. Unless you prefer something else. A resort, perhaps?"

"Affordable sounds great," I said.

He stood and said, "I'll show you the way."

I stepped outside into the hot wind. The man on the dock grinned and reached for my elbow as I stepped onto the dock. He wore a white polo shirt with an official logo and khaki shorts—more appropriate attire than the detective's dark suit.

The detective joined us on the dock. Without asking, he grabbed the handle of my suitcase and began walking away. I hurried after him.

"Do you see that line of trees?" He pointed to a line of towering palms.

"Yes," I answered.

"There's an alley that leads from the marina to the hotel entrance. Do you have a car?"

"No, I took a taxi," I answered. We walked a few yards, and I asked, "When was Sandy arrested?"

"A few hours ago."

How had she texted me in time? Had she known something was about to happen?

"Can I see her?"

He nodded. "Tomorrow. Please come to the station in the morning."

"I'll be there first thing."

#

The hotel was a group of pinkish-gray, two-story buildings with gray metal roofs. The alley was crumbling concrete along the backside of a long stretch of rooms, bordered on the other side by a chain-link fence. Satellite dishes and air conditioning units jutted from the gray stucco walls. The grayness was broken only by bright green sago palms on either side of the path and beach towels fluttering from second-floor railings.

The alley narrowed. I craned my neck, but the building continued out of sight. I glanced over my shoulder. The marina had disappeared. I sped up and rounded the corner. The fence ended at a parking lot, and I spotted an A-frame roof above a steep staircase. I hauled my bag up one step at a time.

At the top, I found a reception office with rattan furniture. A mural of palm fronds and fern leaves spanned two walls—stenciled in a confusing alternating pattern of palm-fern-palm. The once-green paint was grayed as if the leaves were slowly wilting in the heat.

"Hi. Do you have any rooms available?"

"*Oui.* Ari already called." She smiled at my confused look. "I'm Apolline Fournier. Ari is my nephew," she said. "I have only one room. A single. How long will you be staying?"

"I have no idea."

"The room is small, and there's no TV. I can offer you a special rate for three hundred and fifty euros."

"A night?" I asked.

She laughed. "*Non. Ma petit!* You haven't seen the room yet. That's the weekly rate." She typed on an unseen keyboard before she continued, "We have breakfast on the patio each morning." She smiled at me like I'd seen so many French-Caribbean mothers smile at my thin frame. "*Gratis.* Lots of fruit and pastries. Are you here alone?"

That was always the next question. They wanted to fatten me up and marry me off to a son. Or a nephew.

"Yes. I'm alone," I said.

"*Et voila.* Here is the key. Ari should have accompanied you. He could have carried your bag."

I wanted to argue that I didn't need someone to carry my bag, but I simply nodded and left through the side door. I passed a swimming pool and walked along the front side of the same long building. This side had larger balconies with gray plastic furniture, metal railings, and peeling turquoise paint.

My room was a single story that stuck out from the building like a thumb. I used my key and pulled the door open. With a quick glance, I could see everything in the room: a double bed, a small desk, and a worn armchair in the corner. No TV, as advertised. I dragged my bag inside, and the door closed behind me with a soft click.

#

Everything sagged: the armchair and the curtains. Even the wooden desk had a slight bow. The bed was covered with a thin, tropical-themed comforter—the kind that provides no warmth and repels water. It looked as if someone had flattened a parrot and stretched it across the bed. But the bath tile was bleached white, and the towels were soft.

In an alcove across from the bathroom was a tiny kitchenette with a cooktop, a small sink, and a microwave. I opened the single cabinet and found two plates, two bowls, three mismatched pots, and a single skillet—worn but clean.

My phone buzzed with a text from Luke: *Good flight?*

I collapsed into the armchair and sighed. Luke had a habit of sending two-word texts to check up on me. He'd ask, *Good breakfast?* when he'd left an omelet on the counter before he left for work or, *Good hike?* if I'd mentioned taking one. He didn't care if anything was good. He wanted to make sure I'd gotten out of bed, that I'd eaten something, or that I'd left the house.

Good flight? was his way of asking what was wrong with Sandy and how long I'd be gone. But if I told him she'd been arrested for murder, he'd ask follow-up questions, and I didn't know how to answer.

I stared at the phone, considering my response. I typed, *Looking for Sandy,* but then I erased it one letter at a time. That was a lie. I knew where she was.

I'd met Luke the day I'd arrived in Saint Martin. That trip had also been a last-minute decision to help Sandy. When she hadn't met me at the airport, I'd unwisely biked to the market on a mountain road, crashed, and injured my shoulder. Luke had almost run over me in his truck. He'd scooped me up and taken care of me. And he hadn't stopped caring for me.

After thirteen years of self-reliance, living with someone was a difficult transition. It wasn't his fault. Luke was the model roommate. He cooked. He cleaned. He let me operate the remote. I'd enjoyed it at first. It was like being on a luxurious vacation with housekeeping and room service. But I missed doing things for myself. I'd been swallowed up in a blanket of care.

One afternoon, the rain halted work at his job site, and he came home early to find me outside.

"Can't you watch from inside?" he'd asked. "You're going to end up sick."

"I like being outside," I'd answered.

Back then, he still had hope. He hadn't argued. That same day, he'd stepped out into the storm and trekked into the trees on the north side of the house. I watched him pace back and forth. The next day, workmen felled five trees and installed a wooden deck. Three days later, they erected a gazebo with posts on three sides to leave my view unobstructed. Canvas walls were installed—stiff fabric that could be rolled down and tied to the posts.

During the next storm, as lightning tore across the sky and the wind howled through the gaps in the canvas, Luke joined me outside. The storm gripped the fabric, attempting to wrench it from the wooden posts, but the walls held, and we remained dry. He watched me carefully; I knew he was trying to understand. But when he saw the storm reflected in my eyes, he retreated into the house without saying anything.

The cramped hotel room should have been claustrophobic, but it was the opposite. I took a long, deep breath and stretched my arms as far as the wall allowed, dropping my phone onto the bed. I slumped against the sagging chair and tried to ignore my guilt—for not answering his text, leaving abruptly, and being a terrible girlfriend.

My stomach growled. I unzipped my backpack, withdrew my laptop, logged onto the hotel's Wi-Fi, and searched nearby restaurants. Outside, the sky was pink and darkening. Across the street from the motel, I ordered spring rolls and stir-fry noodles from a Vietnamese restaurant and hurried back.

I ate in the armchair, smiling at the green walls as the hot, salty noodles kept slipping off the fork and onto my lap. At home with Luke, I would have struggled to make conversation over dinner. I'd run out of ways to describe the ocean and had nothing else to offer. He was careful not to talk about work, so I didn't feel left out. Dinners had become mostly awkward silence.

My phone buzzed with another text: *Good day?*

I smiled. This two-word question was another routine we'd settled into. I never lied. My answer was the same word every day—on bad days and not-so-bad days.

I texted, *Almost.*

The Caribbean paradise with Luke was supposed to be my happily-ever-after. But my past was a dark cloud that blocked the sunshine. I wasn't capable of good days.

CHAPTER 3

Sunlight leaking through the bottom of the curtain woke me. I stretched my arms and legs to fill the sheets and enjoyed the luxury of having a bed to myself. Then I took a quick shower and dressed.

I opened the fridge, but the smell of rancid peanut oil filled the room, and I slammed the door shut. I walked to the hotel office and found Apolline at the front desk again.

"The room is comfortable?" she asked.

"Yes, thanks. I need to get a few things. Is there a market nearby?"

"*Oui*," she said. "A kilometer or two. Not far. Turn left and follow the road."

"Thanks," I answered.

"Would you like a coffee? You can take it with you."

I nodded.

"*Une minute*," she said and disappeared into an alcove.

Scattered across the counter, pamphlets advertised outings for tourists: windsurfing lessons and fishing charters. I picked up a trifold brochure for a hiking club that met once per month on Sundays. Apolline returned with a cup, and I folded the paper and put it in my pocket.

"Thanks," I said.

Almost an hour later, I dropped my shopping bags inside my room and kicked the door shut. According to my watch, the walk had been just over three miles. Sweat ran down my back, and I stood by the small air conditioning unit in the window and panted.

I fried two eggs and ate them with dry toast because I'd forgotten butter and jam. After the groceries were stowed and my dishes were cleaned and returned to the cupboard, I pulled the hiking brochure out of my pocket and dropped it on the desk. I wasn't a tourist. I needed to visit Sandy. I needed answers.

I returned to the motel office.

"Can you call a taxi for me?" I asked Apolline.

"*Oui.*" She picked up her phone and touched the screen with her index finger. She frowned and then punched the screen more forcefully. "Ten minutes. Turn right at the bottom of the stairs. There's a bench where you can wait."

"Thanks," I said.

#

The police station was a four-story building with a crowded and noisy reception area. I waited in a queue and told the man at the front desk I wanted to visit Sandy Brown. He pointed to a row of blue plastic chairs and told me to wait.

A couple sat to my right, a woman and a man, arguing in French. I caught snippets—mostly from the woman, who didn't bother to whisper. Her car had been stolen, and the man tried to console her, but the gentler he spoke, the angrier she became. To my left was a woman with three kids. The smallest looked about a year old and sat on her lap, and the other two, possibly four and five, huddled on either side of her. They were quiet, and one of the children, a boy, flinched each time the loud woman shouted. I caught his eye and smiled, but he burrowed farther into his mother's hip.

While we waited, a steady stream of people arrived. The man at the desk directed them through a passageway in the center of the wall next to him or a doorway on the far-right side of the reception area that led to a sunny staircase. Nobody was sent in the other direction—down a dim hallway that sloped out of sight. A uniformed officer approached the angry woman and gestured for her to follow him through the far door on the right. I smiled at the little boy, and his shoulders relaxed.

"Anne Wilson?" the man at the front desk bellowed.

"Yes," I answered as I hurried over.

"Follow the corridor." He pointed to the dim hallway. "Someone will meet you."

I could feel the children's wary eyes on my back as I descended into a narrow and windowless hallway lined with dingy photographs of uniformed policemen. After about fifty yards, the hallway ended in a secure gate. I slowed as I reached the bars, but nobody appeared. I didn't notice the doorway to my right until I heard my name.

"Miss Wilson?"

I entered a small room with cheery yellow walls. Behind a single desk sat a young woman in uniform. She had short, curly hair that shone with hair oil meant to prevent frizziness. It wasn't working, but the rounded hairstyle suited her wide-set eyes.

"Please empty your pockets." She pointed to a line of lockers along one wall. I placed my wallet and phone into a locker and set a four-digit code. The little door closed with a snap. "Please sign here," she pointed to a clipboard on her desk. I signed my name, and in the box labeled inmate in French and English, I wrote, *Sandy Brown.*

"Follow me," she said.

We returned to the dim hallway. She unlocked the gate, and I followed her to the other side, glancing behind me as the bars clanged shut. Around a corner, she unlocked a second gate and ushered me through an x-ray machine. At the end of the hallway, she directed me into another artificially sunny room. Inside, on a blue plastic chair, sat Sandy.

Her hair was blonde again and pulled into a tight ponytail at the nape of her neck. Even without makeup, she looked radiant. She wore her own clothes: cutoff jeans and a T-shirt that used to read Led Zeppelin, but the letters had faded to look like broken fence posts.

"Anne!" she called out. "Thanks for coming. C'mon sit. Tell me what you've been up to. How's Luke?"

"Jesus, Sandy," I answered. "We're not at a garden party. They think you killed someone?"

"You're so serious, Anne. Lighten up."

"Lighten up? I just went through two locked doors and an X-ray machine to see you. Tell me what's going on."

She pointed to the only other chair in the room, and I sat. The officer stayed in the doorway, arms crossed, her back to the small room. There were no other doors and no windows.

"I just wanted to have a normal conversation. It's really boring in here," she whined. "Time moves slowly when you have nothing to do. That was the worst thing about prison." She grinned.

"What's funny about any of this?" I asked, glaring at her until her shoulders slumped.

"Okay," she said, dropping her face into her hands and speaking through her fingers. "You're right. I'm in big trouble. It's just—I wasn't sure you'd come. You probably think I belong in here."

"I don't think you belong in here," I said.

"I didn't do this. I didn't have any reason to kill him."

"Start from the beginning. Who was killed?"

"His name was Johan Engel. He was—not a good person. I doubt anyone is upset he's dead." She stood and paced. "A detective interviewed me twice, and both times I learned more than he did." Her voice quieted to whisper. "He was strangled. With one of the dock lines from my boat."

"How do they know it's one of yours?"

She shrugged. "Because they matched? I'm not sure, but they showed me pictures of two dock lines, and they looked just like mine. But that doesn't matter. Who cares where the rope came from? I didn't kill him. I'm not capable of killing any—" She bit her lip and reached for my arm, but I leaned away. She collapsed back into her chair. "I'm sorry," she whispered.

"Stop apologizing," I said, but my voice had gone as cold as the concrete wall behind her. I looked away and swallowed several times until the lump in my throat withered. I heard her sniff, and when I turned back, she was wiping her eyes. "It's not the same thing. That was an accident." I bent forward and held out my hand. She took it and managed a small smile. "We put that behind us."

I wanted to believe my own words—that I'd forgiven her, that we could return to what we were before I found out that she'd been driving the other car the night my family died. But my voice betrayed me, and a chill ran down my spine.

"You shouldn't have to be the one helping me," she said. "I just…didn't know who else to call. I didn't do this, Anne. Someone's setting me up."

"But why?" I asked.

"I don't know."

I glanced over my shoulder at the officer in the hallway. She was looking at her phone, working her thumbs. She didn't seem to be paying attention to our conversation, but I lowered my voice to a whisper. "Does this have anything to do with the…you know? The money?"

She frowned and shook her head. "I don't think so."

"Who knew you'd be here in Guadeloupe?"

She shrugged. "I wasn't even sure when I'd be here. It's not like I was on a schedule. The only person who knew I was arriving in Guadeloupe was Goti. I texted him when I left Roseau—that's the West Coast of Dominica. No. Wait. I also called the marina office to reserve a slip. But I was only stopping in Guadeloupe for a night or two. I was headed to Philipsburg. I thought we could spend some time together. I missed you."

"When did you get here?"

"The day before yesterday. Only a few hours before Engel was killed." She leaned forward and whispered, "Find Goti right away. Slip three-eight-zero. I left something for you in his boat." I nodded. "Thanks, Anne," she said. "I really mean it. I'm glad you're here."

"It's fine, Sandy," I said and stood to leave.

"I don't deserve you," she said.

I turned away, but she caught my arm in her hand and squeezed. When I turned back, her eyes were filled with fear. "I know I have no right to ask, but please help me." I nodded and pulled my arm from her grip, but then her arms were around me in an embrace. I stiffened, but she didn't let go. "I love you," she whispered.

The three words echoed as I fast-walked along the dim corridor. The first time she'd said, "I love you," seven months ago, she'd been lying in a hospital bed. I'd endured her uncharacteristic surge of emotion because I'd saved her life. "I don't deserve you," and "I couldn't ask for a better friend," seemed appropriate to say under the circumstances. I thought her feelings would fade, and I expected our relationship to return to the way things were before I'd learned her truth.

Sandy didn't utter those three words easily. But telling her biggest secret had unlocked others. Trapped in a hospital bed, she had nothing better to do than tell me about her past. She described her time in prison, and when she was braver, she told me stories from her childhood. As a teenager, she'd escaped an abusive home and never returned. I'd always suspected her reasons for not talking about her family, but my imagination hadn't conjured anything close to her reality. Her joy for life was a mask. I recognized it because I wore one too.

Her emotion didn't fade. Each time she told me she loved me, her delivery gained confidence, and her love glowed with a warmth that threatened to melt her mask and make her happiness tangible. Watching the light behind her eyes grow stronger made me shudder.

CHAPTER 4

Outside the police station, the hot sun warmed my bare arms but didn't drive away the darkness closing around me.

I called a taxi and returned to the marina. I passed Sandy's boat and wandered to the farthest point. Across the water, a series of pink roofs stretched across a narrow peninsula—a hotel or condos. Just beyond the pink roofs, the sea showed off its range of blues—pale turquoise over shallow sand and dark teal across deep shipping channels. A smattering of sailboats moored just beyond the marina entrance bobbed in the wake of giant freighters. I collapsed against a dock box, hugged my legs, and watched the sea. The cadence of waves slapping against the dock calmed me—staring at the water was the only time I allowed myself to embrace the darkness.

I wasn't afraid of being loved. I remembered the feeling, and I missed it. After so many years alone, caring about Sandy had been easy. But she'd become my friend under false pretenses. She hadn't been honest until her life was in danger.

I *did* love Sandy, and I hated myself for it. In my darkest moments, I wanted revenge—to take away everyone she loved, but I was the only person who meant anything to her. The realization that she didn't have anyone else always softened my anger into pity. The knowledge that she'd paid a price by going to prison helped, too, as did knowing she'd spent thirteen years searching for a way to make amends. Her blackmail scheme had begun as a way to pay me back, but four million dollars couldn't replace what she'd taken from me the night my family died.

When Sandy told her version of that night, I felt like I'd been there. Her perspective was infinitely worse than the broad strokes the police had drawn—an effort to save a grieving teenager extra suffering. Sandy's need to share the details was selfish. After so many years, she unburdened herself. Her pain eased. She didn't realize that each new truth infected me like a toxic parasite.

For thirteen years, I'd blamed myself. I'd condensed the story into "my family died in a car accident." I didn't want to know the details, but when Sandy finally told me the truth, a tiny part of me was relieved to share the guilt. I'd put them on that road late at night—they were coming home early to deal with a teenage party that had gotten out of hand. But Sandy had crossed the center line and driven them over a bridge.

"I was messed up, Anne," she'd begun with an apology as if somehow being drunk or high justified what happened. "The headlights stayed on," she said. "The car sank slowly into the water, and something waved between the two circles of light. Fingers. Or sections of hair. It's haunted me for years. I wake up screaming and remember the light under the water. *Something* is there, moving, but in my dreams, I never know what it is."

I remembered the horror on her face as she described it. She'd sat forward in her hospital bed and pushed her hair from her face, tucking it behind her ears. Her words had brandished the image within my memories. Her eyes had caught mine, asking permission to continue, and I hadn't stopped her. I regretted it every day since. I should have heard the pain and fear in her voice and walked away. What morbid curiosity forced me to sit there and listen?

"It was windy that night," she'd continued. "No moon. The water was so black, except for the headlights. I ran to the end of the bridge, climbed down to the rocks, and jumped into the water. I guess I thought they'd get out. That I could help them find the beach. The water was choppy. It was hard to swim. I was close to where the car went in when I caught him with my arm."

The word "him" knocked the breath from my lungs, and I sat frozen for a moment, waiting for her next words.

She stared at her hands, her pale skin pink against the white bed sheets. "He was floating. On his back."

My mind screamed, "Who?" But I remained in my chair. Silent except for my hammering heartbeat.

"He was so small."

"James?" I asked in a strangled whisper. "Was it James?"

She nodded to the bed sheets, not daring to look up. "I yanked on him and shouted for help. But there wasn't anyone else on the bridge. I swam for ages, but I misjudged the distance. He was heavy, tugging on my arm, pulling me under. I kept swallowing water, coughing and shouting. But nobody came to help."

A loud buzz startled us as the blood pressure cuff on her left arm filled. She stayed quiet as the pressure grew, but when the whirring stopped, my tension increased with each click. Click. James got out of the car? Click.

Sandy found him? Click. The sound would forever be fused with her next words.

"I let go. It was only a second. But he was gone. I tried to find him. I really tried, Anne. But he was just gone."

When the blood pressure cuff released with a hiss, something inside me broke. I left the hospital, drove home, and stood on the patio at the edge of the cliff with my toes curled around the concrete. The waves reflected a gray sky that day. They moved with a reverence, undulating toward me with a serenity that I longed to feel.

I didn't return to Sandy's hospital room for a week. She'd improved enough to be released, and I offered to drive her to *The Second Chance*. I wanted her to get on the boat and leave the island. I never wanted to see her again.

In her hospital room, an hour passed in uncomfortable silence while we waited for her discharge paperwork. She paced. I stared at my hands until she stopped and crouched in front of me. She was quiet while she waited for me to look her in the eye, and then she said, "I'm sorry."

Her voice was thick with sadness and regret. It liberated my grief, and I cried as I had on that night thirteen years ago—overwhelmed with the knowledge that I would never again feel my mother's arms around me or hear my father's voice. Mia and James would never grow up. I was alone.

I held her gaze. I wanted her to see the pain she'd caused. But she didn't move away. She wrapped her arms around me the way my mother would have. She stroked my hair, and whispered, "I'm so sorry, Anne. I'm so sorry." She repeated her apology over and over as she held me, squeezing as tremors shook my body and rubbing my back when I calmed. I could feel her wet tears on my shoulder, but she never released her grip to wipe them away.

The nurse's squeaky tennis shoes approached and paused in the doorway. For a moment, all three of us were silent, and then I heard a soft scuffle as the nurse quietly left.

Eventually, I pulled away. Sandy handed me a tissue, and I reached for her hand.

"It's okay," I mumbled. "I forgive you."

At the time, I'd meant it. But forgiveness is a process—not a light switch. Sometimes, when I glimpsed pain in her eyes, I thought she'd suffered enough. Other times, I still wanted her to feel the depth of my loss.

#

A passing tugboat blasted its horn and interrupted my self-pity. I stood and retraced my steps, looking for slip three-eight-zero.

The slip was occupied by a wooden sailboat with peeling varnish. The deck was cluttered with coiled ropes, buckets, and netting. Red plastic gas cans sat in a dark puddle in the corner. The deck was visible in a narrow trail from the stern to the hatch, but the dull white paint glistened with faint, oily rainbows. The boat seemed out of place in the sea of pristine white hulls.

"Goti?" I shouted.

"He's not here," said a voice behind me.

I whipped around to find a white-haired man. His beard, also white, hung midway down his chest. He wore a slack tank top, and his skin lay in brown, leathery folds. He was barefoot—which explained his silent approach.

"Do you know where I can find him? Or when he'll be back?"

"Try the closest bar," the man said.

When I reached the marina parking lot, I noticed a brick building with a neon Heineken light in the window. Over the door, a sign read *Salee*. Salty.

I hesitated on the sidewalk and stared at the dark facade and filthy windows. The building looked abandoned. I stepped over the short retaining wall separating the marina's clean concrete sidewalk from the weeds and marched to the door. It opened with a creak.

Inside, two men at the bar rose from a hunch to glance at me before returning to the pint glasses in front of them. The only other person inside was the bartender, a white woman with wide shoulders and short, spiky hair. She was drying glasses and didn't acknowledge me.

"I'm looking for Goti. Is he here?" I asked.

She shook her head. "Not yet. Come back in a few hours." Her husky voice had an American accent—deep Southern, more Louisiana than Florida, but it made me homesick. She turned back to the glasses, and I walked outside.

#

I needed a car. I called a taxi, and the driver suggested a Budget car rental location that turned out to be a fenced lot with a trailer for an office. The man at the counter offered only two options: a bright red Nissan sedan or a two-door, cornflower blue Dacia. I chose the Dacia. It had sporty wheels that seemed too large for the squat SUV, but it looked better equipped to handle the narrow island roads.

I drove away from the rental lot, taking random right and left turns. Aimless driving had been a distraction in Saint Martin. I never worried about being lost on the tiny island—there were a finite number of possible turns, but after twenty minutes of aimless driving in Guadeloupe, I was lost. I pulled into the gravel parking lot of a barbeque restaurant and opened the map app on my phone.

I was on a road that crossed the island, and I was headed west. The map highlighted vista points a few miles farther down the road. I pulled the Dacia back onto the road and climbed into the mountains.

One of the things I loved about Saint Martin was the greenery—especially just after a storm. Miami's foliage paled in comparison—grayed and yellowed versions of Saint Martin's landscape. But even Saint Martin couldn't compete with the lush green forests I found on Guadeloupe.

I rolled down my windows and inhaled the sticky mountain air. When the road became bumpy, I slowed and pulled into a dirt lot with three parked cars. A path marked by a wooden sign led into the trees, and I stepped from the car, stretched my legs, and wandered to the trailhead. Inviting ferns framed the path, providing welcome shade from the hot sun.

Before I met Luke, I'd been a homebody. For over a decade, I followed a daily routine: office, swim, home. But the pool on Luke's back patio was too small for laps, and I hadn't found a substitute. Instead of swimming, I hiked. At first, Luke dragged me to new trails across the island, but alone during weekdays, I explored the hills around our house. Much of the hillside was covered with long grass and cacti. I bought hiking boots to protect my ankles from the thorns hidden within the grass, but many times, I returned home with bleeding legs—scratches from pushing my way through dried brush or tiny slices from the blades of grass.

The vegetation on our hills was minimal—every hike offered a view of the ocean and a constant, cooling breeze. But only a few yards down the trail in Guadeloupe, I was swallowed up by a cocoon of ferns, banana plants, and rubber trees. The sunlight disappeared, and the air was still and stifling. The high walls of greenery closed in around me.

I panicked and turned around. The trailhead was gone. The trail was barely visible. A rustling inside the bushes on my right quickened my pace, and I emerged from the forest in a sprint and returned to the car. I sat inside with the door open, panting and feeling foolish.

I grew up in Southern Florida—the land of panthers, alligators, and cottonmouth snakes. There was nothing to fear on Guadeloupe—no bears or wild boar. But I'd walked into an unfamiliar, dense forest wearing sandals—without even a bottle of water.

The car became too hot. I climbed out and paced. Why was I hiking like a casual holiday-maker? Sandy needed my help. I knew her well enough to know she wasn't lying. She hadn't killed Engel. She didn't deserve to go back to prison for something she didn't do. I was an unlikely friend, but I was her only friend. She needed me.

CHAPTER 5

The bar was lively when I returned. The parking lot was half-full, and most of the tables were occupied. The bartender saw me enter and nodded toward the end of the bar. "Goti!" she called, and then she pointed at me.

A man slid from the last barstool and sauntered toward me.

"You American?" he asked.

I nodded. "I'm a friend of Sandy's. She said you had something for me."

He opened the door and waited for me to step outside. Once the door closed behind him, he said, "Can't talk in there. C'mon."

"Where are we going?" I asked.

"My boat."

"Um," I stammered. "Can you just bring it here?"

"You're as paranoid as she is," he said. He held up both hands. "The marina is full of people at this hour. You don't have to come aboard if you want. Stay on the dock."

"Okay," I acquiesced.

As we walked, I glanced at him, wondering how he and Sandy had become friends. His baseball cap was frayed across the bill, and every visible inch of his skinny black arms was covered in tattoos. He caught me looking, sniffed, and wiped his nose with the back of his hand. When we passed Sandy's boat, he said, "Word is she killed a guy."

"She didn't," I said.

"Yeah, when people get arrested, they never say that. She asked me to hold something for you. In case, you know."

"What is it?"

"Didn't look, you know," he said defensively.

"How did you know Sandy?" I asked.

"She saved my life once. We stay in touch."

He stepped onto his cluttered sailboat and bent down to unlock the hatch. He lifted the wooden cover and gestured for me to follow him.

I hesitated. "You said…"

"Yeah. I know what I said." He smiled. Silver teeth glinted. "Sandy told me she trusted you with her life. She told me the story. I know you saved her—not just when she was locked away. Before that—before you even knew her. Knowing you were out there gave her a reason to get through prison. It gave her life meaning. I understand what that feels like." He paused and then said, "I'm sorry about your family."

I stayed on the dock.

"Sandy wouldn't have told me that until I earned her trust, you know. That must mean something to you. Come aboard. Two minutes. I'll give you the bag, and you can go."

I nodded and stepped aboard. The boat rolled under my weight, and I slipped. He crossed the deck swiftly and caught my arm, holding it until I regained my balance.

"Come below," he said.

He disappeared down a ladder, and I followed him into the darkness. Hot, stale air met me at the bottom. He flipped a switch, and a lamp spilled dim, yellow light across a cluttered chart table. Every surface was covered.

He handed me a backpack made of cheap, imitation leather. Rusted metal studs ran along the two sides. It was heavy, and I grabbed the top handle with both hands.

"Put it on," he said.

I swung it over my right shoulder and struggled to push my left arm through the strap. The weight pulled me off balance, and I held the railing for support.

"Have you seen her?" he asked.

I nodded. "This morning."

"Let me know if she needs anything," he said. I didn't answer. He pushed aside a pile of clothes and sat. I turned to go. "She talks about you all the time, you know," he continued. "When I told her the police were coming, she told me you'd come. She said if anyone could help her, it was you."

"You knew she was going to be arrested?" I asked.

He shrugged. "A friend called to warn me."

"That's how she knew to text me."

"That's when she gave me the backpack," he said. "You know where to find me. Anything you need. Just ask. I owe her, you know."

I climbed the ladder, crossed the deck without slipping, and hopped onto the dock. The backpack straps were loose, so I held them with both hands as I fast-walked to my motel room. I pushed the door closed, locked the deadbolt, and dumped the contents on the bed.

I sank to my knees on the carpet and stared at the neat bundles of cash.

Almost a year ago, Sandy's identity had been stolen and used to launder money by someone she'd known in prison. When Sandy figured it out, she hadn't called the cops. Instead, she'd blackmailed the woman's clients and earned millions—I never asked her how much. She'd promised me the blackmail was over, but as I stared at the hundred-dollar bills, I wondered if she'd been honest. Was this the same money? Or was she still running a blackmail scheme? I counted a hundred tightly-banded bundles. One million dollars sitting on my sad, slouchy motel bed.

A knock on the door startled me, and I quickly scooped the money back into the bag. Had Goti followed me? Had he lied about not looking inside the backpack? A million dollars was a good enough reason to break someone's trust, but it didn't make any sense to steal it *after* he'd given it to me.

"Hello?" I called out. I was rushing—not organizing the bundles well, and I worried it wouldn't fit.

"It's Detective Fournier."

When the backpack was full, I pushed it behind the armchair. Six bundles remained on the bed. I shoved them under my pillow.

"Coming," I said. I took a breath and tried to slow my heart rate before I opened the door.

He stood two feet away with one hand in his pocket and the other behind his back. "I have a few more questions for you," he said. "And I know you're alone here on the island, so I brought dinner." A brown paper sack materialized in his other hand.

"Um," I began, trying to think of an excuse to slam the door in his face.

"I brought cheeseburgers." He brandished the paper bag in my face, and I closed my eyes and smelled fried food.

"I don't really have anywhere for you to sit," I said. "My room doesn't have a table."

"I'll eat on the floor if I have to. It's been a busy day."

I glanced over my shoulder, ensuring the bag was hidden, and then I backed up to hold the door for him. He unpacked food onto the desk and handed me a paper-wrapped burger. Grease stains from melted cheese made my mouth water.

He dropped a smaller paper bag onto the bed and ripped it open to reveal a pile of French fries—not the "chips" I expected. These were skinny fries—gloriously shiny and crispy.

"Is this okay here?" he asked.

"Yeah," I mumbled, a hot fry already inside my mouth.

He smiled. "Are you okay? You seem…stressed."

"You startled me. I wasn't expecting anyone. How did you know where I was?"

"Aunt Apo told me." He took a large bite and chewed for a while before he said, "You went to see Sandy today."

"Yeah, this morning."

"Good, right?" he asked. I nodded because my mouth was full. "My cousin owns this place. He went to university in the States and claims this is the most American burger on the island—more American than McDonald's."

"Are you related to everyone on the island?" I asked.

He laughed. "My father came from a big family. Thirteen kids in all, and twelve of them stayed here. A lot of us left for university. Many of my cousins never returned, but several…" he paused and stared at the ceiling. "Twenty-two cousins live here. I think. What about you? Do you miss your family after moving to Saint Martin?"

"No, my family are all gone."

"Sorry," he said.

"You said you had questions?"

He wiped his fingers on a paper napkin and removed his notebook. "What did Miss Brown do for a living?"

"She used to work in sales for a pharmaceutical company, but now she's…retired. Something happened …and when she didn't check in with work, they fired her." I didn't explain that she couldn't go to work because she'd been locked in a closet for two weeks and almost died of dehydration. I didn't want him to know the rest of the story.

"Her boat, *The Second Chance*, do you know how she paid for that?"

"Did you ask her?" When he didn't answer, I continued, "No idea. We're good friends, but I didn't know anything about her finances or job. We didn't really talk about stuff like that."

"What did you talk about?"

"I'm not sure that's relevant."

An uncomfortable silence settled between us. I wondered if he'd run out of questions or if he was waiting for me to answer. Or maybe he was just waiting for me to stop eating so I wouldn't have to talk with my mouth full.

I considered telling him Sandy's story. I could tell him everything Moreau knew—that Sandy had been kidnapped and had almost died, but she'd gathered valuable evidence. I could explain all of that without mentioning the blackmail. Giving me the thumb drive for the police had potentially put her in danger. Engel's murder could be someone's attempt at revenge. The two things could be related. He should know.

I chewed my burger, thinking of a way to mention Moreau, wondering if Detective Fournier was aware of the special task force, but I remembered Agent Fox's lecture about discretion and decided not to share anything until I called Moreau.

When Fournier spoke again, his tone was more casual. "What other islands have you visited?"

"St. Bart's," I mumbled with a mouthful of fries.

"And what do you think of our beautiful island so far?"

"Compared to what I saw today, Saint Martin is a desert."

He smiled. "Yes. We have a rainforest. And a volcano."

"Um. A dormant volcano?"

He shook his head. "No, it's active."

"Does it ever erupt?"

"Not for fifty years."

While I finished the French fries, he told me about how his father's family had been evacuated almost fifty years ago when the volcano was expected to erupt.

"How can you live next to something like that?" I asked. "Without knowing when it might blow up and kill everyone?"

He smiled. "You're from Miami, yes? So, you're used to hurricanes. When a storm comes, you prepare. It's the same for volcanoes. My family left everything behind, not knowing if they'd have a home to return to."

He kept talking, describing Guadeloupe, but I couldn't focus on his words. He was seated at the desk, and

I wondered if the backpack was visible from that side of the room. If he found it, how would I explain the money?

"Where did you go today?" he asked.

My heart skipped a beat as I remembered my panicked moment in the forest. "I rented a car and drove around. I almost went for a hike, but I wasn't prepared." His eyebrows raised, so I explained, "I didn't have any water."

"You have good instincts. When people go missing on the island, it's usually because they went hiking without telling anyone and got lost."

"But you always find them?"

"Most of the time."

"There aren't any dangerous animals here, right?"

He shook his head. "No. But there are swamps, and you can step in quicksand. If you're out there alone…"

He continued, describing his favorite hiking trails with an animated voice. I nodded occasionally, trying to keep his attention focused on me and away from the backpack. He had a nice face: smooth skin and a strong jawline. He smiled often when he talked about hiking.

But I needed him to leave.

"Thanks for dinner," I said.

He took the hint and gathered the trash into the large paper bag. "I'll be in touch if I have more questions," he said when I opened the door for him.

"I'll be here."

"You should hike the volcano." He tapped the pamphlet on the desk. "It's an amazing view."

I expected him to turn around and walk away, but he stayed in place, staring at me as if trying to make up his mind about something. I held the door open and waited.

"The case against your friend is…" he paused, and I froze, afraid that any movement would break the spell and he wouldn't finish. He took a step backward and stared overhead. I couldn't see what captured his attention: the line of towering palms, or birds, maybe. I held my breath, waiting for him to continue. "We had an anonymous phone call. It feels…too easy. You should hire an attorney for your friend. She'll need a good one."

I nodded. "Thanks," I said.

He took another step backward, and I closed the door.

I waited several minutes with my head resting against the door before I yanked the backpack from its hiding spot. I unpacked the money, counted the stacks again, and repacked them neatly, adding the bundles from beneath my pillow. Then, I shoved the bag into the cupboard behind the mismatched pots and collapsed back into the armchair. There were no notes from Sandy in the backpack. No clues. Just cash.

My phone buzzed with Luke's nightly text: *Good day?*

I wanted to hear his voice. I thought about inviting him to join me in Guadeloupe and pictured him stocking his boat with a loaf of bread and a jar of peanut butter for the trip. But Luke couldn't come without bringing our baggage. We'd have a few hopeful hours and a passionate reunion, but then I'd say the wrong thing, or worse—not say anything, and his face would cloud over.

I wasn't capable of sharing my life with Luke. Or anyone. I'd tried. I'd stood on the edge of the cliff staring into the ocean, searching for a solution. After thirteen years of ignoring my grief, Sandy had dredged it up and paraded it around. The intensity of the pain surprised me. The loss was still raw. I tried to pack it away, but Luke knew my history, and Luke wasn't an emotional ostrich like me. I'd catch him staring, and despite his denial, I knew he felt pity. Pity made me angry. On two separate occasions, Luke suggested that I go to therapy. The first time, I shrugged it off. The second, I answered with a quiet voice that chilled the kitchen, "I will never go to therapy again." After that, he quit giving me advice.

I leaned out of the armchair, grabbed my phone, and texted: *Almost.*

CHAPTER 6

The next morning, I drove to the *Banque des Caraibes*. It was located a few miles away in a congested commercial area. Traffic slowed on the narrow one-way street, and I passed a busy outdoor market that spanned an entire block before I found the bank. Parked cars lined both sides of the street. I crawled three more blocks past storefronts offering clothing and accessories, wireless phones, and cruises to other Caribbean islands. There were more than a handful of attorneys. But no parking spots.

The road dead-ended at the waterfront, and I found a pay-by-the-hour parking lot with open spaces around the corner. The backpack was heavy and conspicuous on the crowded sidewalk. Across the street from the bank, I stood on the curb with several others waiting to cross. Others approached behind, and the crowd compressed around me like an accordion. Someone bumped me— nudging the backpack, and I pulled it from my shoulder and held it against my leg, suppressing the urge to peek inside. When the traffic cleared, I broke free from the crowd, crossed the street at a fast trot, and entered the bank. I slung the bag over my shoulder to hide the sweat stains on the back of my T-shirt and entered a queue behind three people.

While I waited, I rehearsed a story inside my head, but I spoke too fast when it was my turn at the counter. "I need a safety deposit box. I'm visiting a friend, and I don't know how long I'll be here in town, and I want to keep my valuables safe."

I didn't look like someone with anything valuable enough to put inside a safe, but the teller didn't seem to care. He selected a piece of paper and asked several questions—my address and my passport number. I paid a six-month fee in cash for a large box. "One moment," he said. He disappeared through a doorway, and I glanced behind me and tried not to fidget.

Two minutes passed before he reappeared in the lobby. "Follow me, please," he said. We entered a tiny cubicle, and I sighed with relief when I saw the box on the table. He handed me a key. "Please close and lock the box when you are done."

He left, and I unzipped the backpack and withdrew eighty bundles. Eight hundred thousand dollars had been heavy inside the bag, but the stacks didn't look significant in the large metal box. I turned the key in the lock and returned to the lobby. The man was already helping another customer. He gave me a dismissive nod, and I pocketed the key and left the bank.

On the sidewalk outside, I paused. I needed to walk off my nervous energy. And I needed jam for my toast. I followed the crowd across the street and into the market.

The entire block buzzed with irksome gaiety. Music from several radios competed—steel drums and maracas joined a battle of Reggae versus calypso. Families greeted each other with shrieks and kisses on both cheeks. I purchased a baguette and a few bananas and found a jar of the coconut-ginger jam Luke spread on peanut butter sandwiches. The woman behind the table grinned with yellow teeth, but I couldn't return her smile.

The stalls reminded me of Sunday market strolls with Sandy—the highlight of every dull week in Homestead. Our memories were tainted with her truth. She'd unloaded years of guilt by sharing her stories. The telling made her lighter, but after a year of effortless friendship, our conversations now carried complex undertones. Loving her made me guilty; hating her made me empty. Before I'd met her, I'd spent thirteen years burying memories of my family, but her truth uncovered everything—she'd scratched the scab from an old wound.

A vendor approached with armfuls of brightly colored baskets, and I stepped sideways to avoid him and collided with an elderly couple. The woman smiled patiently, but the man frowned. His small, round glasses had slid to the tip of his nose, but he didn't push them up. He lifted his head and peered at me. Elbows jolted me forward and carried me along in the steady stream of the crowd until I managed to slip between two stalls and emerge on a side street.

I returned to my car but stayed inside, rolling down the windows to gulp the salty air. I tore off pieces of bread, dipped them in the ginger jam, and stared at the water, trying to force my mind to go blank, but I couldn't stop thinking about Luke.

I'd texted one word since I'd arrived: *Almost.* Sent twice. How long would he wait for more information? I was being unfair. He deserved more. I pulled my phone from my pocket and texted, *Sandy was arrested for murder. Someone's framing her.*

His response was immediate and unsurprising: *Want me to come?* He was a hero. He couldn't help it. But I didn't want to play the role of damsel in distress. I needed to solve this one myself.

No, I answered. *I'll be home soon.* But it was a lie.

I screwed the cap back on the jam jar and stared at the water until everything went numb again, and then I drove to the police station and waited in the lobby until my name was called.

"Goti came to see me this morning," Sandy said before I sat down. "You can trust him."

"What's the deal with him? How did you meet?" I asked.

She bent her head to hide a shy smile—an uncharacteristic expression for Sandy.

"When I left Saint Martin, the first place I stopped for more than a night was Guadeloupe. It was right after I'd gotten out of the hospital. I wasn't sure I'd ever return. You were so…cold those last few days. It seemed like you wanted me to leave and never come back."

She paused, waiting for me to argue. I didn't.

After a deep sigh, she continued, "I was…in a bad place. I left thinking I'd lost your friendship, and it hurt more than anything I've been through. Harder than leaving home. Harder than—"

"I told you," I interrupted. "It's okay. We got past it."

She smiled. "You said that. But I don't think you meant it." She held up a hand as I started to interrupt again. "When we first met, it was by accident. I'm not sorry about that part. You were the best thing in my life."

I stared at the floor for a long minute before she continued.

"Anyway, I showed up in Guadeloupe feeling sorry for myself with a scary amount of cash hidden in the boat." She mouthed the word cash. "I planned to unload…some of it on every island south of Saint Martin, but by the time I arrived in Guadeloupe, I still had all of it."

She'd left with four million. It had taken us four days to withdraw the cash from safety deposit boxes throughout Saint Martin and find hiding places on the boat. The other four million stayed in Saint Martin. For me. I hadn't touched it.

"I removed a small amount and deposited it but immediately got paranoid. If anyone figured out what I was doing…I freaked and wanted all of it off the boat. It took me three days to open four boxes and ten bank accounts."

"What does any of this have to do with Goti?" I asked.

"He seemed to be hanging around all the time, and I wanted to know why. Once I figured out he lived on his boat, it made more sense, but I was too suspicious to simply ask him. I followed him instead. He did odd jobs in the marina and seemed to know everyone. Every day was different. One day, I watched him change the oil on a boat, get paid in conch, trade the conch for lunch at the bar in the marina, repair lobster nets in exchange for live lobsters, and trade the lobsters for dinner. The next day, he polished all the chrome on a sailboat, and the day after that he climbed a massive mast to fix something.

"He lived in the moment more than anyone I'd ever met. I don't think he ever planned more than a few hours at a time. He got jobs when people stopped by his boat. He never worked early or late. Some days, he didn't work at all. He just fished off the dock for dinner.

"When I figured all that out, I didn't need to follow him anymore, but I was still curious and wanted to meet him. I asked him if he'd clean the bottom of *The Second Chance*—I'd seen him with diving gear. He agreed. I hadn't had it cleaned since I bought the boat, so he was down there a long time. Too long. I worried for a while, and then I jumped in the water to check on him. I found him tangled in his own safety line and running out of air. I cut him loose and dragged him back to the surface.

"He stopped by my boat every day afterward to say thank you." She smiled again—the same coy smile. "He was so sweet. It surprised me. He looks like a thug, right? I offered him a beer. He declined the first couple of times, but when he accepted, we talked for hours. We have a lot in common, and he's a lot older than he looks. He has great stories. He traveled all over the Caribbean before he settled in Guadeloupe. Whenever I'm in Guadeloupe, we hang out. He's my closest friend after you."

"He doesn't do much work on his own boat."

She laughed. "His boat is a death trap." She was quiet for a minute, and then she shouted, "Oh, I just remembered what I was going to tell you—the reason he visited me. Goti recommended an attorney. He said she just arrived a few days ago. She lives on a super-yacht. I told him to set up a meeting. Can you go? Pay her a retainer? In cash."

"Why cash?" I whispered. "Doesn't that seem sketchy?"

She sighed. "Because that's what I have, Anne."

"Okay."

We sat in silence for a few minutes, and then I stood to leave.

"Come back," Sandy said. Her voice was quiet—almost pleading.

I stared at her for a long minute before I answered, "I'll be back."

Exiting through the dim hallway, I considered my own three words: *I'll be back.* Would I? I'd convinced myself I'd left Saint Martin to escape Luke, but was that the whole truth? The second visit to Sandy had been unnecessary, but I'd gone willingly. Why was I helping her?

The open-air market had stirred memories. So much of the past few months I'd been haunted by Sandy's story about James, but before she'd told me everything about that night, there were happy moments. When she wasn't traveling for work, she'd spend weekends lounging in the shade on my back patio while I pulled weeds from my garden. She'd tried to help with the yard work, but after she pulled up an entire row of collards because she thought they were weeds, I made her stay on the patio. She was happy to be in charge of cold drinks. When the afternoon sun made weeding unbearable, I'd join her in the shade, and we'd sip g-and-t's while she told me stories about her travels.

"You have a quiet life," she'd said once.

I'd bristled and answered defensively, "I like my life."

She'd laughed. "I do, too, dummy. I'm here with you every chance I get."

"But you travel to so many places. Your life is way more exciting than mine."

"Maybe." She'd shrugged. "It's exhausting. I look forward to this." She'd gestured to the bed of sprawling tomatoes. That year—the last year I'd grown tomatoes, I'd waited too long to stake them, and they grew wild and unruly. "And you," she'd continued. "I miss you when I'm away."

It had been a rare emotional declaration for her—an uncomfortable moment that I escaped by going inside to refill our glasses. She'd shared real feelings, and I'd walked away and never told her how much I anticipated her visits. For over a year—before I'd met Luke, Sandy had been my best friend. I loved her. Her role in the deaths of my family had changed our relationship, but I still loved her.

CHAPTER 7

Goti wasn't on his boat. I stood staring at the mess on the deck when movement on the next dock caught my eye.

"Can I help you?" a man hollered.

"I'm looking for Goti. Have you seen him?"

"Haven't seen him all day," he answered.

I turned and took a few steps away, but he shouted, "Anything I can help with?"

"No," I yelled back. "Thanks anyway."

I walked along the dock, and he followed, matching my pace and stopping at the end. Waiting for me. I slowed, but he grinned and said, "I was already headed this way."

He wore a tank top and board shorts—the uniform of marina-rats: guys who lived on their boats and didn't seem to have jobs. His short, brown hair had sun-bleached, blonde highlights, and his arms were covered with tiny freckles. His full cheeks gave him a baby face, but I guessed he was in his early twenties.

"Haven't seen you around before," he said. I fought the urge to roll my eyes, but he continued, "Sorry. That probably sounds like a line. It's not. It's just that you're American. Where are you from?"

"Miami," I answered.

"I'm from Biloxi." He sounded excited as if he'd discovered we were neighbors. "Why do you need Goti? Something wrong with your boat?"

"No." I shook my head. "I just have to ask him something."

"Well, he's always around. He was the first guy I met when I got here. Good man. Jack of all trades."

I glanced around before I said, "I'll just try again later."

"If I see him, I'll tell him you were looking for him. What's your name?"

"Anne."

"Nice to meet you, Anne. I'm Jimmy."

He walked away, glancing over his shoulder several times, flashing a wide grin. I waited until he was out of sight before I followed him out of the marina. On the sidewalk next to the parking lot, I ran into Goti.

"*Bonjour*," he said.

"Sandy said you had a recommendation for an attorney?" I asked.

He nodded. "I just came from there. She agreed to meet with you tonight. Six o'clock. Her yacht is La Hormiga—at the far end." He pointed to the other side of the marina, away from his and Sandy's boats.

"Thanks," I said.

"She wants a retainer. Fifty thousand."

My mouth dropped open. "Fifty thousand?" I echoed.

He nodded. "Sandy said you would take care of it."

"Yeah," I said. "Of course."

"Good luck." He jogged away.

I returned to the motel room. I'd hidden the remaining two hundred thousand in equal amounts in four separate places in the room: behind the pots in the cupboard, within the clothes in my suitcase on the floor, tucked into a dusty alcove behind the desk, and under the mattress. I pulled a stack of five bundles from beneath the mattress, wrapped them in a scarf and stuffed the bundle into the bottom of the backpack I'd gotten from Goti.

#

I returned to the bar to wait. The same two men sat on stools with the same pint glasses. The bartender nodded at me as I approached.

"Can I get a gin and tonic, but with soda water instead of tonic?"

"That's a gin and soda," she said.

I laughed, and she scowled. "Sorry," I said. "I'm laughing at myself. A gin and soda. I never thought about it that way. My mom always called it a g-and-t. It's ridiculous that I've called it the wrong thing my entire life. I guess I never thought to order it the right way."

She wore a curious look as if unsure if my stupidity was amusing or not. "Lime?" she asked, and I nodded. She selected a glass, filled it three-quarters full of ice, and measured out the gin. "You're waiting for Goti again?"

"No. Just killing time."

"You're Sandy's friend."

"How did you—"

"Goti told me," she explained. "And you showed up a few hours after she was arrested."

"You knew Sandy?" I asked.

She shrugged. "Someone like Sandy arrives, and you notice. She hung out in here when she was on the island. I liked her. You watch someone long enough, you see who they really are. She's good people. I'm Bertie. Drink's on the house. Take care of Sandy."

"I will. Thanks."

Her words felt like a dismissal. I took my glass to a booth in the corner, shoved the backpack on the bench beside me, and tucked one of the straps under my leg.

Goti hadn't told me the attorney's name, so I couldn't Google her. An attorney who asked for payment in cash was probably not the kind I wanted to hire. I regretted not asking Goti for her qualifications and references, but it was Sandy's decision. And it was her money.

I sipped my drink and glanced at my watch. Should I reach out to Moreau—notify him of the arrest and ask to share her story with Detective Fournier? It was still early enough to catch Moreau in the office, but I hesitated. When Sandy left Saint Martin, I'd never mentioned her at the police station. I wanted them to forget about her, and it had worked. The team had focused on the evidence—not Sandy.

Mentioning her might have sparked Moreau's curiosity about Sandy's involvement with the money launderers. He'd accepted the story about the identity theft and seemed impressed by Sandy's ability to obtain the data and keep it safe. But he was a good detective. If he dug any farther, he'd find the blackmail. She'd been careful with the money trail by keeping it in cash, but there was a trail. And it led to me. Four safety deposit boxes—each with a million dollars. And all four were in my name.

At first, I'd told her to take all of it, but when I visited the first bank and packed six hundred thousand dollars into a shopping bag, I'd reconsidered. I didn't want to return to my lonely life in Homestead. The money was a safety net. With that much cash, I could have any life I wanted.

"It came from really bad people," Sandy had told me. "And they'll use it for terrible things. What I did was like Robin Hood, in a way. You could keep it and use it for something good."

"Like what?" I'd asked.

She'd shrugged. "I don't know. Keep it until you figure it out."

I'd handed over the shopping bag and said, "I'll split it with you. Fifty-fifty."

She'd beamed. At the time, I thought she was happy I was sharing it with her, but the more I thought about how she'd smiled, the more I realized giving me four million dollars had eased some of her guilt. She'd planned the whole stupid blackmail scheme as a way for us to sail off into the sunset of a luxurious life in the tropics, and for a brief time, I'd thought it was possible.

I hit the button on the side of my phone and stared at Moreau's contact details. If Fournier knew the truth about Sandy's good deed, maybe he'd help her.

"*Bonjour*," Moreau answered. "*Ca va?*"

"I'm okay," I said. "I'm in Guadeloupe. Sandy Brown was arrested."

"*C'est dommage*," he said. *Too bad.*

"I was wondering if I should tell the detective about the USB drive. I think she's been set up, and I wonder if there's a connection."

His end of the phone was silent, and I pictured him with pursed lips, thinking.

"*Oui*. I will reach out."

"His name is Fournier."

"*D'accord*. Take care of yourself. Come back to us soon. Special Agent Fox has a new project for you."

"I'll swing by as soon as I get back to Saint Martin. Thanks."

I hung up and sipped my cocktail. I kept one hand firmly gripped on the strap of the backpack. At five minutes before six, I nodded to Bertie and left. The backpack swung back and forth, slapping my back as I walked.

I reached the office, turned right, and kept walking. In the distance, I saw larger yachts, and I headed toward them. On Sandy's side of the marina, most of the power boats had swim steps with easy access from the dock, but the sailboats with taller sterns had step stools or little staircases with metal railings. On this side of the marina, the steps became more elaborate. Names were etched into wooden frames that glistened with fresh varnish. A few were painted to match the boat. I passed a massive, dark gray yacht with a set of five steps covered in plush red carpet.

I neared the end of the marina before I spotted La Hormiga. She was a power boat, short compared to the towering sailboats on either side, but long—two school-buses-end-to-end long. Bluish LED lights glowed along the wide stern.

As I approached, a woman waved. "Anne?" she called out. "She's expecting you."

I stepped aboard La Hormiga. The boat barely registered my weight.

The young woman followed me through a sliding glass door into a massive space with three groups of white leather sofas, each with its own coffee table. Blood-red Persian rugs covered most of the white carpet. Sumptuous red and gold throw pillows complemented the heavy, pleated drapery. Between the windows, wall sconces overflowed with flower arrangements—fresh flowers that filled the space with the perfume of sweet hibiscus. The door closed behind me, and the floral scent was stifling in the humidity.

An older woman sat on the farthest sofa, reading from a bundle of paper in her lap. She had long, dark hair pinned haphazardly on top of her head with a yellow pencil. A few loose strands stuck to her neck. If she heard us approach, she didn't look up.

The young woman didn't speak. She stood only two feet away from the older woman and waited. My eyes darted back and forth between them.

A minute clicked by. She continued to ignore us. She wore a red silk blouse, long-sleeved despite the heat. She reached up to scratch her neck, and a dark patch bloomed on the silk beneath her arm. The top two buttons were undone. Black lace peeked through a gap in the fabric just below the third button, which strained every time she inhaled. With every breath, I expected the button to yield and expose more of her dewy brown skin, but the button held.

She looked expensive. Tiny lines crossed her forehead, and wrinkles on her hands betrayed her age, but the skin on her neck and chest was supple and smooth. I couldn't see her eyes because her head was bowed, but her thick eyebrows were perfect arches. She scratched her neck again with a single French-manicured fingernail and finally glanced up at the young woman.

"Milena," she said in a lethargic voice.

"Senora Rojas, she's here."

Then she saw me. Large brown eyes assessed me, and a subtle sigh confirmed what I already knew—I wasn't much to look at. I crossed my arms, hiding my shrunken chest, and shuffled my feet. But I met her gaze and held it.

She untangled her legs gracefully and stood. Her blouse was tucked into black slacks that hugged wide hips and tapered to her narrow waist. She reached up and pulled the pencil from her hair, and thick, glossy tresses cascaded down her shoulders.

She stood and held out her hand, and I gave her mine. She squeezed it quickly and returned it with not a small amount of disdain. Her skin was soft, her grip firm.

"Sit," she said, and I did.

"My name is Sidero Romano Rojas. You may call me Senora Rojas. Occasionally, I take on a case when it interests me. Milena filled me in with the details of your friend's arrest. A challenge. I accept. Do you have the retainer?"

"Yes," I answered. I pulled the backpack into my lap and reached inside. The young woman, Milena, walked over and discreetly took the stack of hundred-dollar bills.

"Thank you," Milena said quietly.

The ease with which I handed over fifty thousand dollars surprised me. "Why cash?" I asked before I could stop myself.

"I prefer it when I'm not home, and your emissary, Gautier, said it was more…appropriate."

"Where's home?" I asked.

"Venezuela." She drew out the word, creating extra syllables. I'd never considered Venezuela—never had any desire to visit, but in that one sultry word, it became somewhere I longed to go. I caught myself leaning towards her and sat back into the sofa. I let the backpack drop to the ground and pulled a red velvet pillow onto my lap.

"But you can practice here?" I asked.

One of her eyebrows lifted. "Of course."

Before anyone else spoke, another woman appeared —materializing from an unseen staircase as if rising from the floor. She yawned loudly and stretched her lean, muscular arms overhead. Tight, black yoga pants ended just below her knees. The only other thing she wore was a hot pink sports bra. She moved like a sloth, dragging each leg dramatically.

"*Estoy ladillada*," she whined.

"Issy," Senora Rojas hissed. "Go away."

Issy groaned and rolled her eyes but disappeared back into the floor.

"Milena, we'll need a place to work. Book Issy a flight somewhere. *Anywhere.* Let's get started."

"Miss Brown has given us authorization to share certain details with you," Milena remained standing as she addressed me. Her gaze dropped to the notepad in front of her as she continued, "Sandy Brown was arrested yesterday for the murder of Johan Engel, a German national who has lived in Guadeloupe on and off for four years. Engel spends an average of eight months here each year. He is a retired banking executive and owned a villa on Norte-Basse. I'm still compiling his history.

"They allege that Brown strangled Engel with a rope from her boat. Engel's body was found in the marina inside a storage box. The rope was still around Engel's neck, and the size is consistent with the marks on his skin. They matched the rope to others from Brown's boat because they are specialized and only sold in the States. Engel sustained cuts and bruises on his arms and legs. Brown doesn't have an alibi. She claims she was on her boat alone and asleep at the time of the murder."

"Let's work on that," Senora Rojas interrupted. "The lack of an alibi is a problem. Interview everyone. We need someone who saw her that night. Maybe they saw a light in her cabin. Anything. And we need to know how the time of death was determined."

"Motive is weak," Milena continued. "Brown knew Engel from visiting the island, but only through casual meetings. They knew the same people. They hung out in the same places. They did not have a history of a sexual relationship, and I can't find any evidence of a business relationship. Yet. The police don't seem to care about the lack of a motive because the evidence is strong."

"I'm not sure the detective would agree," I said. They both looked at me, surprised, as if they'd forgotten I was in the room. "He told me to get a good attorney."

"He told you? When?" Sidero asked.

"When I arrived, I went to Sandy's boat. He was there, and he asked me a few questions. He told me I couldn't stay on the boat and helped me find a motel room. Last night, he visited my room and told me to get Sandy a good attorney. Not in a flippant way. He said it hesitantly like he thought something was wrong with how easily they'd found the evidence. He seemed suspicious about the call."

Sidero's eyes narrowed. Neither spoke, so I continued, "They had an anonymous call. That's how they knew where to find the body and the rope."

"He came by your room?" Sidero asked.

I shrugged. "Yeah. He said he had questions."

"I need to know everything. Exactly what was said. Milena, notes."

I recounted the conversation but left out the details about his family and hiking trails.

Sidero stood and began fanning herself with her hand. Several rings sparkled, and bracelets jangled as she moved. "*Dios*," she breathed. She paced away from me and then whirled suddenly. I pressed against the back of the sofa. "I can't decide if this helps us or not. If you stay close to him, you might be able to mine him for information. But you could also share our secrets."

"I wouldn't," I said. "I'm not very good at sharing."

She threw her head back and laughed. "*C'est bon,*" she said. "See if you can spend more time with him. Get friendly. Who knows?" Her hands gestured wildly as she spoke. "Now, I need to deal with Isabella. We'll meet again soon. Milena, get her details."

Senora Rojas disappeared without a goodbye.

"Can I get your telephone number?" Milena asked. "Where are you staying?"

"I'm at the motel in the marina. When I can, I'll probably move onto Sandy's boat."

She nodded.

"Is she always this…" I hesitated.

"Intense?"

I smiled. "She's impressive. Beautiful, but a little scary."

"She's the best. Your friend is in good hands," she assured me.

"I didn't get a chance to thank her."

"I'm sure she doesn't care about that. Not even about the money. Just the win."

"I guess that's more important than anything else. Can Sandy get bail? Or whatever that's called here?"

She shook her head. "No, not in a murder case. She will be jailed until the trial. And if she loses…"

She didn't need to finish her thought. I nodded and stepped out the door but turned back to ask, "Is there anything else I can do to help?"

Milena shook her head. "Try not to take the initiative. When she wants you to do something, I'll let you know. It will take me a couple of days to find a place for her to work. I'll book a villa, and then I'll call you."

"Okay."

The breeze in the marina cooled me as I walked toward the motel.

CHAPTER 8

I passed the bar on my way back to my room. I'd been too nervous about the meeting with the attorney to eat anything. I weaved through the crowd to find Bertie. As soon as she saw me, she ignored a man trying to order a drink and mouthed, "Gin and soda." She exaggerated the word soda, mocking me. I smiled. I'd made a friend.

When she brought the cocktail, I asked her, "Do you serve food?"

"Only thing that's edible is the burger."

"Great. I'll take it."

"Sure. I'll open a tab for you. Go find a seat."

I slid into the only open booth and watched the crowd. A group of men stood in a circle, telling stories and roaring with laughter. They were too far away to hear the details, but I could tell they were talking about fishing. I'd been on the boat with Luke enough times to understand their body language—and their excitement.

A couple sat in the booth across from me. They were quiet, staring in opposite directions. The tension between them was palpable.

Several other groups wore matching shirts—long-sleeved, quick-dry material with sailboats on the back.

The men without hats had wind-blown hair and ruddy skin like they'd been sunburned—or windburned.

There were eight barstools, and all of them were filled with men staring at the bar or watching the other patrons in the mirror behind the bottles.

"Here you go," Bertie said as she delivered a plate. Next to it, she laid a paper napkin and plastic silverware. "Comes with sauce on it. But I have ketchup if you want."

"Thanks, I'm fine," I said.

Yellow cheese oozed from beneath a sesame bun. The rest of the plate was filled with fried plantains.

"Let me know if you want another drink," Bertie said.

"Nah, I'll be good with this. Thanks, Bertie."

She nodded curtly, but I caught a hint of a smile.

I picked up the burger and took a bite. The bun was stale, but the juice from the meat dripped down my arm. The sauce was an odd flavor—the color of Thousand Island dressing but with a vinegar tang. After I swallowed the first bite, a peppery heat followed. Not too spicy— just a tangy warmth. Very Caribbean-style.

I finished the burger and watched the crowd. Bertie delivered another cocktail without even asking and slid into the booth across from me.

"Need anything else?" she asked.

"Do you know Senora Rojas? The attorney."

The lines across her forehead deepened. She nodded. "Defense attorney."

"Is she good?"

She raised her right hand and rubbed her thumb across her fingertips. "Big money. But yeah. She's the best. I reckon Sandy wants to hire her?" When I nodded, she continued, "I didn't realize she was in that kind of trouble. What do they have on her?"

"The murdered man was killed with the dock line from Sandy's boat."

"Doesn't mean she was the one holding it," she scoffed. "Well, if she can afford Rojas, it's a good choice. She doesn't lose. But—" She sighed. "Don't get your hopes up. I doubt she'll take Sandy's case."

"She already accepted," I said.

Her eyebrows shot up, and she reclined against the backrest and glared at me.

"What is it?" I asked.

She sighed again. Her fingertips drummed the table in an irregular rhythm before she leaned forward. "Rojas doesn't take charity cases." Her eyes narrowed, and her voice lowered as she asked, "Does Sandy know Rojas? From before?"

"No," I answered. "I don't think so. Goti recommended her. He set it up."

She nodded. Slowly.

"I just gave her a retainer," I said. "Was that a bad idea?"

"No. No. The opposite. I meant it—she's the best. I was just surprised. It's…out of character for her."

"Maybe Goti called in a favor?"

She slapped the table and let out a barking laugh. "Goti? He ain't got a pot to pee in. No way Rojas is doing *him* a favor." She slapped the table a few more times before she let out a long breath and said, "She must have a reason. There's gotta be something in it for her. Just keep that in the back of your head, and everything will be fine."

"Thanks," I said. But I didn't feel reassured.

She scooted out of the booth and returned to her post. I finished my drink and paid. Outside, I headed into the marina and found Goti perched on the edge of a low deck chair on his cluttered boat, trimming his toenails. The clippers snapped once, and he relaxed back into the chair.

"*Bonjour*," he said. "How did the meeting go?"

"That's why I'm here. Can I ask you something?"

"Come aboard." His arm circled in an arc, and the clippers glinted in the overhead marina light.

I thought of his toenails littering the slippery deck. I stayed on the dock. "It's about Senora Rojas. How do you know her?"

"I don't. I did some work on La Hormiga last time she was on the island. That's how I knew she was an attorney. Sandy told me she needed one, and I knew Rojas was here, so I just walked over and asked."

"Thanks," I said.

"Why do you ask?"

"Bertie was surprised Rojas took the case."

"You hired her? Good news."

I nodded. "Yes. Thanks for your help."

As I walked away, I heard the squeak of his chair, but when I looked over my shoulder, he was bent back over his toes.

My phone buzzed as I passed Sandy's boat, and I pulled it from my pocket to read Luke's daily text: *Good day?*

Almost, I answered. And then I typed, *I hired an attorney for Sandy today.*

Coming home? He asked.

Not yet. Soon.

The marina was well-lit. Tall lamps set at regular intervals illuminated wide circles—overlapping at the edges, but *The Second Chance* was dark. The nearest lamp, only a few feet away, was burned out. I stood in the darkness, staring at the black shapes inside the cabin of her boat. Footsteps approached—the slap-slap of sandals against bare feet.

"Did you find Goti?"

It was Jimmy, the man I'd met earlier. He wore the same tank top and shorts. And the same grin.

"Is this your boat?" he asked.

"No. It's my friend's."

"Well, it doesn't look like she's here," he said.

"No. She's not."

"You don't talk much, do you?"

I smiled. "To strange men late at night, you mean? No. I try to avoid it."

He laughed. "Hey, I'm not a stranger. And it's not that late. But I hear you. I'll leave you alone. It's just— this is the second time today I've noticed that you look a little…lost."

"I'm not lost," I answered. But I didn't sound convincing. Was I lost? Why was I staring at Sandy's boat? Did I want to go aboard—to smell her perfume— as if her scent could offer reassurance that hiring Sidero was the right decision? And why did I need assurance? Her freedom was on the line. Not mine.

Jimmy stood next to me, peering into the boat. A minute passed. Then another. And then he whispered, "Is something going to happen?"

I smiled again. "I don't think so. I don't think the boat has the answers."

"I don't even know the question," he said.

I sighed. "Me neither. I think I should go."

"Go where? Home? To Miami?" he asked.

I shook my head. "I know that much. I don't want to go home."

"Then you should stay. There's a lot to enjoy on this island. Have you gone snorkeling? Fishing? Hiking?"

"No. Well, I tried hiking, but I didn't want to go alone."

"I could go with you."

"I don't even know you."

"You're starting to hurt my feelings. I'm Jimmy! We go way back. All the way over—" he swiveled and pointed toward Goti's sailboat. "Over there."

He was teasing me, and his light-hearted banter reminded me of Luke. I missed Luke's humor.

"There's a group hike on the volcano tomorrow," I said. "I was thinking about going."

"You want to hike on a volcano?" he asked. I shrugged. "Okay. Sure. When?"

"I'll meet you in the marina parking lot at eight."

"In the morning?" he asked.

I walked away, waving at him over my shoulder. "See you then!" I called out.

"You know that's really early!" he shouted.

I kept walking. But I was smiling again.

In my room, I showered, put on pajamas, and climbed into bed with my laptop. In a browser window, I typed *Sidero Romero Rojas, attorney*, added *Venezuela*, and hit enter.

Most of the articles in the search results were in Spanish, but I found a profile on a website in English that listed impressive credentials. She'd been a partner at an international law firm based in Caracas before starting her own practice almost twenty years ago. She guest-lectured at several universities. There wasn't any information about her family or social life, and I couldn't find her on Facebook.

I translated a few articles from Spanish. She'd defended a man accused of murder, and he'd been acquitted. Every article described an impressive record of successful acquittals. Sandy was in good hands.

#

The next morning, I woke early and swam thirty laps before I showered and ate breakfast. I checked the hiding places for the money. Everything was exactly as I'd left it. My backpack held my laptop and several books—too heavy to take on a hiking excursion, so I dropped two bottles of water and sunscreen into the backpack Goti had given me, strapped my running belt around my waist, and slid my phone into the secure pocket with two hundred dollar bills.

Jimmy was already waiting when I pulled into the parking lot ten minutes before eight. I had mixed feelings about taking him. He was still a stranger, but I'd be in a larger group—all strangers as well. And Jimmy made me laugh. I could use some humor.

"Still want to climb a volcano?" he asked. "We could change the plan and go snorkeling instead."

"Scared?" I asked.

"Yeah. I can admit I'm scared of volcanos," he said. But he climbed into the passenger seat and grinned. "Let's go."

At the trailhead, I parked next to two already-pink women slathering sunscreen on their arms.

"Is this the place for the volcano hike?" I asked.

One of the women nodded, and the other one answered, "*Oui.* Check in over there." She pointed to a man in a navy polo shirt that stretched across wide shoulders. He wore a large straw hat.

"Hi," Jimmy said as he approached the man. "Can we join the group?"

"Yes, go ahead," the straw-hat man said. "The trail is clearly marked. Follow them."

He pointed to the two pink women as they walked past. Two teenage girls followed them, giggling and shoving each other.

"How far of a hike is it?" I asked.

"Couple hours, maybe. Depends on how fast you are."

That wasn't what I'd meant, but I let it go and followed the women onto a grassy path that ended in a wall of trees. A brief panic returned as I remembered my failed hike, but I heard the two girls giggling ahead of me, and I entered the forest behind Jimmy. A dirt path led through a doorway of ferns.

"Do you hike a lot?" Jimmy asked.

"Yes."

"It's just that you're wearing sneakers. Not hiking boots."

"I didn't pack my boots," I answered.

We walked at a brisk pace, keeping the women within sight. Jimmy stayed alongside when the trail allowed. At times, when the trail narrowed, he led and held branches and waited for me to pass. Every hundred yards, sometimes less, the trail was marked with wooden stakes hammered into the ground or tied to tree trunks.

When the trail began to climb, we caught up with the women. Jimmy greeted them, asking their names, and when they answered in French, he switched to their language, speaking with surprising ease. The women answered with giggling voices.

I trudged along behind. Every time the trail forced me to scramble up a hill, the distance between me and the others grew. Within twenty minutes, I was alone. I paused to drink water. I knew I could jog to catch up with Jimmy—I could hear the occasional shrill voice of one of the women, but I enjoyed the solitude—the cocoon-like feeling of the foliage. My panic had subsided. The trail was clearly marked. If I got into trouble, I could shout for help. So, I lagged even farther behind.

Orchid blooms dotted the trail. Walking slowly allowed me time to take pictures of the flowers and intricately patterned leaves I didn't recognize. A bird wandered past, head bobbing, oblivious to my proximity.

The impenetrable canopy of trees and ferns prevented any breeze, and the humidity became oppressive. I scrambled up a rocky hill and heard running water. The trail widened and led through a grove of trees before it ended at a stream. I searched the muddy banks for footprints, but the trail had disappeared.

In the distance, I heard the roar of a waterfall. I considered crossing the stream, but on the other side, ropey vines hung between the trees like a curtain. My panic returned. I climbed onto a boulder and searched for a marker, but there weren't any. I listened for the women's giggles and Jimmy's voice, but all I heard was rushing water.

"*Bonjour,*" a voice startled me. I whipped around to find a man holding a machete. I stumbled backward on the boulder and lost my balance. My flailing hand caught a vine, and I regained my balance.

"*Non, non,*" the man said, backing away. "*C'est pour les vignes.*" He brandished the knife and grinned.

"For the vines?" I repeated.

"Yes. These trees," he stabbed the air, pointing to the trees on the other side of the stream. "I have to cut the vines. It doesn't take long for the jungle to swallow up the trail."

He walked past me, hopping across the water on flat stones. "Can you help? Drag the vines from the trail."

He reached overhead, yanked a heavy vine, and slashed it with the machete. I stayed on the far side of the stream, watching him, but when a heap of vines covered the trail, I crossed. The vines were heavier than I expected. I had to kneel and push the larger pieces to the trail's edge. The lighter pieces I tossed into the jungle. When the curtain was trimmed into a jagged archway, the man returned the knife to a sheath on his back. I stood panting, hands on hips, sweating.

"Do you have water?" he asked.

I nodded, withdrew a bottle, and drank.

"Thank you for your help. From here, you follow a series of switchbacks that way." He pointed through the trees. The trail was clearly visible—a dirt path through a carpet of green. "Don't follow me. I'm going straight up." He pointed in the air, and I peered at the wall of rock that disappeared in the canopy. "Just follow the trail. If you get nervous, wait. Someone will be along shortly. There are nine hikers behind you."

He grinned again, but he didn't move.

"This way?" I asked.

"Coming alone is brave," he said.

"I'm not alone. It's a group hike."

"You were on your own when I showed up." He waggled his eyebrows, and I was relieved when he hopped onto a ledge and began to climb. I turned away and walked into the trees. The path meandered away from the rocks for several feet and then curved back around a group of boulders.

Around the corner, I lost the path again and panicked until I noticed a series of steps cut into the hillside. As I climbed, the roar of the waterfall receded, and I heard the four women again, chatting in French. I trudged upwards. The trail wound between massive boulders that kept the jungle at bay, but vines hung from the canopy. Once, I felt something brush my shoulder and turned to find a thick vine behind me. I slipped on the wet moss that grew across the flat stones and scratched my knee.

I'd almost reached the top of the hill when I heard voices. A man behind me called, "*Bonjour!*" and overtook me on a wider part of the trail. Eight more men passed, each with a smile and a bright "*Bonjour.*"

Around another corner, Jimmy sat on a rock.

"Hi, Anne," he said.

"Are we there yet?" I asked.

He laughed. "They said it levels out a little. Before we climb again. Ready?"

The trail widened and the foliage thinned. We passed huge trees with shallow roots that snaked across the path, winding over and around each other like mangrove roots but thicker and pale—like appendages of a massive creature. In a few places, the roots were spongy, and I tried to avoid them by placing my feet in the spaces in between.

"Are there any snakes here?" I asked.

"Only in the zoo," Jimmy answered.

"It's so hot," I complained.

"Just a few more minutes," he said.

I plodded along, my ankles sore from placing my feet at odd angles, and when we broke through the canopy, I closed my eyes against the bright sunlight and let the breeze dry the sweat from my face.

"They said it gets steep again but cooler the higher we go, and the view is worthwhile."

We crossed a green meadow with tall grass that tickled my bare legs, and then we climbed a dirt path of switchbacks cut into a hillside.

"Careful," he said. "You don't want to slip here. It's a long way down." He slowed to match my pace, and we kept climbing. My calves burned with each step.

The air cooled and filled with the stink of sulfur. The trail curved, leading around the mountain, and in the distance, I saw a white cloud seeping out of the hill.

"Must be a vent," Jimmy pointed.

"The volcano is venting? While we're on it?"

"Did you not look it up before you came? Who climbs a volcano without making sure it's safe?"

"Did you?" I asked.

"Of course I did," he laughed. "They have guides walking the trail to make sure it's safe, and there's a seismometer at the peak. Let's rest here for a moment." He slid off his backpack and handed me a banana. "I think we're almost there."

"Thanks," I said. "I had a big breakfast, but I'm starving already."

"When we get back down to the trail head, there's a great place for lunch. I mean, if you don't have other plans."

"I don't," I said.

"Why are you here?" he asked.

"Do you mean why am I on the side of a volcano? Or why am I in Guadeloupe?"

He shrugged. "Either, I guess."

"I came here to help my friend," I said.

"The one with the boat?"

"Yes. She was arrested."

"Oh. I heard about that. She killed a guy."

"She didn't!" I exclaimed.

He held up both hands. "*Allegedly* killed a guy." He stood and slung on his backpack. "We should get to the top."

The air became clammy as we climbed, and when we could see the top, the wind chilled my arms.

Chapter 9

The last few feet were the most strenuous. I scrambled on my hands and feet. Several times, Jimmy offered his hand, but I waved him away. Two groups of hikers passed us on their way down, and we pressed against the mossy rock face. Jimmy shouted, "*Bonjour,*" and they repeated the greeting to both of us. I smiled and nodded and appreciated each break.

It took twenty minutes to reach the top. I sat and panted and rubbed my arms against the cold wind. Jimmy handed me a navy blue sweatshirt with *Rebels* in block letters across the front. I pulled it on, letting it fall almost past the hem of my shorts.

"Now we climb down," he shouted over the roar of the wind.

"We just got here!"

"No, not back down. That way," he pointed across the top of the volcano.

"You want to go inside?" I asked.

He laughed. "Just a little. You came all this way."

He used my phone to take a picture of me next to the sign that showed the altitude—fourteen hundred and sixty-seven meters. The smell got worse, and I held a sleeve across my face and tried to breathe through my mouth. We stood at the edge of the crevice and peered down.

"It's not what I was expecting," I said.

"You wanted hot, orange lava?"

"No. I mean, I never want to be that close to lava, but that's what I assumed a volcano looked like."

Below, a basin held a small green pond, large boulders, and grass. It looked like any other hill—aside from the steam.

"From what I read, there's an amazing view when the clouds clear. Want to climb farther down?" He pointed to a rocky trail, and I could see the family of four women carefully descending.

"No!" I shouted back. "Go ahead. I'm going to stay here."

He nodded and jogged after them. I sat cross-legged on the grass and sipped water. Mist swirled around me, depositing water droplets on my face that accumulated enough to run in a stream—like de-salted tears. I could only see a few feet—a bright green hillside disappeared into the curtain of white. I closed my eyes and listened to the howling wind. Several minutes passed before I felt warm sun on my face. My heart quickened, and I opened my eyes to glimpse the impossibly blue sea at the base of the mountain before the wind dropped a fresh shroud.

I stared, willing the clouds to part again. The sea had seemed impossibly far. The peak was higher than I remembered climbing, and I wondered if it had been an optical illusion. Perhaps I'd misjudged the distance. But the clouds remained, and I shivered in the cool air. I stood, brushed off my shorts, and went to find Jimmy.

"Ready to head back down?" he asked.

I nodded, and we trekked down the way we'd come. My footing was more confident, and we descended back to our resting point in only a few minutes. The French-speaking women followed closely behind, chatting. I was focused on placing my feet on the slippery trail and didn't bother translating their words.

The decline was hard on my sore knees, and after another ten minutes, I stopped for a break. I expected the four women to walk ahead, but they stopped, too. Jimmy asked one of them a question in French, and one of the kids answered. They all laughed.

"She said it stinks," Jimmy translated.

They switched to English after that. They told us we'd arrived with the clouds and had missed the view. They'd been at the top for over an hour.

The two girls kept nagging at each other, calling each other names, and giggling. I smiled at them while I stretched. One of the women gave me a sympathetic look and rubbed her right knee.

"I have to go slowly on the way down," she said.

"I was slow on the way up, too," I told her.

The girls' banter turned into a game of tag, and they darted back and forth on the narrow trail like sure-footed goats, almost dancing along the rocky path. I squatted a few times, testing my knees, and I was just about to tell Jimmy I was ready when one of the girls bumped me.

I saw instant fear in her eyes as she slipped. My arm shot out, but I managed to swipe only air before my feet lost traction. Then I was falling. I felt wet grass beneath me and wrapped my arms around my head as I rolled down a steep, grassy slope. My stomach lurched with each rotation, and I grunted as hidden rocks grazed my shoulders and legs. I hit a larger rock, somersaulted several times, and landed on my back. I slid. All I saw was white sky. My arms clawed the hillside—leaves and long blades of grass that sliced my hands and slipped through my grip.

I hit another rock and yelped but slowed enough to dig my feet into a thick tuft of grass and clutch ferns. I lay frozen against the hillside. Afraid to move. Afraid to breathe.

I heard shouting from above, but I didn't answer. I stayed still and listened. Somewhere below me was the girl.

"Hello?" I called out softly.

I waited. I heard a faint rustling, and then a small voice cried, "*Aidez-moi!*" *Help me.*

"I'm coming. Hang on," I said.

I tested my grip on the ferns in my right hand. They held. I shifted my right foot slowly, creeping until I found a rock buried in the grass and pushed against it. The rock held. I dug my hands beneath the grass and found roots. I tugged, but they didn't break free. The soil was soft and wet, and I dug deeper and gripped the root ball.

"I'm coming," I repeated.

I heard more shouting above me. I peered up, but the slope was covered with thick foliage. All I saw was fern fronds jutting from the steep hill. I didn't trust the roots enough to lean away. I began to move down, finding strong roots and using them as handholds. And then I reached her.

She hung from a bramble bush—a stubborn plant growing on the cliff's edge. Just above her, the hillside leveled out into a narrow, rocky ledge. Below her was open air—a drop of maybe thirty feet into the canopy of the rainforest.

"*Aidez-moi*," she said.

"Okay, we can figure this out," I said. "I'm going to shout to see if they can hear us." She gave me a tiny nod. "We're down here!" I shouted.

I heard Jimmy answer, "Hold on, Anne. I'm coming."

"Can you swing your body? Not yet. Let's talk this through before we do anything. I want you to try to swing a leg up, but wait until I have hold of you."

"Hurry."

"Okay, I'll tell you when."

I shifted my weight to the left, closer to her, and searched for strong holds. A thick root jutted from the soil and made an s-turn before disappearing into the ground. I pushed my left leg through the opening. It scratched the skin but fit snugly. I bent my knee, trapping the root, and swiveled until I hung sideways just above her.

"What's your name?" I asked.

"Sofia."

"Okay, Sofia, let go with one of your hands and grab mine. Then, swing your body back and forth until you can get a leg on this ledge. Can you do that?"

She looked down.

"No, don't look down, Sofia. Look at me. *Regardez-moi*. Is that right?"

"*Oui*," she said. She bit her lip.

"I know you don't want to let go. You have to trust me, Sofia. You can do this."

She nodded again and closed her eyes for a moment, and then, in one quick movement, she released the branch and reached for my hand. I gripped it and grabbed her elbow with my other hand. As she rocked her body, I rocked with her. After three short swings, she reached with her foot, but it slipped. She cried out on the next arc, but I shouted, "Use your knee," and she obeyed mid-air.

Her knee caught in a gap between branches with a loud snap. She reached out for my arm with her other hand. I smiled into her frightened eyes and squeezed her arm and hand until her breathing slowed.

"I got you," I said. "Can you pull yourself a little higher?"

She let go of my hands and grabbed the fabric of my shorts. Her fingernails scratched my leg, and her foot caught in the strap of my backpack. As she shook it loose, the strap fell off my shoulder and slid to my wrist. I shifted my weight, trying to catch it, but the swing carried momentum, and it slipped all the way off. It seemed a long time before I heard a soft crash in the forest below.

Sofia settled into the curve of my body. She reached for my hand, and I took it and squeezed.

"Now what?" she asked.

"We stay right here and wait for help."

"*Oui*," she said.

"Do you live here?" I asked. "You've hiked this before?"

She began to cry. She muttered too quickly in French, and I didn't understand anything besides *maman*. I held her hand while she sobbed.

"They're coming," I told her. "You'll be okay."

It was an empty promise. Part of me wondered if Jimmy would really follow me down the hillside. I'd only known him for a day. Would he risk his life to save a stranger?

Sofia sobbed. I lay against the damp ferns and listened to the wind and the distant cry of gulls. The wispy fingers of the clouds cooled my face, and I silently apologized to the roots for thinking they were creepy and malicious.

My fingers ached, and I remembered the stormy night I'd clung to a rock wall, alone and afraid. The next morning, Luke had swept me away, offering refuge and safety. After years of independence, I allowed someone to take care of me, and I liked it. Too much. I'd stopped taking care of myself. I'd become dependent on him. It came easily to him, and he didn't seem to need anything in return. He was happy by nature, easygoing, and quick to laugh. His life was full before he met me—a successful business, hobbies, friends, and family. But in the last few months, his moods soured more often. He didn't laugh as much. Too many nights I escaped the awkward silence by retreating to the gazebo.

I'd run away from Saint Martin to avoid facing the truth: something had to change. Luke had tried to take away my pain, and even though I knew it wasn't possible, I'd let him try. In the last few months, I'd become a passive observer of my own life. The change we needed was me. I had to stop waiting for a solution. I had to stop expecting Luke to fix it. I needed to take responsibility for my own happiness and make my own decisions. I had to let him go.

The clouds parted, and I closed my eyes against the warm sun and breathed in the earthy scent of soil and ferns.

More time passed. My shoulders began to ache, and I felt Sofia stiffen as I shifted my weight. Finally, I heard the squeak of shoes against the wet ferns.

"Anne." Jimmy's voice. He *had* come.

"Took you long enough," I answered.

"Keep talking so I can find you."

"What do you want me to talk about?" I asked.

"Explain why you couldn't stay on the trail?"

I laughed, and Sofia managed a small smile.

"You offered lunch. I was hungry. In a hurry."

His face appeared several feet above us. "You two okay?"

"We'll be fine once we're back on the trail. Sofia, this is Jimmy. He's going to get you back up to the top."

"I'm afraid that's not possible," he said.

"What do you mean?" I asked.

He chuckled. "I found a way here, but going down is easier. Can you shift your weight? Scoot this way? I'll show you."

I helped Sofia find footholds, and I yanked my leg from the curve of the root.

"Careful," Jimmy said.

I moved slowly across the slope until I reached a jagged rock. I tested it, gripping roots with my hands and kicking it with one foot. Shards of rock sheared away and fell. I heard them tumble—rock against rock—not soft, grassy slope. I leaned and peered over the edge to find a wall of stone.

"What's your plan?" I asked.

"Do you enjoy rock climbing?" He grinned.

"You crossed that?" I asked. "How?"

"Slowly."

"I can't do that," I said.

"You don't have to cross it. You have to descend it. And it's not as vertical as it looks."

"No way. There must be another way out of here."

"That hill you went down is too steep. Too wet. I tried, but I started to slip. This is the only way. The stone has natural ledges, and the tree line isn't far. You can do it."

"And Sofia?"

"She can do it too. I'll be here. I'll help you both."

I stared at the wall. Stubborn plants grew in the crevices: blood-red bromeliads, spiky cacti, and moss. A seam ran diagonally—from just below my perch to the far side. It disappeared behind the treetops.

"I see it," I said. "You think we can walk along that ledge." I pointed to the seam. In places, the foot holds would be large enough for my entire shoe, but there were also places where it narrowed to a few inches.

"Exactly," he said. "I'll go first. I'll walk one of you across and come back."

"We go together. You first, then Sofia. I'll follow. One question, though."

"You're wondering how we get to it?" he asked.

"Yeah. It's too far away."

He grinned. "You have to climb up to me first. I'll get you there. It's the worst part, but once you get through it, the rest will seem easy."

I felt Sofia's hand on my leg and turned to find her peering up at me. She looked scared, but also hopeful.

"Did you hear all of that?" I asked.

She nodded. "I can do it."

Sofia climbed first. Her movements were tentative and jerky, but she gained confidence as the ferns held. Within ten minutes, she'd climbed onto the rock face with Jimmy. Then it was my turn. I listened to their voices as I followed. Jimmy's voice was gentle as he urged her forward. Sofia answered with a constant stream of *oui*s—as if she was trying to convince herself she could make the climb.

When I reached the point where I'd seen Sofia stepping onto the rock, Jimmy said, "You can wait there. I'll come back up for you, Anne."

"No," I answered. "Stay with Sofia. I can make it."

I peered below. The wall wasn't vertical. If I kept my body against the stone, I could use gravity to hold me. I dug my left hand deeper within the roots and stretched my right foot onto the rock face, searching for a ledge. I found one and dragged my body across the surface of the rock.

"Good, Anne. Move farther right. You want to walk out another two feet, and then you can start to work your way down."

I focused on Jimmy's voice as I climbed. He was quiet when speaking to Sofia but shouted when he gave me directions. His voice bounced off the rock face and echoed into the jungle below.

"Okay, you're there," Jimmy called out when I'd traversed a few feet of rock. "You can start down now. You're doing great."

I couldn't see them. I couldn't see below me—just up and to the right because my face was pressed against the rock. His voice sounded farther away, and I hoped that meant they were moving faster now that they were within the seam.

I hesitated, considering which leg to move first. I couldn't see my path.

"Start by lowering your right foot six inches," Jimmy yelled.

I lifted my foot away from a tiny ledge and searched for a new foothold. As my weight shifted, the grip on my left hand slipped. I began to slide. The stone scratched the palms of my hands and my left thigh. Sofia's high-pitched scream reverberated across the wall. I clung to the rock, slowing my slide, but my tank top caught and lifted, and a dry branch grazed my skin. As my left hand passed the same branch, I grabbed it. It held. My feet found a wide ledge, and I crouched and rubbed my burning hands.

"Well, that sped things up a bit." Jimmy said.

Sofia giggled, but I saw tears on her cheeks. They were ten feet away—a third of the way along the crevice.

"Take a moment to catch your breath. Give your arms a break," Jimmy said. "I promise that was the worst of it."

"I just want to get off this wall," I said.

"Still hungry?"

"Starving," I answered.

I resumed my climb. In another ten minutes, I reached Sofia, and she greeted me with a careful hug. When the seam descended below the canopy, it widened and became a V-shaped gap that led into a dark wall of rock—a dead end. Below us, the rock curved inward and dropped ten feet to root-covered dirt.

"What now?" I asked.

"It's not that far of a drop," he answered. "But if you hit one of those roots, you could roll an ankle."

"Or break an ankle," I said.

"I think we need to use the Tarzan escape."

I groaned.

"What?" Sofia asked.

"I think he wants to swing on the vines," I explained. "Right? But can you actually swing from those? They're thick. And heavy."

"There's only one way to find out," Jimmy said.

He leaped from the rock and caught the closest vine. His hands closed around it, and his body was a pendulum. But the vine didn't swing. It crashed to the ground and took Jimmy with it. Sofia grabbed my arm while we stared at the entangled heap of vine and root and Jimmy. I held my breath.

He started laughing. He pushed away the broken pieces of vine and stood.

"Are you okay?" I asked.

"That seemed way cooler in my head."

"Well, don't ask us to do that."

He didn't answer. He glanced around and scratched his head several times before he said, "I have another idea."

"Okay," I said.

"The ground is soft. If I can bring in enough branches to cover the roots, you two could drop down."

"That's a terrible idea."

"Why?"

"What if we impale ourselves on a branch? And we can still end up with a broken ankle and be unable to walk away from this stupid volcano. No. I have a better idea."

"I'm all ears."

"See that fallen tree? Find something like that— something you can lift and drag over here. Lean it against the wall for us to climb down."

"Like a ladder?"

"Very funny," I answered. "You know what I mean."

"Okay. I'll look."

He disappeared into the trees, and we heard his footsteps crashing through the foliage.

"I want to get off this wall," Sofia said.

"Me too," I answered.

"I think I can reach that." She pointed to another vine and turned back with wide eyes.

"No," I said.

"He can't move a tree, Anne. It's our only way down. It's not far."

She was right. Jimmy couldn't move a tree trunk, and it would take him hours to build a tower of foliage tall enough. And if it didn't hold, we'd be in the same situation: falling onto the treacherous roots.

"I'll go first," she said.

She stared at the vine for a full minute before she jumped. Her small hands didn't reach around the thick vine, but she clung to it, hanging for a moment before her legs went round and locked together. Then she slid down and landed in the dirt with a soft plop. She beamed up at me. Surprised. Elated.

"Your turn," she called.

I followed her, gripping the vine as my hands met it mid-air, locking my legs together as she'd done, easing my grip to slide.

She tackled me as I hit the ground, her arms went around my neck, and we stayed in the dirt, enjoying the solid feel of being safe on the ground.

We were still on the ground when Jimmy returned, dragging a long branch.

"How'd you get down?" he asked.

"The Tarzan escape," Sofia said. She hopped up and dragged me to my feet.

"I found the trail," Jimmy said. "Let's go get lunch."

CHAPTER 10

Lunch was a Cuban sandwich in the front seat of the blue Dacia. I was too filthy to enter a restaurant. My shorts were streaked with green, and my legs bled from several minor scratches. Jimmy ordered food to go, and we ate on the side of the road.

He offered to clean the cuts on my legs, but after I'd wiped away the worst of the blood, I pushed him away. The scratches were superficial. The skin on my arms had been spared because I'd been wearing his sweatshirt, but I could feel bruises forming on my back and shoulders.

Sofia's injuries were also minor. Jimmy jogged up the trail and brought Sofia's family back down. Her mother bear-hugged me, and Sofia's older sister wouldn't let go of her until they reached the car. They walked arm in arm through the jungle. When we reached the parking lot, Sofia broke free and ran into my arms.

"*Merci*," she murmured into my shoulder.

"You're very brave. Don't ever forget how strong you are."

She pulled out of the embrace and looked up at me with teary eyes. I smiled, the widest, most sincere smile I'd achieved in ages.

"*Merci,* Tarzan," she said to Jimmy.

After we ate, I drove back to the marina.

Jimmy stepped out of the car, but he turned and said, "What are we going to do tomorrow?"

I laughed. Easily. "Nothing. I need to sleep for two days."

Back in my room, I showered for a long time, gingerly scrubbing the dirt from the scratches on my legs. My hair was a tangled mess—small twigs and wilted blades of grass landed on the tile as I shook my ponytail.

After the shower, I wrapped myself in a towel and lay on the bed. I woke two hours later. Purple bruises had bloomed across my shoulders and hips, and the scrapes on my legs were angry-red. I pulled on the only dress I'd packed. It hung below my knees, hiding the worst of the damage. I opened a cold bottle of white wine and poured a generous amount into a mug.

I'd finished two mugs of wine when I heard a knock on the door.

Ari stood outside. He wore long khakis and a green polo shirt that clung to his biceps. His hair shone in the lamplight.

"Are you hungry?" he asked.

I was, but I didn't have to answer because my stomach growled.

He smiled and took a step backward. "Do you need a moment?" he asked.

"No, I answered. I slipped my phone and a credit card into a pocket and followed him to the car.

He drove a few miles—along a familiar road and then turned onto a narrow, one-way road that ended at the beach. He held my arm as we trudged across the sand to a restaurant on the water.

We ordered the same dish: fish of the day in butter sauce served with rice and roasted vegetables. I ordered a glass of Sauvignon Blanc. Ari drank water.

"You hired Sandy an attorney."

It wasn't a question. Something in his tone was critical.

"You told me to get her a good attorney."

He nodded.

"There's something I need to tell you," I said. "I'm not sure if it's relevant or not. A few months ago, Sandy was involved with money launderers—No! Not involved. It wasn't voluntary. They stole her identity, but she turned the tables and gathered information about their clients. I delivered that evidence to the police in Saint Martin."

He was quiet.

"If she's being set up, maybe it's related. Maybe someone found out what she'd done, and this is payback."

"That's a complicated way to get revenge," he said.

"True. I just thought you should know. Also, I work with the police. I'm not a cop or anything. Just a consultant—barely a consultant. I did one project in forensic accounting."

"Thanks for telling me. I can't see how the two things are related."

"Anyway, I told Moreau—Inspector Moreau. I told him about Sandy, and I gave him your name. He said he might reach out."

He nodded. "What happened to your arms? You're bruised."

"I went on the volcano hike today, but I fell."

He leaned forward. "You fell?"

"It's fine. I rolled down a hill. Nothing's broken. I'm just really sore."

He asked about the hike. I described the fall and our descent on the rock face. Our food arrived, and we settled into silence as we ate. When we finished, I stood too quickly and grabbed the table for support.

"Maybe too much wine," I said.

"I was going to suggest we walk on the beach, but…"

I laughed. "I think I've walked enough for one day," I said. "I just want to sit on solid ground."

He wrapped his arm loosely around my waist, and we walked away from the restaurant and stopped at the edge of the dry sand. Light from the restaurant reflected off the frothy surf, but the horizon was dark. It was my least favorite time of day—when the horizon was lost in the blackness. Staring into the void of a moonless, starless night sky chilled me. I sat on the still-warm sand and hugged my knees.

Ari tossed his sandals aside, collapsed next to me, and dug his toes in the sand.

"Do you think she did it?" I asked.

"Sandy? The evidence suggests she did." He spoke quietly, staring into the darkness.

"You think she's capable of that?" I asked. "She's strong, but could she subdue a man, get a rope around his neck, and hold on while he's thrashing around?" He turned to me with a questioning look. "The attorney told me he struggled," I explained. "I saw her. There wasn't a scratch on her."

When he answered, his voice was stern. "Rojas shouldn't be discussing the case with you. You just told me how you clung to a mountain today. Did you know you were strong enough to do that?"

"Our lives were at stake," I said.

He turned away, and his voice was almost lost in the wind and the waves. "Maybe Sandy's life was at stake."

"Are you saying it was self-defense?" I asked.

His hands went into the air before I finished the question. "No. No, that's not what I'm saying. Strangulation is a very rare method of self-defense."

"Rare, but not impossible? You're saying, with all the fighting he did, that he never struck a blow? Not one?"

He sat quietly, and I thought he was about to agree with me, but instead, he said, "No, that's not uncommon. Can I prove it to you?"

"How?"

He moved behind me, and I flinched as his legs brushed against mine. I felt the heat of his body as he pressed against me. His hands went around my neck, and I stiffened and pulled away.

"There. What you just did as I touched you—pulling away like that? That's a normal response. Imagine I had a rope or something similar. If I sat close enough to wrap it around your neck, you'd instinctively pull away, and the rope would tighten. If I twist the rope and pull my body away, you can't touch me."

He pushed away from me.

"Imagine you're struggling to breathe and try to reach me."

I leaned back into the sand and reached back with my arms. The muscles in my upper arms, sore from clinging to the roots, complained as they stretched. I waved my arms in increasingly wide arcs. He was right. I clawed at the sand, but I couldn't reach him.

"Okay," I agreed. He moved to sit beside me, and I continued, "He was killed on the dock? By Sandy's boat?"

"I can't answer that." His voice was cold. He'd already shared more than he wanted.

"None of that matters anyway because she didn't do it," I said.

"Why do you think there might be a connection to the money laundering?"

I hesitated. I couldn't tell him about the blackmail—for two reasons: I didn't want him to know about the money, and I didn't know any of the details. Sandy told me she'd only asked for small amounts of money, but I wondered if any of her victims had a motive to hurt her.

The two things were probably not connected. Setting her up for murder *was* a complicated way to get revenge. And unlikely. She'd arrived only hours before the murder, and only two people had known she was coming: Goti and someone in the marina office.

"I don't know," I admitted.

"Tell me what happened."

"Someone Sandy knew in prison long ago used her identity to launder money. Sandy figured it out and followed them. She took a huge risk—she almost died."

"That's what caused the kidney damage? The reason she needs dialysis?"

"What?" I asked. "No, she's better now."

"She gets daily dialysis. We had to bring her equipment to the station. We didn't have a dialysis machine." He stared at my shocked expression. "You didn't know?"

"I thought she recovered."

"She needs a transplant."

"What?" I stared at the wet sand at my feet. "Is she dying?"

"I think she's okay as long as she has the treatments.

That's all I know. You should ask her."

We were quiet for several minutes, listening to the waves. Tinkling glass and muffled laughter crossed the sand. A couple walked past, arm-in-arm and barefoot.

"Before Saint Martin, did you always live in Miami?" he asked.

"Yes, well, actually, a small town outside of Miami called Homestead."

"Did you like it?" It was a simple question, but the answer was so complex. I hesitated. He laughed softly. "I take it you didn't?"

"I did once. I had a happy childhood," I said.

He was quiet for a moment. "And something happened? Sorry. You don't have to talk about it. Just making conversation."

Could I make conversation? For so many years, I'd shied away from social situations. I'd been so isolated when I met Sandy. And I thought she'd understood. She avoided talking about *that thing that happened* as much as I did. With other people—people who weren't *trying* to avoid it, the topic ruined every attempt at a normal conversation. The pity was unavoidable.

"I think I need to talk about it," I said. "I buried it for so long—pretended that I was, I don't know, not healed exactly, but *past it*. A few months ago, I had to confront it all over again, and now the pain feels fresh—just as it did thirteen years ago." I took a deep breath. "That's when my family died. My parents and my brother and sister died in a car accident. They drove over a bridge, and they all drowned." With my left hand, I drew small circles in the sand, and I wondered if he could hear my heart racing. "Sandy was driving the other car," I finished.

He whistled softly. "You must be the most forgiving person in the world. To be friends with her after something like that."

"She didn't tell me for a long time—after we'd already become friends. Hating her won't bring my family back. Homestead…has too many bad memories now. I moved to Saint Martin to make better ones."

"You made a memory today," he said.

"Yes, I did," I said. "When Sofia hugged me today, seeing the gratitude in her eyes—that was a good memory."

"I think you're being too hard on yourself. Give yourself time to heal."

I searched for another topic—something to lighten the mood, but I couldn't think of anything. When Ari spoke, his voice was almost a whisper. "I feel like I'm on the wrong side of this case."

"Because you think Sandy didn't do it?"

"If it was her, she did me a favor. A year ago, a close friend died of an overdose." I held my breath until he continued, "Engel was her dealer."

\#

Ari dropped me at the hotel, but I was too restless to return to the armchair. The alley was welcoming at night. Bright lights spilled from the windows and crossed the pavement. I wandered past the bar and into the marina, heading towards Sandy's boat without really meaning to.

My phone buzzed with Luke's nightly text, *Good day?*

I stepped aboard *The Second Chance,*sat in the chair on the deck, and hit the call button.

"Hi," he answered, surprised. "How's it going over there?"

"Okay."

"How can I help?"

"I went over a cliff today."

"Literally?"

I nodded even though he couldn't see me. "I hiked to the top of the volcano, but on the way back down, I slipped and fell. It was a life-flashing-before-your-eyes moment." I heard the sound of the sliding glass door from his end of the phone, and I pictured him stepping onto the patio barefoot. "I've been waiting around for something to happen. At least, that's what I told myself. But that was a lie. I was waiting for something inside of me to heal. I had an epiphany up on that hill today. It's time for me to start being honest. With you but also with myself."

"Okay," he said.

"You don't make me happy. You try harder than anyone I've ever met, but you *can't* make me happy. I have to figure it out for myself."

"Okay," he said. Just like that. He was giving up. And I was letting him.

"Happy is probably the wrong word," I continued. "I might be broken enough that happy isn't possible for me. But you shouldn't have to be miserable too. On that hill today I realized how much I love you." I paused. "Enough to let you go."

I heard the waves crash against the rocks below him, and I closed my eyes and longed to be there on the patio next to him. I heard his smile when he spoke.

"Is this a if-you-love-something-set-it-free thing?" he asked.

It was a classic Luke response. In any situation, he found humor and lightened the mood. "I know telling me was hard for you," he continued. "I appreciate your honesty. I hope you know I'm here to help, but I'll stay out of your way while you need space."

I didn't answer. A sob caught in my throat. Tears splattered the boat deck.

"I love you," he said.

"I know," I answered.

"Call me whenever you need to, okay?"

"Okay. Bye."

I hung up the phone. The decision I'd made on the hill had seemed inspired. It felt as if the universe agreed— the sun had shone in solidarity, but after saying it out loud in the darkness, it didn't feel like the right thing to do. He was better off without me, but I wasn't better off without him.

I wiped my tears and stood. When I reached Bertie's bar, the green neon sign was a flickering invitation, but I hesitated. The door opened. Two men stumbled out, laughing and leaning on each other for support. I wanted company, but not the loud kind. Even in the dim interior, my swollen eyes would betray me. I headed to the motel. I had white wine in my fridge.

#

Ari stood in front of my door, staring at his feet.

"Hi," I said. "Why are you back? Has something happened?"

He shook his head. "I drove away, and I was thinking…" I unlocked the door and backed against it.

Leaving it wide open. "The way our conversation ended…I shouldn't have said any of that. I wanted to check on you," he continued. "To make sure you were okay." He stepped inside.

"I'm okay," I said. I slid away from the door, and it closed with a soft click.

He touched my cheek with the back of his hand. "Were you crying?"

I blinked several times. "Just a little."

"You had a dramatic day. Sometimes, we're like the volcano. We need to find a way to vent the steam, or we'll explode. I know how you felt. Like life was suddenly more precious?"

"Something like that."

He pulled me into an embrace. I pressed my face against his shoulder and felt his breathing change.

"I should go," he said.

He didn't move right away, and when he did, he pulled away only far enough to stare into my face for a moment. Then his hands dropped from my shoulders, and he stepped to the door.

The light was off. The room glowed in red light from the clock on the microwave. He was a dark silhouette. His hand remained on the doorknob for a long minute before he returned to me. He mumbled something in French into my neck. A warm flush burned along my spine as his lips brushed my skin. His hands went around me, tighter this time, holding me as his body pressed against mine, knocking me off balance. I was unsteady from too much wine, and I began to fall. This time, I didn't try to save myself. I just gave in and let him catch me as his mouth closed over mine.

Chapter 11

My phone woke me, buzzing with repeated texts from Milena. I squinted to read the first one, *Time to work,* and blinked several times before I could read the next: an address and a Google pin. As I stared at the phone, it buzzed again, and a line of four emojis of clapping hands appeared. I groaned and pulled the pillow over my head.

I didn't drink wine often, and I remembered why. The headache. I dragged myself from bed and chugged half of a bottle of water. Every muscle in my body ached.

I showered—to loosen my sore muscles and to rinse away the guilt from kissing Ari. I hadn't explicitly broken things off with Luke. It had been unsaid—hanging on the edges of the conversation. I hadn't said the actual words.

When Ari's lips closed over mine, the ambiguity hadn't mattered. I wanted to push aside the melancholy of losing Luke and feel something better, but Ari's lips made me ache for Luke. I tried to force Luke from my thoughts and surrender to Ari's passion, but he sensed my hesitation and pulled away. He mumbled an apology and left. I collapsed on the bed in a heap of shame and hot tears.

After the shower, I toweled off and examined my legs. Scabs had softened in the hot water, but the redness had faded. I pulled on the dress I'd worn the night before and swallowed two painkillers I found at the bottom of my backpack. After a breakfast of two fried eggs and toast with jam, I felt better.

I checked my phone, but it had been quiet other than Milena's texts. Nothing from Luke.

The sporty Dacia climbed hills and careened around hairpin turns until the road dead-ended at the address Milena sent. I parked next to a black Land Rover in a circular driveway and walked to a railing at the edge of the drive. Below, a black metal roof protruded from the steep hillside.

I descended a staircase onto a concrete patio and stepped into the shade. The walls of the house were cold concrete—silvery-gray, but the massive door was black and glossy with a polished gold handle. Two fans, mounted within the overhang, spun lazily overhead. The faint breeze lifted goosebumps along my arms, and I hugged myself as the door opened inward.

"Hi, Anne," Milena said.

"Wow. This house."

She leaned toward me and whispered, "It might be the ugliest villa on the island, so I knew *she'd* like it." I smiled. She gestured for me to follow her, and then she continued in a normal voice. "Watch your step in here."

I tiptoed across oversized squares of white marble tile that reflected so much sunlight I used my hand to shield my eyes. I didn't notice Milena stop ahead of me and bumped into her. She giggled, and I squinted against the sunlight and said, "Hangover."

She nodded knowingly. "Wait here. I'll get you a water."

I stayed put, squinting. Honed, white marble framed a yawning black fireplace. Stark, white walls contrasted with a single painting—minimal black brush strokes against a gray canvas. Two sofas, covered in sumptuous white leather, were flanked by side tables with white metal frames. Bulbous white lamps appeared to levitate over the invisible glass surface. The only blemish was a white shag rug that had yellowed in the sunlight.

"Wow," I breathed.

Milena smirked as she returned with a bottle of sparkling water. "Don't sit."

"Yeah, I'd be afraid to."

She led me into the next room. Two large whiteboards were propped on oversized dining room chairs that matched the glossy finish of the front door. The table was a slab of clear glass over a simple black metal frame. A rainbow of highlighters and post-it notes strewn across the table seemed offensive in the monochromatic house—like muddy footprints across the pristine, white tile floor.

"Hi," I greeted Sidero. She sat cross-legged in a wide chair at the head of the table. Her bare, brown legs stuck out between the arms of the chair, and her head was bent over a large book in her lap. She wore an oversized, crisp white button-down shirt. I marveled at her posture. Straight and powerful—like someone who did Pilates. She removed her large reading glasses and set them on the book in front of her.

"Anne," she said.

It took me a moment to register my own name. Her accent turned it into something exotic.

"You're welcome to stay here," she said. She set the book on the table and straightened her legs in one graceful movement. I glanced away. The shirt was the only thing she wore. "Before you agree, you should know that I never stop working, and I'm a terrible roommate." She stood and walked to the board. "We're short-staffed at the moment, so I'm hoping we can count on you for some of the legwork. Milena cleared it with Sandy."

"Of course. I'm not sure how I can help."

"Milena made a list of the boats near *The Second Chance* and managed to interview several of the owners. Your first job is to help track down the others. Yes?"

I nodded. Milena crept up behind me and handed me a legal pad. On the top sheet was a list of twenty boat names.

"It's imperative that you share everything with me. If a fishmonger approaches you at the market, I want to know about it. However, I will not share everything with you. My goal is winning this case—not keeping you informed. If you need an update on our progress, ask Milena. Or stay here and listen."

She stared at the board as she talked, but then she turned and held my gaze.

"I have something to share," I said.

"Please do." She opened a dry erase marker and gestured for me to sit.

"You asked me to get close to Detective Fournier. I had dinner with him last night."

"Brava!" Sidero shouted. "You are full of surprises. So much progress in one day. Tell me what you learned."

"Not a lot. He's guarded. I don't think he believes Sandy is guilty. The lack of motive bothers him, but he argued that she's physically capable. He wouldn't talk about where Engel was killed. He'd been talking freely up to that point, and when I asked him about it, he clammed up."

"Interesting. Stay close. See what else you can learn."

"There's something else. He has a personal connection to the case."

One of her perfect eyebrows lifted.

"A friend of his, someone I think he cared a lot about, died from an overdose, and Engel was her dealer. Did you know that about Engel? About the drugs?"

Her eyes narrowed, but she didn't answer. She turned to the board and tapped on the white surface with the black marker several times before she capped it and settled back into her chair. She pulled the book back into her lap.

Milena gestured for me to follow her, and we passed the white room again and entered a kitchen full of gleaming stainless steel.

"She likes to be alone when she works," Milena said.

"Well, I have my instructions." I held up the pad of paper. "Any chance you can coach me on what to ask? Or what not to ask?"

"It's on the next page. I made a list of questions. It's best to ask the same questions to ensure you get the same answers."

She'd written five questions. At the bottom of the page, I read, *Let them talk if they want to, but only ask these five questions.*

She walked me to the front door. "If you need anything, just ask. I know Sidero invited you to stay here, but I—" She looked over her shoulder and lowered her voice. "I wouldn't. I *have* to be here. You don't."

When I stepped onto the concrete patio, she closed the door behind me.

#

I drove down the hill and followed my phone's instructions to return to the marina. When I pulled into the parking lot, my phone rang.

"Wylda!" I shouted.

"I'm reminding you about lunch tomorrow. I know you lose track of the days."

"I can't make it. I'm out of town."

"Where?"

I sighed. "I'm in Guadeloupe. Sandy was arrested."

"*Cherie!* Why didn't you say?"

I hesitated. I'd met Wylda when I'd first arrived in Saint Martin because she was Sandy's friend, but Wylda didn't know anything about Sandy's past. My friendship with Wylda was the one thing in my life that Sandy's secrets hadn't tainted. I never meant to become friends with her. A few weeks after Sandy left the island, I returned to Wylda's salon for a haircut. She welcomed me with a bear hug.

"Your hair is fine," she said. "But you look like you need a cocktail."

She locked up the salon, led me around the block to a taco shack, and ordered two margaritas. She squeezed her wide hips into a patio chair and said, "Tell me."

"Tell you what?" I asked.

The taco shack had three tables—all placed at the edge of the street. The only thing between a steady stream of traffic and the tables was a rotting wooden railing. I watched the cars speed past. A driver honked and swerved as a pedestrian stepped out onto the road. The next car slowed to allow the person to cross, and several more cars honked their disapproval. The taco shack was an unlikely place for a quiet chat, but something in Wylda's calm smile made me drag a chair to the farthest corner—away from the road and sit.

"Sandy came to see me before she left, so I know she's gone. Why are you still here?" she asked.

"I met someone," I said. "I'm…staying."

"You don't sound sure." She frowned. "Isn't it too fast?

She barely knew me, but she'd known the truth before I did. It *had* been too fast. I'd made too many changes in my life too quickly, and now I was retreating.

I stared out at the line of boats in the marina. "Luke and I broke up last night," I said.

"Oh, *Cherie.*"

"You were right all along. I shouldn't have moved in with him so soon."

"I said that before I met Luke. Before I saw the two of you together. I was wrong, Anne. And you're wrong now." She tsk-tsk'd—solace and chastisement with one click of her tongue.

"He's better off. Anyway, I have to stay here and help Sandy. I'll call you when I get back to Saint Martin."

"Take care of yourself, Anne."

"Thanks. Talk soon."

I thought about Wylda's words. *You're wrong now.* Was I making a huge mistake by letting Luke go? I thought about his wide smile. His curly hair. He was perfect—a great cook, a successful builder. And he was *fun*—more fun than anyone I'd ever met—even Sandy. He'd taught me how to fish, how to kayak, and he'd tried to teach me to surf.

I felt homesick. Sandy's boat was a few hundred yards away. The police weren't watching it—I'd boarded it last night. I could use my keys, start the engine, and drive away. I could still fix things with Luke. If I told him everything about Sandy. If I told him about the money.

I wiped the sweat from my forehead and stepped out of the hot car.

Leaving would mean deserting Sandy. I'd agreed to help Sidero with Sandy's defense. Her boat wasn't going anywhere. I could leave anytime. I picked up the legal pad from the passenger seat and headed into the marina.

CHAPTER 12

Milena's list included slip numbers. I wondered how she'd had time to create a comprehensive list. The first boat on the list was called *Dreaming*. I stood on the dock and called, "Hello?" but nobody appeared. The second boat, *Pier Pressure,* was also unoccupied. And the third. I paced the dock, making a small x next to each boat name but never spoke to anybody. It took me over an hour to accomplish nothing more than a sunburn.

I headed to the bar.

"Hi, Bertie," I called out from the doorway.

"Cocktail?" She winked.

I shook my head. "Too early for me." I lowered my voice and glanced at the two men at the end of the bar. They stared into their usual pint glasses and didn't seem to notice me.

"What's going on?" she asked.

I climbed onto the stool and sipped the soda water she placed in front of me. "I'm supposed to talk to a bunch of boat owners, but none of them are around. So, I figured I'd hang out here where it's cool. And dark. I was getting burned."

"Are you selling something?"

"No," I laughed. "This is for Sandy's case."

"You could try the restaurant. And you'll have better luck in the evenings. Most people are at work right now. And some keep their boats here year-round but live elsewhere. Try the office. And wear sunscreen."

I laughed. "I lost my sunscreen over a cliff."

She leaned on the bar. "I'm guessing there's a story behind that."

I shrugged. "Yesterday, I hiked the volcano. My sunscreen went over a cliff. I'm lucky that's all I lost. I fell—that's why my legs are all scratched up."

"You know I can't see your legs, right?" she teased. "All day, I serve legless people. It's like y'all just float in here." She grabbed a small bottle from the counter behind her and slid it across the bar. "Take mine. I don't need it. I live in this cave."

"Thanks."

I applied sunscreen to my face, chest, and arms while Bertie refilled my water.

"You okay?" she asked. She leaned closer. "Your eyes are red and puffy, and you seem on edge."

"I didn't realize it was that obvious." I sighed. "I'm hungover."

"Well, I have a good ear if you need to share."

I blinked furiously and sipped my drink. "I'm a mess, I guess. I broke up with my boyfriend last night."

"I thought you were here alone," she said.

"I am," I answered.

"You broke up over the phone?"

"It felt like the right thing to do at the time."

"And the drinking happened after?" she asked.

I shook my head. "No. Before."

"So, you got a little drunk and made a phone call. And now you're regretting it?"

I nodded.

"You know what makes me feel better when I've gone and done something real dumb?"

"What?" I asked. Something about Bertie's accent—how she pronounced dumb as if it had two syllables: *da-um* made me smile.

"Pie," she said.

"You serve pie?" I asked.

"Hey now, this might not be a fancy place, but I have standards."

I laughed. "Pie is your standard?"

"You betcha. Pecan pie. Always cheers me up. Hang on, I'll warm us up two pieces."

She disappeared and returned with two plates. Atop wide slices of pie sat two generous scoops of vanilla ice cream.

"Wow," I said.

The buttery sugar of the pie mixed with the creamy vanilla and dissolved in my mouth.

"You feel better already, don't you?"

I nodded. "It's impossible to feel sad when you're eating this. Do you make it yourself?"

"Yes'm. Just like my momma used to."

"Where are you from?"

"Alabama originally, but I lived in New Orleans thirty years before moving here. You?"

"Miami, but I live in Saint Martin now—at least I did before the break up. I'm not sure what I'm going to do now."

"Eat more pie. You'll figure it out."

I laughed. "I don't think pie can fix me, but this is the best thing I've eaten in a long time. Reminds me of home." I took another bite. "Do you work every day?"

"I have three days off startin' tomorrow. Do I need to remind you what your drink is called so you can order it when I'm not here?"

I grinned. "Funny. What are your plans for three whole days?"

"Not a godamn thing." She tossed a dishcloth into the sink and raised both arms in celebration, even though the sink was only six feet away. She reminded me of Wylda. Physically, the only thing the two women had in common was their height and width, but Bertie exuded the same calm confidence. They were both comfortable in their own skin.

One of two men at the end of the bar raised his glass. It was a half-hearted gesture, and Bertie rolled her eyes and stepped away to serve him. I finished my second glass of water, tucked a twenty-dollar bill under my empty plate, and headed to the marina office.

Inside, I found the same blonde woman I'd met when I first arrived.

"Bonjour," her voice sang out as I entered.

"I'm wondering if you can help me. I need to ask these people a few questions, but none are on their boats. Do you know if they are even on the island? Or if they live somewhere else?" I showed her the list. "I'm not trying to harass them or anything. I just want to ask if they know anything about the night of the murder. I'm here trying to help my friend—the one who was arrested."

"Oh," she said, shaking her head. "I can't share those details with you." She sounded uncertain.

"I'm working with an attorney. Senora Rojas. I'm sure she can file the paperwork to make the request more formal, but it would really help me out if you can look it up now." She chewed on her lip for a moment. "I don't need personal information. I already have their names. I just need to know if they were here or not."

She looked at the list. "*Oui,*" she shrugged. Her long fingernails tapped against the keyboard. "Three-one-five—that boat is for sale. It's listed with a broker, and the owners live off-island. The next one is a rental. I have access to their Airbnb records." She typed again and then said, "It was unoccupied."

She looked up each boat, working in order on the list. I took notes as she called out the information. When she'd finished, only three boats remained. She confirmed that the owners had been around during the past few days. I circled those slip numbers.

"I can't tell you how to contact them. Just show up. Eventually, you'll catch them. They are here often."

I tried the three slips again before I texted Milena, *I narrowed the list to three options, but no luck yet. I'll try again tomorrow.*

Below my text to Milena were Luke's last two words, *Good day?* I let the screen go dark and wandered to the far end of the marina. I sat and dangled my legs over the edge.

I wanted to call him. But that was unfair. I'd asked for space. I couldn't use him to recover from our break-up.

"Hi," someone behind me said. Jimmy's voice.

"Hi, Tarzan," I answered. He sat next to me, his flip-flops dangling.

"Are you looking for Goti?" he asked. I shook my head. "Why are you here? Did you run out of volcanos to fall off of?"

"I was working. Trying to help my friend."

"How is she?" he asked.

"Fine, I guess. I didn't go see her today."

"And how are you helping her by sitting here?" He grinned.

"Do you know who Engel was?"

"The guy who died?" I nodded and waited for his answer. "Didn't know him. But rumor is he was a bad dude."

"I need to know more about him."

"To figure out who really killed him? That's how you're going to help her?"

A small fishing boat cruised past, leaving a v-shaped wake that rolled towards our dock.

"Yes," I answered. "That's a good plan, right?"

"That's a terrible plan, Anne. I mentioned that Engel was not a good dude, didn't I? So whoever killed him—assuming it wasn't your friend, is probably just as bad. Seems like a good way to get yourself killed, too. And that would piss me off. Because I worked really hard making sure you didn't die yesterday."

"But why would someone kill Engel? He was a drug dealer. Was it a turf war? Theft gone wrong? What?"

He shook his head and laughed. "You've been watching too much TV."

"Okay, why then?"

"Maybe there wasn't a reason. Maybe he was just in the wrong place at the wrong time."

"Doesn't seem likely. He was strangled. He was a big

guy, and that would have taken a lot of effort. If someone was just trying to get rid of him, why not just push him into the water? Seems like someone was angry at him."

"Whoa. Intense."

"Sorry," I mumbled. "I have no idea why I'm even telling you any of this."

"Because I asked," he said. "And we shared a life-changing experience yesterday. I saved your life. You trust me." He grinned again. "But figuring out who killed him seems like a job for the cops."

"Yeah, you're right." I stood, and he joined me. We walked back to the parking lot. "Anyway, thanks for the chat."

"Anytime," he said. "Most interesting conversation I've had in a while."

"Thanks, Tarzan."

"That name's not gonna stick, is it?" he called out after me.

#

I walked to my car and drove to the police station. After another forty-minute wait, I was escorted behind the locked gates.

Sandy slid into her plastic chair with a tired, worried expression. "Milena visited. Seems like I made the right choice."

I shrugged and sat across from her. "I paid the retainer. I assumed that's what the backpack was for."

"No, dummy. The backpack was an escape plan."

"For you?"

"No. For you. Someone set me up. I'm not sure if you're safe, so keep the backpack close."

"I lost it."

"What?" she shouted.

"*Just* the backpack. Not the contents."

"Jesus, Anne. You gave me a heart attack. As long as the you-know-what is safe."

"In a bank."

She smiled. "I taught you well."

"Why didn't you tell me about the dialysis?"

"How'd you find out?" she asked.

"So you *were* trying to hide it."

"I found out during those last few days in the hospital. When you disappeared." She paused. "It's no big deal. As long as I run the machine every night, I'm fine. Really."

"For how long?"

She shrugged. "Forever. Until it doesn't work anymore, at least."

"Why didn't you want me to know?"

"Because, I figured you'd want to give me a kidney or something, and I can't take anything else away from you. I've only ever wanted to give you something back, but I keep messing things up."

"How do you even know I'm a match?"

She laughed softly, but it broke the tension. "You are in every other way," she said. When I didn't say anything, she said, "You seem…different today. Weird." I ignored her, and she stared at me for a long minute. "What happened?"

I sighed. "I broke up with Luke," I told her. "And then I kissed Ari, the guy who arrested you."

Her hand moved to cover her mouth as her jaw dropped, and then she laughed.

"Go, Anne! I think you should visit all the islands. Every time you arrive at a new one, you jump into bed with the first guy—"

I cut her off. "I didn't…Look. Do you need anything? If you don't, I'll just go."

"No," she pleaded. "Please don't go. I won't laugh. I'm not making fun of you. I'm just surprised. I thought Luke was…I don't know. The One. Or whatever. Please tell me about it. I'm stuck in here, and it's boring. I *need* your stories."

"You promise not to make fun of me?"

"Promise. I'm so impressed by you right now. This is a whole different Anne in front of me. And I like it."

"I'm the same boring Anne underneath. I just lost my mind for a minute. I'm not sure what happened with Ari. He was just there when I needed someone."

She sat quietly, but her body buzzed with anticipation.

I told her about the hike. I tried to describe what I felt on the cliff with Sofia, but I tripped over the words. She clapped when I described sliding down the vines.

"Was it just the adrenaline? Or did you think he was hot the first time you met him? You have a thing for cops, don't you?"

I shrugged.

"You did think he was hot!"

"He's good-looking, I guess. I'm not sure I thought about it when I first met him, though. I was in shock. But he looks good in a suit, and the French accent is…"

She asked about Luke, and when I ran out of ways to avoid answering, I stood up. "I gotta go. I'll visit again, but I can't come every day. My priority has to be helping the attorney build your case." I paused. "There's nothing more about Engel, is there? Something you haven't told me that could help?"

She bit her lip, and I sat back down.

"I knew him," she said. "I partied with him a couple of times. He liked me. But nothing ever happened between us. I wasn't interested. But sometimes, he followed me."

"Did you see him that day? The day he died?"

She shook her head. "Sometimes he'd show up when I moored. He always seemed to know when I arrived."

"He was stalking you?" I asked.

"Not exactly. He was interested and wasn't the kind of guy who takes no for an answer. He thought he was a bigshot."

"Who do you think killed him?"

"I don't know!" The officer glared from the hallway, and she leaned closer and lowered her voice, "I really have no idea."

"We need to figure it out. It might be the only way to get you out of here."

"Goti knows everybody. He can help you."

I nodded and stood to leave. "You okay? You need anything?"

She shook her head.

CHAPTER 13

The next morning, I swam before I visited the boats in the marina again. No one appeared, so I ordered Vietnamese noodles and returned to my room. In the hotel office, I borrowed a roll of tape from Apolline, and I used the wall in my room the way I'd seen a team of detectives use the whiteboard in the police station's conference room. At the center, I taped a page with *Engel* written in all caps. Three other pages read, *Sandy's dock line, the dock box,* and *drugs.* I added the missing pieces: *Motive? Opportunity?*

But all I did was stare at the pages. Putting them on the wall hadn't helped.

Late afternoon, I visited the marina again, but the three boats were still empty. On the way back to the motel, I passed Goti and waved.

"*Bonjour,*" he called out.

"*Bonjour,*" I answered.

"How is the attorney?" he asked. I shrugged. "Sandy is a local hero. Nobody is really sorry that Engel died."

"Because he was a drug dealer?"

He glanced over his shoulder and whispered loudly, "Where did you hear that?"

"The cops, actually. You knew him well?" I asked.

He took a step closer. "Be careful about what you say about Engel."

I wanted to point out that Engel wasn't a threat any longer, but Goti motioned for me to follow him through the parking lot and behind a group of sago palms. The palms weren't tall enough to hide us, and I hesitated. When he insisted, I followed. He didn't speak until I settled on a narrow stump next to him.

"Engel was like a lot of Europeans that move here. He came on vacation, but he couldn't leave, you know. He loved the island life. He was a dealer back in Germany. Small time, but when he got here, he got into the club scene, selling weed, or E. Never anything hard. Two years ago, he got into something…bigger. He built a network to service the tourists."

He peered through the palm trees before he continued.

"I know everything about this island, but I don't know how he moved his product. I know his guys. They aren't smart, but they never get caught. Someone trained them."

"But you don't know who."

He leaned in, and his exaggerated whisper made me want to giggle. "Nobody knows. And don't go looking for that answer because it will get you killed, just like Engel."

I shifted on the stump. It was difficult to take him seriously while hiding behind a group of trees that didn't prevent anyone from overhearing our conversation. But I could see through the trees. No one was within earshot.

"If Engel's gone, who's taking over for him?"

"Smart question. Also a dangerous question." He shook his head. "Even if I knew the answer, I wouldn't tell you. You're here to help Sandy, and you can't do that if you're dead."

"Sandy said Engel liked her."

"Sandy was a disco ball—the sparkliest thing in every room, and Engel liked pretty things. He made a lot of money fast and liked spending it. He thought he could buy her. But she seemed to know what kind of guy he was and steered clear. Every time she returned to Guadeloupe, he'd find out and show up. He has spies everywhere."

"But he's gone."

"Someone took over his network," he answered. "Engel wasn't violent, but I wonder if he got tired of waiting for her." A wave of regret crossed his face. "Maybe that's why she killed him."

"She didn't kill him, Goti."

"No?"

"No, of course not. Someone's framing her, and I can figure out who if I know why. Was Sandy a convenient scapegoat, or did someone want her out of the way? Or maybe both." He squinted, but he didn't answer. "Do you know where the body was found?" I asked.

He hopped down from his stump. "Follow me."

I hurried after him, rubbing my backside. We walked through the marina, turning left, right, and left again. We walked parallel to the motel for a minute, and then Goti stopped and pointed to a dock box that was roped off with police tape.

" *Voila*," he said.

"Inside that?" I asked, and he nodded. "But it's nowhere near Sandy's boat." He didn't answer. "If she strangled him with one of her dock lines, she'd have done it near her boat. She couldn't have carried him all this way."

"Yes, she could." He looked around, spotted what he needed, and pointed. "See that cart? She could have gotten him inside and rolled him here."

"So, she killed him all the way over there," I pointed in the general direction of *The Second Chance*. "And then she lifted him into a cart, rolled him here, and lifted him out of the cart and into that dock box?"

He shrugged.

"Why? She had a boat. And it was nighttime. Why didn't she dump him at sea? And then leave the island? It doesn't make any sense."

He didn't answer.

"If she killed him here and threw him in the dock box just because he was too heavy to take him anywhere else, why was her dock line here? Did she bring it with her?"

He remained quiet. I scanned the dock and noticed *La Lune*—one of the boats on my list.

"Thanks for your help Goti," I said.

#

I returned to the motel room and stared at my notebook pages. The conversation with Goti had reinforced what I was missing. I tore out another page and added it to the wall with three more questions: *Why put Engel in a dock box? Why use Sandy's dock line? Why frame Sandy?*

There was a connection between the dock line and the reason to frame Sandy. Someone had either intentionally killed Engel to frame her, or the murder had been impulsive, and Sandy's dock line had already been there. But why? The answer seemed pivotal. If I could figure out why he'd been killed with Sandy's dock line, I could figure everything else out.

When the evening light turned the wall from mint-chip ice cream to split pea soup, I made toast and ate in bed, trying not to think about Luke. I left my phone on the desk, and it remained quiet.

#

In the morning, I was staring at the pages on the wall when a knock at the door startled me. "Housekeeping," the voice called.

"One minute," I said, straightening my clothes and smoothing my hair. The woman outside the door was short and almost as wide as she was tall.

She grinned and repeated, "Housekeeping?"

"Can you come back in about fifteen minutes?" I asked.

She shrugged. "*Oui.*"

I closed the door and showered, gathering my toiletries into a neat pile on the counter. I dressed in clean shorts and a tank top and shoved my dirty clothes into the plastic takeout bag from the previous day. I pulled two books from my backpack to make room for the remaining cash and slid my laptop inside.

I walked to the motel office. "Apolline?" I asked the empty front desk.

A girl emerged from a back office. "*Vous aidez?*" She asked. *Can I help you?*

"Do you have a laundry room?"

"No, but you can use the machines in the marina. I can give you a map to the office—"

"Thanks," I interrupted. "I know the way."

The perky blonde from the marina office unlocked the laundry room and propped the door open with a brick. She showed me how to use the machines and translated the French labels.

"Okay?" she asked after she'd done everything except load my dirty clothes into the machine.

"Yes, thank you."

Her ponytail swished as she left. I started the machine and sat down. My phone buzzed with a text from Wylda: *Thinking of you. Be safe.* I didn't know how to respond. She didn't know the history between me and Sandy, and I enjoyed how our conversations weren't tainted with the truth. Her giggle was one of the only good things in my life, and I didn't want my darkness to overshadow her delight. But that meant I had nothing to share with her.

There were still no texts from Luke.

I left the washing machine chug-chugging and walked to *La Lune*. A man stood on the deck, and I quickened my step.

"Hello!" I shouted.

He watched me approach. Even from a distance, I saw his forehead crease in annoyance. I smiled wide and waved.

"Can I ask you a few questions?"

He stood in the doorway, one arm raised against the metal frame, his body poised to walk inside and ignore me.

"Please? I'm just trying to help a friend," I said. His expression softened. He nodded and relaxed, but he stayed in the doorway. I didn't want to board the boat without an invitation, but the wide deck separated us. I hopped onto the swim step so I didn't have to shout.

"There was an incident here in the marina. A man died. Were you here that night?"

"Yes, I heard. He was a friend of yours?"

I shook my head. "I didn't know him. Did you? Johan Engel?"

"Engel?" he repeated. "Everyone knew who he was. I didn't realize…" His voice trailed off, and he stared into the distance. He wore a lavender golf shirt, unzipped at the neck to reveal a thick silver chain and curly black hair. He took a step towards me and leaned against the rail. The boat rocked under his weight, and my hand shot out to maintain my balance. I stepped back to the concrete dock. One side of his mouth lifted in a subtle smile.

"You're not a boat person?" He studied my face, and I tried to remain expressionless. Milena had coached me not to offer information. I was supposed to ask five simple questions, but I wasn't following the script. "I saw him on Wednesday night. I remember because I'd come down to check on the lines after Tuesday's storm. I had a late tee-time that day and didn't arrive until after dark."

I stayed quiet, watching him remember.

"He wasn't alone. Another man was there. Over there." He pointed across my left shoulder. "There was a Beneteau in that empty slip. I've never seen it before. Can't remember the name. Maybe a forty-footer? Shorter than the slip. Didn't quite fill it."

"Did you recognize the other man?" I asked. Still off script.

He shook his head. "He was shorter. Dark skinned. Wide like a barrel. Bushy beard. They were arguing. Loudly.

The other man shouted *finis*, but I don't remember the rest. I wasn't paying attention. I was already late getting home, so I was in a hurry."

"Do you know what time that was?"

"I arrived at half past six and was here about twenty minutes. I can check. My wife called me." He pulled his phone from his pocket. "Here it is. Six-fifty-three. I told her I was just leaving, and I locked the door and left."

"Thanks," I said.

"When I walked past, the smaller man hit Engel. That surprised me. Engel was the kind of guy you avoided. Dangerous. Not aggressive, but not very smart. It's easy to get on the wrong side of someone like that. Someone with the balls to confront Engel…I didn't stick around to watch. I went home."

"Can I ask your name?"

"Remy Castillon," he said.

"Have you spoken to the police?"

"No. I hadn't realized I had anything to tell them. I've been away."

"You'll want to speak with Detective Fournier." He nodded. "Is there anything else that might be helpful?"

He thought for a moment and then said, "I don't think so. How do I get in touch if I think of anything else?"

I gave him my cell number. "Thank you for your time," I said. And then I hurried back to the laundry room.

Chapter 14

Within the privacy of the humid room, I dialed Milena's cell.

"I found a witness. One of the boats you asked me to check out. The boat name is *La Lune*. The owner is Remy Castillon. He was there that night. He saw Engel arguing with someone."

"Slow down. Let me get something to write with," she said.

I told her everything I'd learned.

"When will you be here?" she asked.

"I'm in the marina doing laundry. I can't leave until it's done. I might be there in…an hour?"

"Okay, see you then." She hung up.

I called Ari and related the highlights to his voicemail.

Finding a witness felt like a turning point in the case—a way to prove that someone else had been in the marina fighting with Engel. The heat in the laundry room drove me outside, and I paced the walkway.

An hour passed slowly before Ari returned my call.

"How are you?" he asked.

"I'm fine," I answered quickly. "Look, we don't have to talk about what happened the other night. Just forget it. Did you get my message?"

"Yes, of course. Remy already called. He's going to stop by the station tomorrow and make a full statement."

"That's great," I said.

"I appreciate you informing me, but you need to stay out of this. It's not safe."

I bristled. "If I hadn't gotten involved, would you even have a lead right now?" I walked as I talked, stomping along the dock. "I got the impression you didn't really believe Sandy was guilty, but you're not actually doing anything to find out who killed Engel, are you?"

I stopped talking to catch my breath.

"Let's meet later and talk. Okay?"

"I don't have time. I have to meet with Sandy's attorney. Just do me a favor and follow up on Remy's statement. Someone else was with Engel that night—someone that probably killed him. You have to find him."

"I'll follow up on it. I promise."

"Thanks," I spat into the phone and hung up on him.

My excitement about finding a lead had quickly been replaced with restless anger. I marched through the marina until I ran out of dock.

#

I folded my dry clothes and returned to the motel. As I passed the office, I waved to Apolline through the window but slowed as I reached my room. My door was open—not wide open, but the door wasn't latched.

Housekeeping? Perhaps she was still inside, cleaning. Or perhaps she'd simply walked away without ensuring the door latched properly. Then, I saw chipped paint and wood splinters on the ground. Someone had broken into my room. I was still three doors away, frozen in place. A doorknob rattled, startling me. A man's face appeared in the nearest doorway, and I turned and ran back to the office.

"Apolline!" I shouted from the doorway. "Someone broke into my room."

Her face registered shock only for an instant, and then she picked up her phone.

"Ari," she spoke with a commanding voice in French, too quickly for me to understand. She hung up and pocketed her phone. "Show me."

I followed her. She walked with purpose, unafraid, and I jogged to keep up. When she saw the splintered frame, she frowned. "When did this happen?"

"Just now. I was only gone for two hours—maybe less. I went to the marina to do laundry."

"We'll wait in the office," she said. We walked back to the office, but she kept glancing over her shoulder as if she expected someone to burst from the room. She made coffee, and we sat silently, waiting.

Ari arrived with two uniformed officers. Apolline and I waited outside, but I could see the damage as they entered. The bed was stripped, the bedding piled in the corner. The seat cushion on the armchair had been removed and sliced. Stuffing jutted out, spilling across the floor. Cupboards were open, their contents scattered. Shards of ceramic plate lay amidst the pots and pans. The two mugs sat upright and intact in the middle of the mess.

Ari gestured for me to enter the room. "Can you tell us what is missing?"

The tattered remains of my suitcase lay on the far side of the bed. My clothes were scattered across the floor. I bent to pick up a pair of shorts, but Ari barked, "Leave it."

I retreated outside.

"Was anything taken?" he asked.

"I'm not sure. I don't think so."

He pointed to the wall where I'd taped my notebook pages—my lame attempt to solve Sandy's case on my own. The pages had been torn, but some of the tape had stuck to the wall. Tiny white pieces of paper were all that remained of my research. "What was on this wall?" he asked.

I shrugged and turned away. "Housekeeping arrived," I told Apolline. She frowned again, and I explained. "My trash is gone, and it smells better. Like bleach."

"Where were you?" Ari asked.

"I was doing laundry in the marina. Has this happened before?" I asked.

Apolline's brow knit tightly. "Never."

"Do you know what they were after?" Ari asked. His eyes darted between me and the bits of tape on the wall.

"No idea," I said. But there were only two options: they were after the money, or someone wanted to know how much I knew. The notebook pages had all been removed. They weren't ripped up and thrown on the floor. They were gone. "Can I take anything from the bathroom?"

"No, I'm sorry."

"You'll have to find another hotel," Apolline said. She and Ari exchanged a glance, and I thought he was about to argue.

"I don't want to stay here," I said. "I have another place. I'll be fine."

I texted Milena, *Can I stay at the villa?* Her immediate response was, *Of course* with another emoji of clapping hands.

"Can I go?" I called out to Ari. He appeared in the doorway and glared. I held his gaze until Apolline stepped in front of him. She patted my shoulder as she passed. When I looked back at Ari, he was still staring. Apolline's sandals slapped against her wide feet. When the sound faded, Ari's shoulders dropped, and he said, "I'm sorry."

"About losing my toothbrush?"

He smiled and stepped from the room but stayed more than an arm's length away. He needed distance.

"About the other night," he began. "It was a lovely night, but it was a mistake. I can't get involved with you."

"I'm not looking for a repeat," I said.

"Thank you for understanding."

I backed away, and he followed me to my car. When the path narrowed, he walked behind me, as if afraid of an accidental touch. He held the car door as I slid inside.

"You have somewhere safe to go?" he asked. I nodded. "Stay in touch. Stop investigating. Act like any other tourist. Just enjoy the island."

"Okay," I lied.

He closed the door and watched me drive away.

He knew I was avoiding his questions. He'd been in the room enough times to know the tape hadn't been there before. If he asked Apolline about it, she'd tell him I'd borrowed the tape yesterday. His words, *stop investigating* meant he knew I'd been working on Sandy's case, so why hadn't he pressed me for more details? Because he was embarrassed about the kiss? Or was he upset I'd found a potential witness before he did?

They'd taken my notes. Was there a connection between the break-in and my conversation with Remy Castillon? Was I being watched? Two people knew where I was staying: Ari and Milena. I hadn't even told Goti my room number. Whoever broke in was following me.

My tires screeched as I turned too sharply into the parking lot of a market. I needed a toothbrush. I'd lost all my toiletries: the fancy lavender shampoo from Wylda, my hairbrush, and my favorite lip gloss.

I wandered the aisles, selecting a toothbrush and toothpaste, and yanking a white tank top with Guadeloupe scrawled at the base of a crooked palm tree. If Ari didn't return the rest of my clothes, I'd run out in three days. At the end of the wine aisle, I paused at a display of cheap rubber flip-flops. I only had one pair of shoes—well-worn leather sandals. I needed a different store—one with decent footwear. I couldn't run in sandals.

#

When I arrived at the villa, Milena's reaction to the news of the break-in was to feed me. She pushed me into a chair at the kitchen table and presented a steaming plate of rice and black beans.

"You shouldn't be on your own," she said. "You could have been hurt. Or worse." I bristled, but I took a bite of beans. They were seasoned with too much lime and pepper, and I coughed until Milena handed me a glass of water.

"Great work at the marina—finding a witness," she said.

I nodded. "Detective Fournier said he's already been in touch. He will make a formal statement."

She frowned. "That's not how we do things. We don't share information with the police." She reached across the table and patted my hand. "But maybe you did the right thing."

I ate a few bites of rice before I confessed that I wasn't hungry and pushed the plate away. Milena cleaned the dishes, and then we toured the rooms downstairs. My bedroom was a small cell with a twin bed and a nightside, but the single window offered a view of the ocean in the distance.

"I can get you an extra blanket if you need it," Milena said. "Sidero sleeps upstairs, and she runs the air conditioning all night. It's freezing down here. Take this," she handed me a shawl, and I wrapped it around my shoulders. It was soft—perhaps cashmere and felt warm against my chilled skin.

Milena returned to the dining room to work, and I escaped outside. A steep, concrete staircase led below the house. Tall beams supported a wide deck off the living room that shaded a forest of ferns. I descended until I reached a terrace with a sunny wooden platform. A rainbow of colored ceramic pots was a whimsical contrast to the anemic interior of the house. Several green-gray succulents had grown too large for their containers and had collapsed and rooted between the wooden slats.

Farther down the hill, a sandy path led to a gazebo— grayed and splintered with age. A bench ran along the perimeter. I stepped inside cautiously, testing the strength of the floorboards, and peered over the railing. The hillside was vertical—a twenty-foot drop before it leveled into a copse of cannas. I settled on the bench. Trees on either side of the gazebo framed the silvery sea, and I thought of Luke.

The first evening after he built my gazebo, we ate dinner there, sitting on the wooden platform with our plates in our laps.

"What do you think?" he'd asked.

"I love it," I told him. And I had. It meant so much to me. He'd built it as a refuge—an attempt to pull me away from the cliff's edge. The gazebo was his way of supporting me. He knew I was working through something and wanted to give me a safe place to accomplish it.

"What do you want in here?" he'd asked.

"One comfy chair," I'd answered.

He hadn't been able to hide his pain. He'd expected me to invite him to share the space. He'd offered it as a way for me to open up. I'd known what he was asking and given him a selfish answer.

The gazebo should have been the thing that brought us closer together. I loved him more for building it. My heart ached with the knowledge that someone cared that much for me. But instead of thanking him, I'd used his offering as another means of pushing him away. The gazebo became our breaking point.

CHAPTER 15

An hour later, I climbed the stairs and returned inside. I wandered through the house and walked out onto the back deck. The gazebo seemed far away—a warm refuge from the coldness of the house.

My phone rang, and Wylda's wide smile appeared on the screen. I remembered the day I'd taken the picture. Her green eyes had twinkled in the sunlight, and I'd wanted to capture her laughter and carry it in my pocket.

"Hey," I answered her call.

"*Cherie*, what's wrong?"

I hesitated and imagined her wrapping her arms around me, pulling me into a warm hug. I thought of her softness, the way her body yielded, and the way she always smelled of the salon: a combination of lavender shampoo and Barbicide.

"Someone broke into my hotel room today," I said.

She gasped, "Are you okay?"

"I'm fine. I wasn't there, and they didn't take anything. The worst part was everyone's reaction. I could tell that sort of thing doesn't happen there, which means I was targeted. Someone wants me to go home."

"Because of Sandy?"

"Yes."

"Are you coming home?"

"What home? I sold my house. I gave up my entire life for Luke. But we don't fit together. I can't go back there. I don't have anywhere to go."

She let out a long "Oh," that caught at the back of her throat and erupted in a warm purr. "Anne. You have friends here. You can stay with me. But I don't think you should. I think you need to talk to Luke. *Talk* to him. You hold everything inside. That's not fair to him. And it's not fair to you either."

I twirled the fringe of the shawl as she spoke.

"*Cherie*, you don't have to carry everything alone. Luke loves you. I see the way he looks at you. He treats you as if you're a fragile thing." She let out another long sigh. "*Moi aussi.* But you're not fragile. If you and Luke are going to work, you have to talk—to share everything with him. Stop holding onto whatever it is. He can handle it. And with his help, you'll be able to work through it. He helped you before, *oui?* Why don't you trust him?"

"It's not that I don't trust him. I promised Sandy I'd keep her secret."

"Does Sandy understand the cost of her secret?"

"I don't know," I mumbled.

"Sandy would do anything for you. I think you're blaming it on her, but you're the one holding back, pulling away from Luke because you're afraid of letting someone love you."

I nodded.

Her voice softened. "*Talk* to Luke."

"Okay," I said.

"Call me every day. I want to know that you're safe."

"Okay," I repeated.

Scuffling feet rounded the corner, and Sidero appeared.

"That sounded dramatic," she said.

She wore a long sweater with a wide neck that hung from one shoulder. Just below the hem, white linen shorts ended near the top of her brown thighs. The sweater draped across her body, and I resisted the urge to reach out and touch the fabric.

"That was my friend," I said.

"Sounds like she did all the talking. Who is Luke?"

"My boyfriend—ex-boyfriend, I mean."

One of her eyebrows raised. "Recently?"

"Yes, a few days ago."

"What was her advice?"

"To talk to him. There are things I haven't told him."

Sidero chuckled. "I'm not sure I agree. We all need to have our secrets, don't we? But maybe your friend is right. He's important to you, this Luke?"

I didn't answer.

"I think yes," she mused. "You should listen to her. Go back to Saint Martin. Spend time with him. Don't worry about the case. We've got things in hand. We can manage without you."

She was right. I'd hired her. I should trust her to do the job. I should return to Luke, tell him the truth, and try to work things out. But I'd made a promise to Sandy. Despite my complicated feelings, I owed it to her—or to myself. To follow through.

"No," I said. "I have to stay."

"She must be a very good friend to deserve so much from you." I was quiet again. "Come back inside, Anne.

Join me for a drink." I followed her into the living room. She patted the couch beside her. "Sit." I hesitated, staring at the pristine white leather, and she laughed. "Sit!"

I sank into the cold leather and drew the shawl tighter around my shoulders. Milena brought two glasses of red wine and handed me one. Sidero motioned for her to sit with a slight nod, and Milena obeyed and sat across from us. She perched on the edge of the other sofa.

"It's really awkward to drink red wine in this room," I said.

One side of Milena's mouth lifted in a shy smile, and she nodded.

"Milena is single too," Sidero said. "For how long now?"

A dark look crossed Milena's face as she answered, "Two years."

Sidero didn't seem to notice Milena's discomfort. "I'm single for the moment. Until Izzy returns. We're three single ladies. *Salud!*" She raised her glass too quickly. I held my breath as wine sloshed, but it stayed inside the glass. I clinked my glass against hers in a careful toast. Milena raised her glass to the air between us.

"What's next?" I asked.

Sidero waved with her free hand. "No. No work tonight. Just single ladies having a glass of wine. Or two." Her words were slurred, and I wondered how many glasses she'd already had. It was late afternoon—a little early to be drunk. "Tell us about your Luke," Sidero said.

I described the first time Luke took me fishing— when I'd caught the biggest fish I'd ever seen.

"My arms were sore for days afterward." I paused, remembering how I'd collapsed on the deck with Sandy's letter of confession. I gulped wine to clear the lump in my throat.

Milena rescued me. "I used to fish in the river but never caught anything like that. Did you eat it?" she asked.

I nodded. "It was the best thing I've ever tasted."

Milena refilled our glasses.

Sidero scowled. "I would have thrown it back in and gone to a restaurant. I don't like to get my hands dirty anymore."

"I thought I'd hate that part, but it would have been irresponsible to catch a fish and let someone else clean it. I wanted to respect the fish."

They both laughed at that.

"Respect the fish," Sidero echoed.

"That was the day I fell in love with Luke. It was hard work, reeling and reeling, and my arms ached. I asked him to help me, but he told me I could handle it. He believed in me."

"He sounds dreamy," Milena said.

"Yeah," I agreed. He was dreamy. Tall and tan, he was often shirtless and sandy. Always sweaty. He never stopped moving. He worked all day, sometimes leaving a job site early to join a game of beach volleyball. He'd arrive home with the shopping and cook dinner. Some nights after we ate, we'd take the kayaks out and bob in the waves under the sunset.

Every morning, he slid from bed in the darkness and went for a run. When we moved in, I worried about him for the first month of morning runs. The road was narrow and shoulder-less, and he ran in the darkness. But he returned every morning, and my uneasiness subsided.

During that first month, he'd wrap his sweaty arms around me when he returned, forcing me to join him in the shower, and I began every day with a honeymoon glow. Hopeful. Until the glow faded.

"You miss him?" Milena asked.

"I do. He was always happy and interested in everything. It got annoying sometimes, you know? It was like living with a puppy that follows you everywhere and wants to play all the time. Before him, my life was dull and quiet, and I liked his energy. He kept me busy."

"Being alone in that hotel room must have been lonely," Milena said.

"Actually, it was nice being alone," I said. "I lived alone for so long before Luke, and I think I missed it. Maybe the transition to living with him was too abrupt. Maybe I needed to ease into it."

Milena shrugged. "Sometimes things just don't work out. Maybe the timing was bad."

"What happened with your boyfriend?" I asked.

She shrugged. "I traveled too much." She stood and walked to the kitchen, calling out, "Be right back," over her shoulder. I heard anger in her voice—her job had caused the breakup.

Sidero leaned toward me, yawning as she said, "He wasn't right for her." Her musky scent of leather and patchouli mixed with the red wine. Her head rested against my shoulder, and she whispered, "Maybe Luke isn't right for you either. Plenty of fish in the sea." Her hot breath tickled the tiny hairs on my neck. "Respect the fish," she said, quivering as she chuckled.

Milena returned with a fresh bottle, but she rolled her eyes when she saw Sidero slumped against me. She set the bottle on the table and plucked the two empty ones.

In the doorway, she turned and said, "Come find me if you need anything, Anne."

"Thanks, Milena," I said.

Sidero raised a hand and gave her an elegant wave. "Tell me another story," she murmured. Her head rose, and she finished her glass, but she settled back into my arm and stretched her legs onto the sofa.

"About what?" I asked.

"Anything. Just talk. I like listening to you. You're so *American*. Tell me about how you met Sandy."

"It was an accident. We'd both stopped to taste honey at a farmer's market stall. Sandy spilled honey on me."

"Honey. Is that your secret?" she asked.

"Sorry?"

"It's the reason you're so sweet."

I rolled my eyes. "It's too chilly in here," I said. "I'm going outside."

She groaned with disapproval. I eased a white pillow under her head as I rose from the sofa. Her eyes remained closed, and she held out her empty glass. I took it and set it on the table.

"Good night," I said softly.

Her hand raised again, but her wave was limp and lifeless.

I filled my glass and exited through the front door. I descended the long staircase, stopping to sip wine. I tasted black cherry and vanilla and fresh-cut pine. The combination reminded me of the cherry cup cookies my mother used to bake for Christmas because of their festive dark red filling. Cherries weren't in season in December, so she used canned cherry filling. The cookies were too syrupy and sweet, but my mother loved them. She loved anything with cherries.

"I don't know why I don't make these year-round," she'd say. When fresh cherries were available in the summer, she'd make cherry pie or cobbler served with vanilla ice cream. My stomach grumbled. I wanted to drive down the hill and sample Bertie's buttery pecan pie again, but I'd had too much wine.

I dropped the shawl on the gazebo bench and peered at the ocean. The ripples were faint lines, moving in slow motion, too distant. I longed for my own gazebo, the one Luke built, where I could hear waves crashing against the rocks and taste the salt in the air.

I finished the wine but didn't want to risk waking Sidero, so I stayed on the bench, staring at the sea until the sun began to slip into the water, watching the horizon change from pink to orange.

When I finally stood, the hillside was black. I climbed the stairs, holding the railing in the darkness, but when the stairway ended on the garden terrace, I lost my handhold. I moved slowly, arm outstretched, until I reached the next set of steps. Light from the downstairs window flickered as something moved. I shuddered, thinking someone had been watching me.

In my room, I locked the door and climbed into bed.

Chapter 16

I emerged in the morning with a headache. Milena offered me coffee and a plate of *arepas* oozing with cheese, scrambled eggs, and spicy chorizo.

"You slept alone?" she asked with narrowed eyes.

"Of course," I answered.

"She can be…persuasive."

"I'm not—" I hesitated. "Maybe you have the wrong idea about me and Sandy," I said. "We're just friends."

"That wouldn't matter to her." Her voice was soft, and she didn't meet my gaze. "She hates being alone. Whenever Izzy leaves—" She shrugged. "It's always the new person, so I figured she'd try it on with you."

I shook my head. "I left her on the couch and went outside. She seemed…sleepy."

"Drunk, you mean."

I endured a long, awkward minute, and then I asked, "Has she tried it with you?"

She was turned away, rinsing a mug, and her shoulders tensed. She set the mug on a dishtowel but didn't turn around.

"She doesn't drink wine often," she said. "Normally, it's tequila. She can drink tequila like water. Wine makes her hungover. That's why she went to the boat early this morning. She's detoxing in the sauna."

She stared out the window. Another quiet moment passed as she collected my plate and scraped the uneaten food into the bin. "It's my day off," she said in a forced-perky voice, "Are you busy? You don't have to, but do you want to do something with me?"

I watched her stack the remaining plates into the dishwasher. I wanted to pry, to rephrase my question about Sidero's advances, but Milena seemed shy—like a turtle ready to withdraw.

"I don't have plans today," I said.

"If you want to hang out," she began. She whirled and looked me in the eye. "We could go to the zoo." She grinned.

I laughed, "The zoo?"

"No, no. We don't have to," she said. She turned back to the sink and wiped the counter with a cloth. Her shoulders dropped. "That's too weird, right? Maybe something else."

"Milena," I said. "Do you want to go to the zoo?"

"Okay, yes," she said, facing me again. "I *really* want to go to the zoo."

I smiled. "Let's do it. Let's go to the zoo. It can't be any stranger than anything else I've done since I got here."

Milena squealed. "I'll be ready in ten minutes."

I finished my coffee and returned downstairs to change. My backpack sat on the floor, slumped against the wall. I withdrew my laptop and tossed it on the bed, but I left the money inside. A hundred and fifty-thousand dollars wasn't heavy, but it bulged against the thin nylon fabric. I regretted not depositing the rest in the bank.

"Anne?" Milena called from the hallway. "Ready?"

I pulled on the backpack and answered, "Coming."

In the driveway, a man in a long-sleeved shirt paced. His bald head glistened. I remembered Remy's description of the man who'd argued with Engel: barrel-chested with a black beard. The man raised his head in a short nod.

Milena whispered, "He's new. Sidero increased security this morning because of your break-in."

"Is she worried it could happen again?" I asked.

She gripped my forearm and pulled me to the car. When we were inside, she said, "I shouldn't have said that. It's not because of you. Sometimes, when Sidero rents a villa, she hires extra security. She feels safer on the boat."

"Safe from what?" I asked.

She ignored me and fumbled with her seatbelt, and I started the Dacia and pulled away from the villa.

"I've been to the zoo in Martinique and the one in Caracas. What about you?" she asked.

"I went to the Miami zoo when I was a kid, but that's it. What's your deal with zoos?"

"I wanted to be a veterinarian," she answered. "Or do something with animals."

"What happened?"

"My father wanted me to be an attorney. He paid for law school."

"Was your father also an attorney?"

"No," she snorted, surprised by my question. "My family are…farmers. I was lucky to go to university. My father worked his entire life to save enough money."

"It's hard to argue with his decision if he's paying for it."

"Exactly. So, I became an attorney. Better than being a farmer."

"You could change your mind, though, right? Go back to school?"

She shook her head. "I work for Sidero now." Her tone carried a curious finality.

"But not forever," I said.

She stared out the passenger window for a few minutes, and I wondered if she was admiring the view of the mountains on either side of the road or if I'd said something wrong. I was still curious about her relationship with Sidero but needed a more delicate approach. Perhaps she'd relax inside the zoo, and I'd find an opening.

"What animals do they have here?" I asked.

"Panthers," she answered. Her voice was flatter, deflated.

"What kinds of animals are you interested in?"

She turned back to face me. "I don't know," she said. "All of them, I guess."

"If you worked in a zoo, which animal would you most like to take care of?"

I could feel her excitement renew. "I always enjoyed taking care of our animals. My mother would get upset with me for bringing home creatures. I found a wounded capybara once and hid it in the barn. And a sloth and several monkeys. My mom always found them and made me release them.

"I saw an elephant once. In the Caracas Zoo. Someone was cleaning the cage, and the elephant kept touching him. It was so gentle but playful. I wanted to be the guy in that cage. I wanted my own elephant."

"Well, you'd have to work in a zoo to have your own elephant. I doubt they make good pets."

She laughed and turned back to her window, but this time, she leaned forward with anticipation as I pulled into the zoo's parking lot.

Milena insisted on paying my admission, almost skipping through the gate. Inside, a canopy of trees sheltered us from the heat. Ferns on either side of the path threatened to reclaim the space. Small enclosures for the animals had been carved out of the jungle.

We passed raccoons, red pandas, and monkeys. Milena's excitement was contagious. We stayed in the lemur house for a while, laughing and pointing.

"So many of them remind me of my family," she said.

"Their little shocked faces are so cute," I said. "They have so much personality. That one," I pointed to the far corner. "He's quite vain, isn't he?" The lemur sat apart from the rest, cleaning his fur and watching his reflection in the glass. "And that one," I pointed to the other side of their cage, "He's a bully."

Milena shook her head. "That one's a she."

"How do you know?"

"Because they have female-dominated societies, and she's clearly in charge."

"Good for them," I said.

"Not sure that's any better," she said softly. But she noticed my raised eyebrows and continued, "My father was…overbearing. When I left home, I thought I wanted something different. But now I work for Sidero. She's the boss. It's different. But it's not better."

"Milena, when I asked you about Sidero earlier, you never answered my question."

Her face clouded over for a moment, but she recovered quickly and pulled my arm. "Come on!"

I hadn't misunderstood her reaction. She didn't want to talk about it.

We exited the lemur house and continued along the concrete path. "The next part is supposed to be amazing!" she shouted.

I ran to keep up with her, and we stopped at the base of a wooden staircase.

"Are you afraid of heights?" she asked. I shook my head. "I read about this online."

We climbed to the top and reached a platform built between two trees—like a treehouse. A rope bridge stretched to a platform in the distance. She peered below and grinned.

"We're going to cross that?" I asked.

Three teenage girls stomped up the steps behind us and crossed the bridge at a trot. The ropes wobbled, and the girls giggled and shrieked with delight.

"C'mon!" Milena shouted. She stepped onto the narrow slats of wood.

I followed. As Milena moved, the bridge bounced underfoot, and I hesitated and clung to the thick wire support.

"Just don't look down," she called out.

I hadn't been looking down, but as soon as she told me not to, I couldn't resist peering over the ropes. The concrete path had disappeared, replaced by a carpet of impenetrable jungle—a solid layer of treetops just below the bridge. Above me, the towering kapok and rubber trees formed a lacy canopy. The bridge spanned the space between.

To my right, a huge coconut palm blocked the view. It was lopsided—one side had been cut away to make room for the bridge. Milena landed on the tower on the far side, and I placed one foot in front of the other, letting go of the wire only long enough to reset my grip. The ropes swayed as I walked. At the halfway point, when I'd passed the coconut palm, the view cleared, and I stopped again and stared into the trees.

I saw another bridge far in the distance—much higher than where I stood. I watched a person move across—too far away to know whether it was a man or a woman. The bridge crossed above the highest trees. From my vantage point, the person appeared to be walking in the sky.

"Coming!" I called out. I sped up, my steps more confident, my hands steadier. I wanted to go to the bridge in the sky. I needed to see *that* view.

"You okay?" Milena asked as I stepped onto the solid wooden surface and let out a long breath.

"Yeah. Let's keep going."

The ropes led us away from the highest bridge, and I lost sight of it. We paused on the towers to let others pass and peered below to view animal enclosures. Palm trunks emerged from cannas and banana leaves and stretched high overhead, exploding into fronds shaped like giant fans or peacock feathers. But the majestic palms were dwarfed compared to the rubber trees. Vines snaked down the thick, odd-shaped trunks and hung from unseen branches.

Finally, we climbed two narrow flights of stairs and emerged onto a shaky tower in the treetops. A hot wind blew hair across my face. I froze, unable to let go of the railing with either hand and squinted into the sun, allowing the wind to push my hair from my eyes. The wind gusted again, and Milena shrieked and grabbed my forearm. Her small hand was strong, and I winced as her thumb squeezed a bruise.

"Do you think it's safe?" she asked.

"Why are you asking me? This was your idea!" I shouted over the wind.

I peered down at the framework of the tower and counted five sections of crisscrossed wooden supports nailed into each of the four sides before the tower disappeared into the jungle below. The gaps in the diagonal planks of the platform were wide enough to see open air below. I kept my phone in my pocket, worried that it would slip through a crack and disappear into the jungle.

Milena flashed a nervous smile and let go of my arm. "You go first," she said.

I nodded and stepped around her, gripping the railing on the other side, and stopped at the bridge. The ropes wiggled in my hand, and I took a deep breath and waited for a fresh dizzy spell to subside.

I stepped onto the shaky wood plank. The bridge swayed, and my stomach lurched. I took another step. And another. I found a rhythm—like riding a wave. Step. Sway. Step. Sway. It was terrifying. And thrilling.

When the bridge trembled out of tempo, my knees wobbled. I glanced over my shoulder to see Milena swaying on the first step, her eyes squeezed shut.

"Wait 'til I get to the middle!" I shouted.

She nodded, and I continued, but the rhythm seemed impaired by her presence on the planks. I glanced over my shoulder several times, worried that someone would bounce onto the bridge behind me or that Milena would move.

When I reached the mid-point, I called, "Your turn!" and held on while the bridge bounced underfoot. She screamed several times as she crossed, and then she was next to me.

"Wow," she said, her voice barely audible above the wind.

"I've never seen so many trees," I answered. "I've been to the Everglades so many times. I thought that was a forest, but this—it's just solid trees as far as we can see."

She smiled, "For me, it's like home."

"Really?"

"Yes, where I'm from—it's very much like this."

"I thought you said your family were farmers?"

She nodded. "We must clear the trees."

"That's crazy. I can't imagine seeing such a forest," I let go of the rope long enough to gesture to the horizon, "and decide to start a farm."

She laughed, but it was half-hearted. "If the other decision is to starve…" Her voice trailed off. We stood in silence for a while.

"Milena, I know this might be uncomfortable to talk about. Is Sidero taking advantage of you?"

She shrugged.

"I'm not judging you. I just want you to know you can talk about it. If you need to."

Her face was expressionless.

"She's—" she began. She bit her lip, and I waited. "I'm Catholic. It's a sin."

"Because she's a woman?" I asked.

She nodded.

"I'm not Catholic," I said. "I don't agree that it's wrong."

She turned to look at me. "No?"

"Two consenting women—there's nothing wrong with that." I paused. "But it's wrong if you don't want her to do that."

"My body likes it," she whispered.

I let go of the rope and gently touched her shoulder. "Doesn't matter. It's still not okay for her to make you do that."

She nodded and chewed her lip again. I couldn't tell if she wanted to say more or was trying not to cry. I waited. I stood beside her, one hand on her shoulder as we swayed with the treetops.

"I'm okay," she finally said. "Let's climb down."

The concrete path felt strange underfoot. Our footsteps were heavy. We meandered the walkway, but after the thrilling heights and her emotional admission, the napping cats and slow-moving tortoise couldn't hold our attention.

The only animal we stopped to watch was the jaguar, TiMal. He paced at the edge of his enclosure, rubbing his solid body along the chain link. When the fence ended and he stepped into a patch of sunlight, he paused and lifted his massive head. His velvety coat shimmered. He'd appeared solid black, but the sunlight highlighted an intricate pattern of darker spots.

"That's why I wanted to come," Milena whispered. "To see him."

TiMal basked in the sunlight for a moment and then turned and continued a slow saunter, rubbing his other side against the fence. We watched him pace for several minutes, and when Milena finally moved away, I followed.

"He was worth the trip," I said.

In the parking lot, Milena suggested lunch. I agreed, relieved that she still felt comfortable with me. She directed me a few miles down the coast road to a seafood restaurant at the top of a hill that overlooked the beach in both directions. We settled into sun-bleached teak chairs on the back deck.

"I didn't know you were an attorney," I said. "When I met you, I assumed you were Sidero's assistant." Her brow furrowed, and I quickly asked, "How did you start working for her?"

She sighed and leaned on the table with both elbows. "My father could barely afford my school fees. I needed a job to pay for living expenses, so I worked as an assistant to a professor in the legal department at the university. I applied for jobs when I graduated, but…no offers came. One day, Sidero was at the university for a guest lecture, and she offered me a job."

She paused and stared at her clasped hands for a moment.

"I knew who Senora Rojas was—everyone in the department knew who she was. She won high-profile cases. It was a dream job. It felt like I'd skipped all the grunt work that comes with working in a big firm, but I should have known it was too good to be true. The only legal work I did was favors for her friends—insignificant things like real estate disputes and registering foreign corporations." She sat back and looked directly at me. "So, I suppose you're right. I am an assistant."

"But someone like her must have connections. Something that could lead to another job?" I asked.

She shook her head. "In the past two years, she's become more and more isolated. There haven't been any lectures. No big cases. We move around a lot—staying in a harbor for a week at a time at most. We're stuck in a loop, stopping at every island from here to Grenada. We never go farther north, and we never go farther south."

"You never go home?"

She shook her head again, but this time, she smiled. "It's different now. Your friend's case means we're staying in Guadeloupe. We settled into the villa, and I get to do actual legal work. It's exciting." She covered her mouth with both hands. "Sorry. That's insensitive."

"It's fine. I know what you mean. What do you think Sandy's chances are?" I asked. "You said having Remy's testimony would create reasonable doubt. Is it enough to get her out of jail?"

She shook her head. "They found DNA evidence."

"What? How?"

"Sorry. I shouldn't have mentioned it, but don't get discouraged. Sidero has a perfect record. Whatever her other faults…she will find a way to win the case. Whatever it takes."

Her last sentence was delivered under her breath. I considered asking what she'd meant, but our food arrived, and she switched the conversation back to the zoo.

"Thanks for coming with me," she began. "My favorite part was the lemurs. What about you?"

"The rope bridges," I answered. After a few more moments of silence, I said, "I can hear the passion in your voice when you talk about animals. Why don't you pursue it?"

"I can't leave Sidero."

Perhaps she made too much money to walk away. Perhaps her family in Venezuela depended on her earnings. Part of me wanted to respect her privacy. She was an adult. She could make her own decisions, but another part of me was angry—the part of me that Sandy had awakened.

Sandy wouldn't have remained silent. She would have pushed Milena until she got answers. The two women had similar backgrounds; they'd both escaped poverty for a chance of a better future. But that was the only thing they shared. Sandy hadn't endured abuse. She'd run away.

"I ran so fast, I was halfway to Silver Springs by the time the screen door slammed shut." Sandy's backwater-drawl returned when she talked about her childhood. "I left with the clothes on my back and enough bus fare for Miami."

Sandy's strength was what I most admired about her. For over a year, I never knew why we'd become friends so easily, but I understood once she'd shared her secrets. We were both broken. We knew grief and loss. Unlike Milena, Sandy's experiences hadn't weakened her. She was hardened. Unbreakable. She'd run away from home and never looked back. She'd experienced setbacks—she'd spent five years in prison. But she'd never stopped fighting.

Milena was different. She was fragile and resigned. If she'd once been a fighter, she'd used it all up. I wondered what had drained the life from her.

"Milena, why do you stay with her?" I asked. "Because you need the money? I have money. If I helped you, would you leave?"

She was quiet for a moment before she answered. "You don't have enough." I opened my mouth to argue, but she continued, "She'd find me. She'd kill me."

My jaw dropped. She stood and walked out of the restaurant. I paid for lunch and followed her to the car. Her arms were crossed. Her face was stoic, and she didn't meet my eye. She was done talking.

I drove back to the villa. In the driveway, I said, "I can't stay here."

She nodded. "I understand. Thanks for going with me today," she said. "Where will you go?"

"No idea. A hotel, maybe? Or a short-term rental. When I was in the marina office, I heard the girl talking about Airbnb rentals. I'll try there first. I'll text you when I figure it out."

I packed my things. She met me at the door and held it open. As I walked past her, I said, "I can help, Milena. Please think about it."

"Thanks," she said. "I wish I had a friend like you. Sandy's very lucky."

She closed the door.

Chapter 17

The same girl sat behind the desk in the marina office.

"Hi, I'm Anne," I told her. "I'm sorry, I haven't asked your name."

"I'm Claire."

"When I was here before, you mentioned rentals. You said that some people rented their boats out?"

"*Bien sure*," she said. "Are you looking for a place to stay?"

"Yes. I don't want to stay at the motel any longer. I need something today, if possible."

She turned to her computer screen and typed as she spoke. "Let's see what we can find for you. It's the off-season, so there should be something available."

She muttered in French as she searched the listings.

"Is it just you?" she asked.

"Yes," I answered.

"I don't have anything today. But you can leave me your details, and I'll call you if I find something."

I left my phone number and walked back to the car. I passed the short palms where Goti and I had spoken, and I perched on an uncomfortable stump and booked a hotel room on my phone.

The hotel was a sprawling resort. White buildings rose from a white sand beach that curved around a shallow, turquoise cove. A path snaked around pools filled with bloated tourists, thatched-roof tiki bars, and misting porticos. In my room, I dropped my belongings on the bed and opened the sliding glass door to a narrow balcony.

The poolside was a hive of activity. Watchful moms with brave toddlers sat on wide pool steps. A volleyball bounced over a net that stretched the width of the pool. A dozen heads bobbed on either side.

I left the bag of clothes on the bed and took my backpack with the money and my laptop. I paid cash in the hotel gift shop for an overpriced two-piece suit, a sarong with a pattern of fuchsia hibiscus, and a wide-brimmed straw hat. I stretched a towel across an empty lounge chair beside a woman hidden behind a paperback.

On a new notebook page, I wrote, *Why break-in? What were they after?* No one could have known about the notebook pages on my wall. They were looking for something else.

A man in a white polo shirt and crisp khaki shorts stopped next to my lounge chair and clapped. "You look too serious!" He cocked his head and giggled. "No working allowed by the pool. We're just about to start a new game of volleyball. Will you join us?"

"Uh," I said. "No, thanks."

"Okay. Well, I'll be back. I'll find an activity for you." He pointed at me and grinned. He moved on, and I heard him clapping as he found his next victim. I turned back to my notebook and wrote, *Money.*

Who knew about the money? Goti? Sandy trusted Goti, and she didn't easily trust anyone—not after what happened in Saint Martin. If he hadn't told anyone, perhaps someone had seen me at the bank. Or maybe the break-in had nothing to do with the cash. They'd ripped the notebook pages off the wall. Maybe the break-in was tied to Sandy's arrest.

There was another explanation—one I'd been ignoring. I shivered in the late afternoon heat. What if someone knew about the blackmail? If one of Sandy's blackmail victims had tracked her down, they'd be looking for more than a couple hundred-thousand dollars. They would be looking for revenge. But how would they have found her?

I pulled out my laptop and searched for news about Sandy's arrest. The story had appeared on a local news service the day after she'd been arrested. It was succinct—ten sentences about Engel's death and Sandy's arrest. The story had been copied onto several news sites. One enterprising blog included a picture of her. It was a headshot—perhaps downloaded from the pharmaceutical company's website where she'd worked.

She'd assured me the blackmail couldn't be traced back to her. But if she'd used her phone or been seen, someone could find her. And if they knew who she was, connecting me to her wouldn't have been difficult. I'd dropped her name enough times since I'd been in Guadeloupe—at Bertie's bar and at dinner with Ari.

Three children approached the couple next to me. They gathered their belongings and walked away. Two more families walked past, small children trotting along behind their parents.

"The buffet opens in ten minutes," said the woman to my right. "There's probably a line queuing up now."

She was fair and freckled and middle-aged. Her legs were tucked beneath a towel despite the large umbrella shading our chairs.

Two women stopped near her. The shorter one was pink and huffing—like she'd hurried across the sand, jogging to keep up with her tall, athletic friend who wore wide linen pants and a tight racerback tank-top that showed off enviable muscle tone. The woman in the chair completed the set—average height and weight. She looked like a stay-at-home mom who didn't enjoy tennis enough to compensate for a regular diet of fast food.

"C'mon," the shortest one wheezed. "We want to get a good table." She waddled along behind the tall one, turning several times to make sure the third woman was following.

The woman in the chair snapped her book shut and said, "Enjoy the quiet. This is my favorite time of day—when the kiddos head inside, and I can finally hear myself think." The chair groaned as she rose.

"Enjoy the buffet," I answered.

She grinned as if we shared a private joke about buffets.

A parade of families passed, hungry children, weary parents. When only a handful of people were left poolside, I stuffed my notebook into the backpack and headed to my room.

I couldn't brave the buffet alone. I ordered room service and waited ninety minutes for a dry roast beef sandwich and a limp salad while I flipped channels. The glass patio door barely muffled sounds from the pool deck. A second shift of splashing began, and voices from the crowded poolside bar bounced between the buildings as the sun set.

Sleep was elusive. Thundering footsteps rattled the mirror on the wall above my head, and muffled voices echoed along the hallway. Every time a door slammed, I sat upright. The hotel had seemed a safe haven, but I longed for silence.

#

In the morning, I grabbed a coffee and a chocolate muffin in the hotel lobby and headed to the police station.

"Hi," I said from the doorway.

"Jesus, Anne. Do you know how long it's been? Time moves so slowly in here."

A flush bloomed across my cheeks. I took a long breath, letting it out slowly, and glanced down the hallway. I wanted to retreat but couldn't get through two locked gates without an explanation.

I turned back to Sandy, not bothering to hide my anger. She sank into a chair and covered her mouth with her hand.

"How could you possibly be upset with me? After everything you've…" My voice trailed off.

Neither of us spoke. In the distance, I heard the metallic clang of a gate. A woman shouted in French. Footsteps receded. Sandy was trapped. In prison. In a foreign country.

"Sorry," I said.

"You're right," she answered. "You have every right to be mad."

"I've been angry with you for so long," I said.

She stayed quiet, holding her face in her hands.

"I want to let it go. I've tried to forget it, but I can't." I took another long breath, holding the air in my lungs

for a four count before I let it escape. "It's because of…
James," I whispered.

Her face contorted into something awful—
something that looked like it crawled from the deep pit
of grief inside me. Months ago, when she'd told me the
story, her face had been impassive, and I'd misread it as
apathy. But sitting in the blue plastic chair, devoid of
makeup, her shocked expression told the real story. Her
grief was as acute as mine. Tears streamed down her face,
and she didn't wipe them away.

"I'm so sorry, Anne," she blubbered. Her shoulders
trembled, and she wrapped her hands around her upper
arms and squeezed as if to hold herself together.

"I'm so angry. Because you told me. And because you
didn't save him." I blinked away hot tears. "I didn't think
I could forgive you for that. For letting go of him." I lost
control and couldn't speak for a moment. "When my
family died, I felt so guilty. For so many years. I thought it
was my fault. And then I found out what you'd done, and
I had someone else to blame. It made me feel better for a
little while. But then you told me about James."

She nodded.

"When you let go, you left him alone—" my voice
cracked. "All alone in the dark. And James—" a sob
threatened to choke me, but I swallowed it and
continued, "James was afraid of the dark. He would have
been so scared. How could you let go?"

She slid from her chair and kneeled before me,
laying her head in my lap. "I'm sorry," she repeated over
and over. "I'm sorry. I'm sorry."

After several long breaths, I reached out to stroke her
hair. "It's okay, Sandy."

It wasn't okay. But it was better. Voicing it allowed me to let go—a tiny bit.

I took a deep breath and dragged her chair closer. She sat. I held her hands in mine while she recovered. She coughed several times, and I retrieved a cup of water from a cooler in the corner and watched her gulp. She glanced at me, her eyes red and swollen, but she didn't speak.

"We need to find you another attorney," I said.

"Why?"

"Because Sidero is a monster. She's abusing Milena."

"Jesus," she breathed.

"I'll work on finding someone else. Also, there's an update," I told her. "I found a witness—a man who saw someone arguing with Engel the night he died. They were fighting. Ari—Detective Fournier, I mean, is going to talk to him. It's good news."

She stood and paced the small room twice before she spoke. "Even when you feel that way about me, you still helped?"

I nodded and managed a small smile. "Yeah."

"You're a really good person. I don't deserve you."

"You've said that before."

"It's true," she said.

"Being angry at you doesn't mean I hate you." She swiveled to look at me, and I smiled again. "Okay, yeah. There were moments I hated you. But I'm still here. I'm still going to help you." I took another deep breath. "I think there's another problem. Someone broke into my hotel room."

"What?" Her voice was too loud, and the guard glared at her.

"It's fine," I said. "I wasn't there. I was doing laundry. I had my backpack with the... you know."

"I thought you put that in the bank," she whispered loudly.

"Most of it."

"Don't worry about finding another attorney. I'll figure it out. Take the money. Go home. The boat has fuel. I always fill it up as soon as I enter a harbor."

"I can't leave you here alone."

"Isn't it what I deserve?"

I hesitated, but I'd come this far with the truth. "Sometimes I feel that way. But I need you. You understand what I've lost. I didn't know that before, but now I see that's why we were so close. Because you *understood*. Nobody else gets it."

She took my hands in hers. "How could anyone as smart as you be so stupid?" She shook my hands. "Luke understands, too."

I pulled away from her. "Back to the break-in. I was wondering if it had something to do with the—" I glanced at the guard and mouthed, "blackmail."

"You think they were after the…money?" she asked.

I nodded. "What else? There was a story online about your arrest, and they included a picture of you. Maybe someone recognized you."

She chewed on her thumbnail. "I don't see how. I was too careful. But I guess it's possible. It's hard to avoid every camera. Even more of a reason for you to leave."

"Would it matter? If they broke into my room, they already know I'm involved. They could follow me anywhere."

"But at home, you have Luke."

"Not anymore," I reminded her.

"Don't be so stubborn. Don't throw away what you have with him. It's the real deal."

"Too late."

She laughed. The sound reverberated off the yellow walls. "It's never going to be too late for Luke. That man is smitten. He'd do anything for you."

"He built me a gazebo."

She laughed again. "Exactly. Who does that?"

"I'm not leaving," I said. "Not until I know you're going to be okay."

"You can't save me this time, Anne."

"What do you mean?" I asked.

"They found my hair on Engel's body. Milena came here yesterday to ask me the same question over and over. Had I seen Engel that day? I swear, I didn't. I remember exactly what I did. Claire—she works in the marina, she helped me set the mooring when I arrived. I saw Goti. I went to the office to pay slip fees and had dinner at the bar."

"Bertie's?" I asked.

She nodded. "After that, I stayed on the boat. I never saw Engel. She kept pushing—like she wanted me to make something up. Maybe I bumped into him at the bar or in the office. But none of that is true, and I don't want to lie. I don't know why, but someone set me up, and they did a really good job. I'm stuck here. You need to let it go, Anne."

"No," I said. I sprung up and paced the room. "If I figure out who killed Engel, the police will have to let you go."

She caught my arm as I passed her chair. "It's too dangerous," she said.

I backed against the far wall. "It doesn't have to be dangerous. Engel had enemies. He was a drug dealer, right? Odds are, someone wanted him dead."

"Where are you going with this?"

"Where did Engel hang out?"

She bit her lip and narrowed her eyes. "There's a bar called *La Lumiere*. He was there most of the time—unless he was hosting a party. What are you thinking? You're going to barge in and start asking questions?"

"It's a bar. I'll go for a drink."

"Not looking like that, you're not," she said.

I looked down at my cutoff shorts. Frayed strands hung from the worn edges. "I need to shop anyway. I'll get new clothes," I said. "Better clothes."

"Do you remember everything I taught you?"

"What do you mean?"

"Never drink anything someone else buys you," she said. "Ask for bottled water. Any good bartender will give you one if you ask. Act bored. If anyone approaches you, just tell them you're supposed to meet your boyfriend. Act haughty. A bad attitude will keep most of them away, and it will explain why you keep checking your phone. If someone hassles you, go sit at the bar. Get the bartender's attention, order another drink, tip generously, and ask them to call you a taxi. Don't wait outside. Never stand around outside alone."

"Jesus, Sandy—"

"No, Anne," she cut me off. "Don't take this lightly. If you're going to do this, you need to be careful. You need to be someone other than you. You're too nice. Too trusting. You need to be paranoid. Or don't do it."

I returned to my chair. "Okay. I'll be you. Tell me what to do."

"Someone else needs to know about this. Someone who you can check in with." She stared at the yellow wall for a minute. "Goti might be too protective. You met Bertie?" I nodded, and she snapped her fingers. "Go talk to Bertie. Tell her what you're doing. Make a plan to check in with her daily." She shook her head. "I still don't like this. Have you talked to Luke?"

"No."

"Promise me you'll go see Bertie before you do anything."

"I promise," I said.

CHAPTER 18

"I was going to call you," Claire exclaimed when I entered the marina office. "I found a rental for you." She grabbed a key from a small cabinet behind her desk and motioned for me to follow her. "It's not much, but it's clean and well-maintained."

Claire walked fast. I barely glanced at Sandy's boat as we marched past.

The boat was called *Solitude*—the same word in both French and English. She was a small trawler with outdoor carpet on the aft deck, a wood-paneled galley, and a tiny cabin with a fan-shaped bunk.

"It's small," Claire said.

"It's perfect," I answered.

She showed me how to use the appliances—a mini microwave tucked beneath the dinette seat, an under-counter fridge, and a two-burner stove.

We had to take turns peering into the head because the hallway was so narrow. "I'd use the showers in the marina if I were you," she said. "There's an access card on the keychain."

After the tour, she stepped back onto the dock and stood with hands on hips. "Well?"

"I'll take it."

"Great. Come back to the office, and we'll handle the paperwork. It's available for five nights."

After I signed her forms and gave her a credit card, I retrieved my shopping bag of clothes from the car.

"Hello," a voice called from across the parking lot. I whirled to find Jimmy waving as he approached.

I smiled. "Do you work in the marina? You're always here."

He shrugged. "No better place." He took one of my shopping bags. "Where you headed?"

"I rented a boat for a few nights."

"Good choice," he said as I stopped at the *Solitude*.

"Thanks," I said. "See you around."

I stowed my things in the bunk and scooted into the dinette with my notebook.

Engel, I'd written in the center of the page. Then I'd drawn arrows from his name to *drugs* and *network*. Someone took over his network. That person had motive to kill him. I wrote: *Find the replacement, find the killer.*

How did I find the head of a drug network?

#

The bar was empty except for a new bartender and the two regulars. The one at the end of the bar gave me a subtle nod, and I smiled back. I was a regular now.

The bartender looked up as I approached. He was much younger than Bertie. He had a neat beard and thick glasses.

"Hi," I said. "I know it's Bertie's day off, but I need to ask her something. Any chance you can give me her number?"

"No," he answered.

"She's okay," the guy at the end of the bar slurred. "They're friends."

The bartender scowled at him, but he picked up his phone.

"I'll text her and ask. What's your name?"

"Anne," I told him.

He typed for a moment and then stared at his phone until we all heard a *ping* in response. "What's your number?"

I rattled off the digits. My phone buzzed in my pocket. *Come see me,* Bertie texted. And she sent an address.

"Thanks," I told the bartender. I gave the old guy at the end of the bar a wide grin and left.

#

Bertie's house was third in a line of canary-yellow bungalows. I parked on the street and knocked on her pink door.

"Come in," Bertie shouted. "In the back."

I let myself in and navigated a tiny, cluttered living room to find an equally messy kitchen. At the back, through an open sliding patio door, I found Bertie in the garden.

She looked different—younger, livelier. The dim lighting in the bar had given her a sallow glow, accentuating every wrinkle, but her skin was a healthy pink in the sunlight.

"Hi, Anne. Gregori *can* make a gin-and-soda. You didn't have to come all the way here."

"I didn't come for a cocktail."

"Shame. I already mixed them."

"Well," I smiled. "If you already mixed them."

"Sit."

She disappeared inside. I heard clinking, and she returned with a plastic pitcher and two tall glasses with lime wedges on the rims. She poured the drinks and settled into a patio chair.

"Margaritas," she said. "Tequila is better for day drinking. Why are you here?"

"I need help, but it's sensitive. And possibly very dangerous."

"Sounds fun."

"Feel free to tell me no, but I'm wondering if you know anything about how—" I paused, unsure how to ask the question.

"How?" she prodded.

"Not sure how to ask. You know how sometimes the question is difficult when you don't already know the answer?"

"Spit it out, girl."

"How do I find the head of a drug network?"

She choked on her drink and coughed into her hand. "I wasn't expecting that."

"I know. I'm sorry to just show up here and ask questions like this. I swear, if you don't want to be any part of this, I'll finish my drink and go."

She chuckled. "So, if I want to kick you out, I have to wait for you to finish your drink?" She cocked her head. "This has something to do with Sandy?"

"Yes. Sandy is being framed for Engel's murder. I'm sure of it. I just found out what role Engel played here, so it makes sense that if he was killed for a specific reason—and that reason doesn't involve Sandy, I can prove she's innocent."

"That's quite a reach. Ball-sy. Digging up a bunch of dirt on dealers in order to free Sandy. You didn't oversell the dangerous part. You don't think this all sounds like a bad idea?"

"Yeah, it does. But it's my only idea so far."

She chuckled again, and I watched her think for a moment.

"I don't know everything," she began slowly. "I'll tell you what I do know because I think you need to hear it. These aren't nice people. This isn't something you should get involved with."

"I understand," I said. "I already got that lecture from Sandy. She doesn't think I should do it either. But she told me if I did, I had to tell you what I was doing."

"I came here three years ago," she began her story. "Used my retirement to buy the bar. Found out later it had a certain reputation, and I spent the first few months letting everyone know there was a new sheriff in town. That's how I met Engel. Caught him dealing out of the men's room and threw him out. He still hung around the marina and occasionally ventured into the bar, but he behaved himself.

"Recently, he'd become more…flashy. Rumor was he bought a fancy villa. He threw wild parties. I knew he'd gotten into something bigger, but as long as it stayed out of my bar, I didn't care. And I didn't give it much thought. I like my life. It's quiet. I deserve quiet."

She sipped her drink before she continued.

"Engel was never in charge. Couldn't have been. He didn't have enough sense to pound sand down a rathole."

She ignored my raised eyebrows. "I don't know who was." She paused for another drink. "I liked Sandy. I've seen women like her—bright and shiny to hide how broken they are on the inside. She had something unique about her. It looked a lot like hope."

I looked at my hands in my lap. Bertie was like an x-ray machine. She'd nailed Sandy.

"And me?" I asked quietly.

She smiled. "You're something different. Broken on the outside. You seem fragile. Like a strong wind could blow away that lanky little body of yours. But that's not true, is it? Everyone that's ever met you underestimates you."

"Not everyone."

I grinned at her. She rolled her eyes. "Doesn't matter if you're scrappy. Here's the hard truth, girlie: I don't know who took over for Engel. Maybe you're on the right track to figuring it out. It's a strong motive for murder. But you can't go poking around. You'll get yourself killed. Best thing is to let the cops figure it out."

"But they aren't even looking for anyone else. They have evidence that Sandy did it. End of story."

She sighed. "I understand you want to help your friend."

"I'm all she's got."

"C'mon inside. I need to eat. I think better on a full stomach."

We moved into the kitchen while she prepared lunch: jerk chicken, collard greens, and coleslaw. While we were eating, my phone buzzed with a text from Ari.

Need to see you. He texted a location, and I agreed to meet him in thirty minutes.

On my way out the door, Bertie cautioned me once more. "Don't go poking your nose into it."

"Okay," I answered, but she didn't look convinced.

#

Ari was waiting by the door to the restaurant, arms folded. Clear intentions. No more kissing. Fine with me.

"Where are you staying?" he asked. We stood in the entryway, waiting to be seated.

"On a boat. A rental. Can I move onto Sandy's boat after that?" He scowled and shook his head. "I don't understand," I continued. "You know Engel wasn't killed on her boat. In fact, he wasn't killed anywhere near her boat. Why do you consider the boat a crime scene?"

"How do you know where Engel was killed?" He sounded more angry than surprised. When I didn't answer, he scowled again. "Stop investigating."

A hostess interrupted his lecture and seated us at the back of the restaurant, away from the other tables. She probably heard the anger in his voice.

I waited until she left us alone. "I'm here to help Sandy. And I've done more to help her than you have."

"It's not my job to help her."

"But it *is* your job to catch the person who did this, and we both know it wasn't Sandy."

He sighed. "Has anyone ever told you how stubborn you are?" Before I could retort, he held his hands in the air. "Hold on, I have news. But before I tell you, you have to promise that you will take the warning seriously. Someone was sending you a message when they broke into your hotel room." He leaned forward across the table. "I believe you. I agree that Sandy's innocent. But I can't let her go until I have more proof. And she's safer in jail. Promise me you'll trust me to solve this."

He glared at me. I wanted to believe him. But he was on the wrong side. "Okay, I'll take it seriously," I said. "What changed? Why do you believe me now?"

"I always believed you, but now…"

"What?" I asked.

He sat back in his chair as a waitress approached. He ordered a curry dish, and I asked for a glass of water.

"What?" I demanded after the waitress left.

"Remy Castillon was killed."

The restaurant began to spin, and I leaned against the table. "What?" I asked. "How?"

"I think the better question is why. He died a few hours after speaking to you. That's not a coincidence. Remy was a good guy. Successful. Well-liked. Someone didn't want him talking to me. His death looked like an accident, and I wouldn't have questioned it, but the timing was too…convenient. So, I dug a little deeper. He was murdered."

The waitress arrived with water, and I gulped half the glass. Bertie's margaritas had dulled everything. I needed to flush the tequila from my system and clear my head.

"I need to hear it again. Your entire conversation with Remy. Every detail," Ari said.

"There won't be anything new." I thought about the way Remy had described the other man: short, wide, with a beard. "He said he was surprised when the other man hit Engel. Because Engel was dangerous. He thought the other guy was either more dangerous or really stupid."

"Did he say where he hit him?"

I shook my head, "No. He hurried away."

"And they were on a boat?" he prompted.

"Yes, but Remy didn't know the name. He knew the make. It started with a b—Beneteau? He thought it was too short in the slip. But that's it. He didn't tell me anything else."

"He knew Engel?"

"By reputation only."

The waitress set a plate in front of Ari and asked me again if I wanted anything to eat. I declined.

"How did he die?" I asked.

He ignored my question. He took a bite and chewed slowly, studying my face. I tried to look determined, but I didn't really want to know how Remy died. It was my fault he was dead. No—not my fault. I hadn't killed him. But if I hadn't tracked him down and spoken to him, would he still be alive?

"How did he die?" I asked again.

"I can't tell you that."

He continued asking questions as he ate, trying to get me to remember new details about my conversation with Remy. I asked if he had any leads, if he knew who was responsible, and what were his next steps. He didn't answer.

When he finished eating, he dropped cash on the table, and we walked outside.

"I'll follow you back," he said. I turned to shake my head. "Just to make sure you get there safely. And then I'll walk away."

"I don't need a babysitter," I said.

I didn't want him to follow me home. I didn't want him nosing around. If someone killed Remy, it meant I was on the right track. The break-in at the motel wasn't about the money. Someone was sending me a message. I was getting closer to the truth.

Chapter 19

I returned to the boat, locked the door, and collapsed on the bed. I wanted to call Luke again, but I was afraid I'd ask him to come. I texted him instead.

Hi.

I stared at the phone until it buzzed.

Hi yourself, he wrote. And then, *Found a new property to develop today. Great view.*

He thought it was the house. That I couldn't settle into the house. He thought he could build another house—just for me. The magnitude of his love overwhelmed me.

Don't move. I texted back. *It's not the house.*

I panicked when I couldn't find the words to explain it fast enough. My phone stayed silent. I knew he was staring at my words, *It's not the house,* I hoped he wasn't jumping to the obvious conclusion that if it wasn't the house, the problem was him.

It's me. I typed. *I'm broken.*

My phone buzzed right away. *Yes. But anything that's broken can be mended.*

He thought he could fix me.

But then he texted, *…with enough duct tape.*

You want to duct tape me back together? I asked.

Sometimes. So you can't run away.

I laughed.

Let me be your duct tape, he wrote.

After months of watching me sink farther into my own selfish depression, he still wanted me.

I texted back, *OK* and set down the phone.

Was his optimism enough to compensate for my melancholy? Would he be satisfied with moments of happiness in the sea of my isolation? How much longer would he react with compassion when my mood soured unexpectedly?

We'd had good days, but something always triggered my grief. Like the day he'd taken me to see his job site. We'd stared at the concrete slab, and he'd described the future walls, the windows, and details like the flooring. He could see the full potential of the house—what it would *feel* like to live there once it was full of personal belongings. Once someone made it into a home.

After, we'd hiked to a secluded beach. He'd set down a blanket, but the privacy was irresistible, and we'd stripped and gone into the water. I swam just beyond the break and floated, arms and legs outstretched. Vulnerable. A daring and luscious feeling. The waves carried all my weight for a time.

When I swam closer to shore, Luke kneeled in the water and pulled me against him. The soft waves lifted and lowered me in a regular rhythm. He sank deeper and deeper within the soft sand until the waves crashed over my shoulders and into his face. He didn't let go until I moaned and dropped my head against his shoulder. Then he released me, and the next wave deposited me onto the sand.

I left the beach in a warm glow. Smiling. Hopeful. But it was short-lived. On the way home, we stopped at a gas station. Luke pumped gas, and I looked out my window and saw a little boy in the back of a silver SUV. He was seven, maybe eight. He looked right at me, met my gaze, and smiled. My warm glow disappeared, replaced with coldness as I remembered James.

Luke sensed the change in the car. He'd given me an odd look as we walked into the house, and he hadn't argued when I retreated to the gazebo. He silently delivered a glass of wine into my hand and returned to the house. He never asked for an explanation, and I never gave one.

How many times could he endure my mood swings? I wondered if he thought of me as the house—unfinished but with potential. Perhaps he was in love with the version of me he saw in his mind—the finished, furnished version, and he only endured the real me because he hoped for something better.

Could he duct tape me together long enough for me to heal? Could I heal? It was unfair to make him wait. That was the real reason I'd run away—because I couldn't bear to drag him farther into my depression. If I wanted to be with him—and I did, I had to change. The only solution was for me to let go of the darkness. I had to truly forgive Sandy. I had to forgive myself.

And I had to tell Luke the truth.

#

Bertie's margarita wore off, leaving me with a dry mouth and a headache. I carried my floppy hat and a bottle of water up to the deck and collapsed in a chair. The sun sank behind a bank of clouds on the horizon, but blazing crimson rays shone through—as if the sun was trying to burn a hole through the clouds.

The marina calmed in the darkness. The birds nested. The soft lapping of waves against the hull replaced the noisy clanging and squelching. I stayed on the deck until the moon appeared. I wondered if Luke was on the patio, watching the moon rise.

He picked up on the first ring.

"Hi," he said. Just hi. As if none of the past few days had happened.

"I miss you," I said. "And I'm sorry."

"I miss you, too. And I understand. At least I'm trying to. I know you had to face some tough stuff, and it takes time to deal with it. Your friendship with Sandy is…complicated."

"I need to tell you the truth."

"Okay," he said.

"Sandy blackmailed those people. The ones that—"

"I figured," he interrupted. "It didn't take a genius to work that out."

"Right. Well, I promised her I wouldn't tell you. But now she might spend the rest of her life in prison for a murder she didn't commit. It just doesn't seem like her secret matters anymore."

He was quiet, and I heard creaking. He was on the patio.

"Don't rock the chair like that," I said. "You're going to break it."

He chuckled, and I heard the chair legs scratch as he stood up. "I'll go up to your gazebo. I've been in there the last few nights."

The phone was quiet, and I pictured him tiptoeing across the flagstone path he'd installed. Some of the steps were too small for his feet, so he had to walk on his strong, lithe toes. I heard the sigh of the cushions as he settled into the chair. He remained quiet, waiting.

"Those last few days Sandy was in the hospital, she unloaded a lifetime of secrets. She told me everything. About her childhood. Why she went to prison."

As I spoke, the moon hovered just above the palm trees—a giant disc of light. A warm breeze caressed my bare shoulders. I stood and leaned against the metal railing as I told him about James. "I felt like I lost him all over again, and the second time hurt so much more. Because she could have saved him."

Luke was silent. The moon stared, unblinking. Most nights, the moon had been there, watching as I sat on the edge of the patio, peering into the black waves. The moon remembered.

"Some days I wanted to jump," I continued. "I wanted the waves to carry me away to the same place James went. I'm so sad. All the time. And so angry. I don't know what to do with it all."

"Why are you there?" he asked gently. "Why did you show up to help her after that?"

"I don't know."

"You do know," he said. "You used it as an excuse to run away from us."

"Yes. I was unhappy, and I knew I was making you miserable."

"I didn't know how to help you." He sighed. "I think you need to talk to someone. A professional."

Hours ago, the suggestion would have provoked fresh anger, but I was too tired. "I did that once," I admitted.

"I know," he said. I bit my lip at the concern in his voice. "But it doesn't have to be that way again. You're a different person now. You're in control. Nobody is going to lock you away without your consent. You're stronger than you were back then."

"Am I?"

"Yes."

"Are you watching the moon?" I asked.

"Yes," he said. "I wish you were here."

"You're right—I was running away. But I made a promise to Sandy. Even if our relationship is complicated, I'm still her friend. Her only friend. She's in real trouble, and if I help her, it gives me a chance to fix everything."

"That's backwards. She should be helping you. You saved her life. You kept her secret. You don't owe her anything."

"I know. You're right. But fixing this gives Sandy and me a chance to start over. Maybe we can figure out how to be close again. Her friendship meant so much to me. It's worth fighting for."

"I want us to be worth fighting for too."

I nodded because words felt impossible. But after a few deep breaths, I managed to say, "We are. I'll come home. Soon."

"I'll be here waiting as long as it takes. I love you, Anne."

"I love you, too."

The moon danced across the water as I ended the call.

#

In the morning, I sat on the top deck of *Solitude* with my notebook.

Become Sandy, I wrote. I needed a new wardrobe. Would it be enough? Could I become Sandy just by dressing like her? Would it be enough to simply act like Sandy?

My plan was to go to a bar and hang out. So many tourists would be doing exactly the same thing. It didn't feel dangerous. But Sandy's reaction was out of character. Perhaps there was something she hadn't told me.

A few minutes after nine, I dialed Moreau's number.

"Anne," he said. "How are things in Guadeloupe?"

"Not great. They have DNA evidence against Sandy. I hired an attorney. But I have a question, and it might seem strange."

"*Oui*," he said.

"What do you know about the drug scene in Guadeloupe? Who are the players?"

The phone was silent, and I pulled it from my ear to make sure I hadn't dropped the call.

"Are you still there?" I asked.

He sighed. "What have you gotten yourself into this time?"

"Nothing. Yet. It's just that I have this theory about who really killed Engel. I wondered if you had any insight."

"Anne, get on a plane and come home." His voice was stern.

"I will. Soon."

"Come home. I will help. From here. Once I know you aren't doing something…stupid."

I smiled. "I guess I don't have a very good track record. I promise I haven't done anything yet."

"Good. Come to the station, and we'll talk about it."

"Okay," I said. "See you soon."

I hung up the phone but didn't book a plane ticket. I grabbed the keys to the Dacia and went shopping.

I entered a boutique with a window display of short dresses.

"*Bonjour,*" said the saleswoman.

"I'm looking for something to blend into the crowd—not draw attention."

She nodded and disappeared around a display. "One moment." She returned with a stack of dresses piled over one arm, and I followed her to the dressing room.

I squeezed into a simple black dress that hugged my narrow frame, but the saleswoman frowned. "*Non,*" she said. "You need ruffles. Or a belt. You're too skinny." She brought more options. The next dress was tight across my hips, but the top had a wrap-around style, and the midsection was missing. The mirror showed a version of me with a waist.

"*Oui!*" she shouted.

"It's not too much?" I asked.

The next four were terrible. She sensed my aversion to dresses and paired wide, flouncy shorts with glittery, sequined tops. She selected five pieces, including the dress with the bare midsection, and then we moved on to shoes. I found silver, cork-soled, slingback sandals with a short heel and tested them by sprinting to the front door.

She laughed. "Are you afraid that dress is going to attract the wrong kind of man?"

I smiled. "That's exactly what I'm hoping for."

We shopped for jewelry while she told me which clubs to visit, which bartenders poured generously, and which places to avoid altogether. I asked why.

"Because you're just looking for easy fun. You're new in town. You want to meet someone. Places like *La Lumière* are not right for you. That's just for locals."

I kept her talking while we picked out a multi-strand silver necklace and two pairs of hoop earrings. She wrapped everything up, and I returned to *Solitude* and lay on a towel on the deck. I couldn't nap. My head swirled with the cautionary words of Sandy, Bertie, and Moreau. I was going to a bar for a few drinks. What was the big deal?

I ate dinner on the top deck. After the sun set, I showered, took time to carefully blow dry my hair, and then I dressed in my new clothes.

Chapter 20

Strings of white bulbs hung from a wooden framework that held triangular canvas sections that provided shade in the daylight. The canopy reflected the light at night, and I squinted as I ordered a drink. When it arrived, I slipped into the dim recess and sat alone at a bistro table with a view of the bar.

I waited and watched.

In Miami, Sandy dressed me up and dragged me from the comfort of my couch to noisy bars. I didn't like the feeling of strangers careening into me on the dance floor, and the loud music gave me a headache, but I enjoyed watching Sandy. She was magnetic. All eyes followed her around the room. I'd never captured anyone's attention on my own, but I reveled in a temporary spotlight by her side.

The music in *La Lumiere* was a mixture of reggae and pop, and the beat was constant and infectious—even my rhythm-challenged hips twitched involuntarily. Trios of ladies with wide smiles danced with their arms overhead. Men navigated the tiny islands of women, occasionally nabbing a partner. The dance floor swayed in constant motion like sea grass in a tide.

I pretended to nurse my drink and studied each exchange, waiting for a lingering handshake or a subversive nod. Nothing happened.

"*Bonjour*," a man said as he slid into the seat across from me.

"Hi," I answered coolly.

"You look lonely over here," he said.

I smiled—a small, polite smile I hoped he read as *please go away*. "I'm waiting for my boyfriend."

"Do you want to dance while you wait?" he asked.

"No. Thanks," I answered.

He slid off the stool and pointed across the bar. "I'll be over there if you change your mind."

A few minutes later, a women separated from her trio and approached me.

"Hey," she said. "I remember you. We're staying at the same hotel. Do you want to join me and my friends?" She gestured to the two women on the dance floor, and I recognized the duo. The short woman's bright pink skin glowed hot under the harsh lights, and the tall one wore a scowl.

"Maybe the guys will leave you alone if you're with us?" she said.

I shrugged. "Sure. Thanks."

I carried my drink to their table, holding it low and allowing half of it to spill while I walked.

"I'm Mandy," the first woman said. "And these are my friends: Pauline and Dot." The three of them smiled at me expectantly. Pauline was the tall one.

"I'm Anne."

"I haven't seen you around the hotel," Mandy said.

"I was only there one night," I explained.

"Where are you from?"

A nervous laugh escaped my throat. "Saint Martin."

"Ohmygod," the woman called Dot slurred. One word. Ohmygod. "Amazing. So fancy. You're so lucky."

I smiled. I was supposed to be Sandy tonight, so if I seemed fancy, I was succeeding. "Yeah," I said. "So lucky. And you guys? Where are you from?"

"Milwaukee," Mandy answered. "Our friend just moved here. She invited us to visit, but she ditched us." My eyebrows raised, and she continued, "She cannot be away from her new boyfriend."

"She paid for the entire trip," Dot argued. "And you don't even really like her anyway."

"Shut up, Dot," Pauline said.

"Can I buy you guys a round? It's the least I can do," I asked. Dot shrieked and clapped, Pauline shrugged, and Mandy hugged me. I ordered rum punches from a passing waitress. "Very native," I said.

"So, what is there to do here?" Mandy asked.

"I don't know. The normal tourist stuff. Parasailing, hiking. The beach. There's a zoo."

Pauline snorted. "A zoo?"

"It was better than I thought it would be. I also hiked the volcano. But I haven't done anything else since I got here."

"Why are you here?" Mandy asked.

"I'm visiting a friend."

"Is she here?" Dot asked.

"No, I'm on my own tonight," I said.

Their drinks arrived, and they were distracted by clinking their plastic glasses and shouting, "Cheers." Then Dot pulled Pauline back to the dance floor.

"Thanks for coming over," Mandy said. "I really wanted to talk to someone normal. Dot's smashed, and Pauline, well, I've had better conversations with my pet hamster."

"You have a pet hamster?"

She smiled. "My kid's pet. But it's grown on me. You have kids?" I shook my head. "Like Dot said. Lucky." She sighed. "Kidding. I love my kid. But I'm a single mom, and your life looks amazing. You live in paradise. No kids. Beautiful clothes. Men hit on you. That's why I invited you over, actually. Cause that guy talked to you. I've been here for two hours. Nothing."

I laughed. "Sorry," I said, when she looked hurt. "I'm not laughing at you. It's just—your perspective is…refreshing. The truth is my life isn't amazing." Her face fell, disappointed that her image of me was flawed. "Never mind that," I said. "Let's get you hit on."

I thought of all the lectures I'd received from Sandy at every nightclub we visited.

"Pull your shoulders back," I said, taking on more of a dramatic southern drawl. Playing Sandy's part. "Smile. And…let your hair down." She reached up and pulled her hair out of a bun at the back of her head. It fell past her shoulders. Wavy and messy. "Better. Now, stop looking like a mom. Get out there and dance—not with your friends. Give someone room to get to you. If you see someone you like, look him directly in the eye and smile."

She bounced onto the dance floor, and I watched her follow my instructions—Sandy's advice. I stayed at their table. The three of them came and went, sipping drinks and dancing. Two men approached and began dancing with them, and Pauline quickly peeled away and returned to the table. I was happy to be stuck with Pauline. She was quiet, and I felt camouflaged while I continued scanning the room.

I bought the trio another round of rum punches. When Pauline announced that she wanted to leave, I told Mandy I'd share a taxi so she and Dot could stay. Mandy gave me a bear hug and winked.

"Be safe," I called out as I left.

When the taxi dropped me at the marina entrance, I slipped off my shoes and walked barefoot to the *Solitude*.

#

I slept late and spent a lazy day on the boat. That night, I dressed in a new outfit and went to a different bar that the saleswoman had mentioned. I didn't make new friends. I sat in the corner until I got bored and approached the bartender to order a fresh drink. I turned to find Goti behind me.

"What are you doing?" he asked.

I shrugged. "Just having a drink."

"No, you're not. You look…different. Like Sandy."

"I couldn't come here looking like I usually do," I said.

"Are you alone?" He looked around the bar. "You're going to get yourself in trouble."

"I'm just having a drink, Goti," I said, angrier than I intended.

"I don't believe you. I know why you're here, and it's a bad idea. Let's go."

His bossy tone made me angry, but my feet hurt. I wanted to return to the boat and put on my pajamas.

"Okay," I agreed. I followed him out to the parking lot. He stopped next to a scooter. "Oh," I said. "On that?"

He grinned and handed me a helmet.

I fastened the strap under my chin and climbed onto the seat behind him. I gripped his sides, squeezing tighter as the scooter took off and sped down a hill. He drove too fast, weaving around cars and speeding through congested roundabouts. I tried to lean as he did, but my instincts fought it, and he tapped my hand a few times reassuringly.

We arrived at the marina within minutes.

I tossed the helmet at him. "You're a terrible driver."

"Tell me what you were doing at that place."

"Just watching drunk tourists. I guess I'm not cut out for surveillance. It's boring. I don't know why Sandy and Bertie were worried. Nothing happened."

"Bertie," he said. "Was this her idea?"

"No. It was my idea."

"You know she's supposed to be some badass cop from the States? Rumor is she took down an entire cartel by herself."

"Really?"

"Go back to your boat. Stop playing cop."

"How did you know I was on a boat?"

He grinned again and shrugged. "I know everything."

He sped away.

#

The next night, I returned to *La Lumiere* but left early with sore feet and no leads. Instead of walking back to the *Solitude*, I went to the bar.

"Why do you look like that?" Bertie asked.

"Don't you start," I said. "What do you have to eat?"

"Special tonight is fish and chips."

"Okay. And a drink, please."

As she mixed a drink, I looked around the bar. "It's quiet in here tonight."

"Yeah, it's nice."

"Goti told me you used to be a badass cop. How come you didn't tell me that?"

She chuckled, the sound a deep grumble. "Rumors. You know how the truth changes the more it's told?"

"What is the truth?"

"I was Secret Service." Sadness swept across her face and settled on the bar between us. I remained quiet. "Yeah, I used to be Badass Bertie. I put away some bad guys. Not anymore."

"What happened?"

"I retired," she said. She wanted to end the conversation, and I knew that feeling. I didn't ask her for more.

But she offered it. "My partner got killed. My fault. I wasn't paying attention. Someone got the jump on us, and he got killed."

"Did you quit?"

"No. I stayed to avenge him. I felt like if I put enough of the bad guys away, it might balance things. Took me years to understand it would never be enough. Nothing was going to even that out. Nothing was going to make it better. I had to make my own peace. And then I quit. Came here. Bought the bar."

"Badass Bertie," I said with a smile. "Suits you."

"I earned the nickname. But I never had another partner after that. I was reckless. Took risks. Nobody wanted anything to do with me. That was fine with me—that whole lone wolf thing suited me just fine."

"You're still a lone wolf, Bertie."

"No, I'm not," she chuckled. "Those two over there. They're my pack now." I laughed. "And you. You're in my pack," she said.

She spent several minutes refilling drinks for the two regulars at the end of the bar. Then she disappeared into the kitchen and arrived with a heaping plate of fried food and a bottle of ketchup.

She climbed onto the stool next to me and selected a potato wedge. She blew on it gently before she took a bite.

"Frank. That was my partner. We'd been together for years. Working in financial crimes. We had a lead on an offshore company moving money through the fish hatcheries in the Gulf. Easy to spot. The numbers didn't make any sense, but impossible to prove. We knew they had to be laundering money, but we couldn't figure out whose money it was. That's usually the way we track down the launderers—by following the trail of cash. But in this case, even though we knew it was moving, we had no idea where from.

"We'd done everything by the book. Warrants, searches. We watched that place night and day for months. We halted shipments of packaging materials, equipment, and chemicals. We searched everything. There was no cash anywhere. Frank was the one who solved it. We were on an overnight shift, trying to gag down stale, leftover pizza. We were parked in the spot with the best vantage point—right next to a ditch downhill from the facility. Just after a storm, that ditch would stink to high hell.

"Anyway, it was two in the morning. Neither of us could sleep because of the stench, so we were chatting. About nothing, really. Then Frank says, "I can't eat catfish anymore. The prices are so goddamn high." And that got me thinking. Day after day, that place shipped out catfish. But supply was down. Prices were sky-high.

"We stopped a shipment going out. Had to destroy half a crate of perfectly good catfish before we found the cash. They sealed it inside plastic bags and stuffed it inside the fish. The shipments went to local restaurants that deposited the cash and washed it back to the hatchery as payment for the supply. Brilliant plan. Right under our noses. Once we knew what we were looking for, we figured out how the cash arrived.

"We took down the entire laundering operation— the hatchery, the restaurants, and a local bank that facilitated everything. But the source was slippery. They'd used middlemen, and the guys in the hatchery never knew who'd hired them. The funds were all routed back to offshore accounts. Untraceable. Took Frank and me another year to find them. We figured they'd approach another hatchery, so we watched and waited."

She paused to eat more fries.

"We were too impulsive. Frank called for backup, but I didn't want to wait. Not after all that time. Turned into a bloodbath. Frank and I were pinned down. One of the employees at the hatchery had been caught in the crossfire. Frank wanted to go, pull her out. Asked me to cover."

She sighed.

"He saved that woman. Backup arrived. We moved in to clear the rest of the building. Ugh," she rolled her eyes. "I'll never forget the stench. Put me off fish forever.

You buy fish at the store but never really think about where it comes from or what it takes to get it all sealed up nice and tight in that plastic wrap. Honestly, I think we're better off not knowing."

She wrinkled her nose at my plate, but she ate another fry.

"Frank and I—we'd been partners for years. And then one day, I stopped to peer into a fish tank, and he got his head shot off."

I didn't know what to say. There's no appropriate response. Sorry you got your partner killed? Better luck next time? "I'm sorry," doesn't cover it. Nothing will capture the magnitude of guilt that Bertie carried with her.

"Did Frank have a family?" I asked.

"Three kids."

"Sorry, Bertie."

"His wife visited me here a year ago. Two of his kids are in college now. The youngest is…well, she's probably in college now too." Bertie sniffed. "She hugged me. Said she missed me. Hoped I was doing okay. She sat here and told me all about the kids, how well they're doin'. She wasn't angry. She doesn't hate me."

"Maybe she doesn't think it was your fault."

"It was my fault, though. And I told her that. How can she hug me after that?"

I laughed softly. "It's complicated."

She turned to me with a curious look.

I licked my lips and took a sip before I said, "Sandy killed my entire family. It was a car accident. She didn't tell me for over a year after I met her."

Bertie whistled. We sat staring at the bar for a long minute. I took another bite of fish and asked, "Is this catfish?"

She laughed. A cathartic belly laugh. She slapped the bar several times. I blinked and took a few long breaths.

"It's complicated," she repeated, nodding. "Seems like an understatement. And I assume you don't want to tell me your story?"

I shrugged. "Eventually. There are parts I can't tell you. It's Sandy's story, really."

She nodded again. "I think another drink. I'll join you this time."

She rounded the bar, but before pouring the gin, she leaned closer and whispered, "It *is* catfish."

She returned to the stool next to me with two gin-and-sodas. I waited until she'd finished her drink before I said, "What's the trick to surveillance? How do you stay there without getting bored?"

She glanced at me with narrowed eyes. "Why are you asking?"

I shrugged.

"I told you to leave it to the cops."

"I can't trust them to do anything," I said. Her cheeks puffed—like a steam engine building momentum, but before she could lecture me again, I said, "I found a witness, but he was killed. Detective Fournier said he believes me—that Sandy isn't guilty, but he isn't doing anything."

"How do you know? Do you have him under surveillance, too?"

"No. Of course not. I just know. He won't answer my questions. He doesn't care about finding the truth."

"Or maybe he's good at his job. He's not *supposed* to answer your questions."

"It's not like I'm inexperienced," I said. "I work for the police in Saint Martin."

I was stretching the truth.

"And what is it that you do there, girlie?" She'd seen right through me.

"Forensic accounting," I admitted. "But—"

"But nothing. You sit at a desk and stare at numbers. You're not a cop. Stop acting like one."

"But Sandy's going to spend the rest of her life in jail unless I do something."

She pursed her lips.

"That's why you're dressed like that," she said. "You think you're going to spend a few nights in a club and uncover the entire criminal network on the island?" She chuckled. "There's a better way."

"What?"

"Follow the money," she said. "Isn't that what you're good at?"

Chapter 21

I slept late again. My shoulders were sore, my leg muscles tight from so much standing. I stretched and jogged through the marina, hoping to loosen up. Then I visited the boutique and bought a pair of flats and more jewelry.

In the afternoon, I sat in the galley with my notebook.

Follow the money, Bertie had said. But how? I didn't have a trail to follow.

When the sun set, I slipped into the slinky dress and took a taxi to *La Lumiere.* My transformation into Sandy was complete. Heads swiveled. Men ogled. Women glared. I ordered a gin and soda from the bar, and a man appeared at my side.

"*Vouloir dancer?*"

"No, thank you," I answered politely. "I'm waiting for friends."

I took my drink and meandered through the crowd. Faces parted to let me pass, wide, jeering smiles. Elbows and hips jostled me, spilling my drink, and I twitched as a hand cupped my rear end.

The bar was more crowded than the previous nights. There was no safe space from the sea of bodies, no dark corner to hide. And the crowd meant I couldn't watch the room. I'd never spot anything. I turned and began to move toward the door.

"Anne!" a voice shouted. "Over here!"

Mandy waved frantically and pushed her way through the crowd, towing a sleek man at least a decade younger than her.

"Anne," she breathed. "I'm so glad I spotted you."

"Hi, Mandy. Where are your friends?"

"Our friend, the one who moved here, she's throwing this huge party because it's our last night here. But Federico didn't want to go, so I came here instead."

"It's your last night, and you ditched your friends?"

She looked crestfallen. "Federico didn't want to go," she mock-pouted and turned to the man behind her. "Anne, this is Federico."

I gave him a polite nod. He whispered something in Mandy's ear and wandered away. "He's going to get a drink," she told me.

"How did you meet him?" I asked.

"I met him the other night. And then we spent a few days in my hotel room."

"He wants you all to himself?"

"He didn't want to go to that party because he says my friend's boyfriend is a—" She leaned into my ear and whispered loudly, "a drug dealer." Her breath smelled of sweet rum. I raised my eyebrows. "I know, right?" she continued. "I should have known. The flashy car, the mansion. But it's not like her to get involved with someone like that. It's probably the money. She doesn't like to work." She rolled her eyes. "I'm not sure why we are even friends."

"Still, tonight's your last night on the island?" She nodded. "It's your last chance to see her before you go home."

"Am I a bad friend for ditching her?"

I didn't answer.

"But I don't want to go alone," she whined. "Will you go with me?"

I counted to ten before I answered with a nonchalant "Okay," and a casual shrug.

"I'll tell Federico. Hopefully, he won't meet someone else."

"Maybe you will," I said.

She grinned.

#

The taxi turned down a narrow lane filled with parked cars. Unless a neighbor was also entertaining, Mandy's friend was not hosting a small gathering. The road ended in a single massive gate. There were no neighbors.

I stepped from the car and tugged at my dress. Two wide men in black suit coats guarded the entrance. I balled both my hands into fists as we approached the gate.

"I'm not invited," I whispered to Mandy.

"You're my plus-one," she said.

She gave one of the men her name and linked her arm through mine. The other man eyed my bare midriff and sneered, but the gate opened. On the other side, a golf cart shuttled us up the long driveway.

"Ostentatious, right?" Mandy whispered.

The house appeared small at first. A wide, brightly lit portico was flanked by tall foliage that hid the rest of the house. The front door was open, and we walked inside and through a round foyer with a gilded chandelier.

"That's ostentatious," I said.

From the foyer, four hallways diverged like legs on a water bug. In the center of the room, a fountain bubbled. Mandy released my arm and gave me a shove. She skipped around the left side. I walked around to the right. The room opened onto a patio, and we descended a few steps to the pool deck.

People milled around a long pool, talking and laughing in small groups.

"C'mon, let's find Pauline and Dot." Mandy pulled on my arm, and I followed her, weaving between groups of people. I noticed several stares, mostly from men who stared at my dress.

"There they are," she said, pointing to a line of dark silhouettes on a lawn.

"How can you tell?" I asked.

"Elizabeth. She got fake boobs a few years ago. See the chick that looks so top-heavy she might fall over? That's Elizabeth. And you can see Dot and Pauline, right? C'mon."

I followed her down another set of steps. The villa was situated on a plateau just above the ocean. I could hear waves crashing against rocks.

"Anne, this is Elizabeth. And her boyfriend, Armando Gonzalez." Nobody said anything. "This is Anne. We met a few nights ago, and I invited her. I hope that's okay."

One of Armando's sculpted eyebrows raised, but he said, "Yes, you are very welcome."

"You have a lovely house," I said.

Elizabeth gave me a thin smile. "It is lovely, thanks. We still don't feel very settled, do we, baby?" She reached out and stroked his jacket.

"Did you just move here?" I asked.

"Recently, yes," Armando answered. "Shall we find you some champagne?" He raised a hand in a small wave, and a waiter appeared with a tray of champagne flutes.

"Don't mind if I do," Mandy said.

"I thought you weren't coming," Pauline said. "You've been holed up with that oily Italian for days."

"He's French," Mandy pouted.

"Whatever," Pauline said.

"Please make yourselves at home," Armando said. He walked away.

Elizabeth peered after him.

"I still can't believe you live here, Beth," Dot finally spoke.

"It's Elizabeth—not Beth. And I really need to go find Armando." She hurried away.

"Why did we come here?" Pauline asked.

Dot answered, "You were the only one who wanted to. You wanted to get another look at this house. We all knew she'd ditch us. She can't let Armando out of her sight."

"I told you there's something wrong there," Pauline said.

"I enjoyed the free trip," Dot whined. "And Mandy certainly enjoyed the last couple of days. We're headed home tomorrow. Why worry?"

"Because there's something not right about him."

"You're just jealous."

"No, I'm not. I'm telling you, the way she obsesses over him, it's not normal. She can't be away from him for more than five seconds."

Mandy finally chimed in, "Pauline, Beth's a big girl. She can make her own choices."

"What if this isn't a choice?"

"What are you saying? That she's being held here against her will? You saw what just happened. He walked away. She followed. She wants to be here. Who wouldn't? This place is dreamy," Dot said.

"Don't be so naive, Dot. That guy doesn't run a hedge fund. He's not an attorney. He's a—" Pauline said.

"Okay, I think we need to mingle a little bit," Mandy said loudly. And then she whispered. "Stop it, Pauline. Enjoy the champagne for an hour. We owe Beth that much. Then we'll go."

Pauline's scowl deepened, but she nodded.

We separated. Dot and Pauline went one way. Mandy and I went another. We agreed to stay in pairs and meet in an hour in the foyer.

"How long has Elizabeth been here?" I asked.

"They just moved in like two weeks ago. She called the next day and invited us."

"How did she meet this guy?"

Mandy pulled me onto a bench. "She was on a business trip to Puerto Rico. She met him in a bar. It was love at first sight. She never came home. She traveled with him for weeks—even went to his hometown in Caracas or somewhere down south. When she invited us, we were curious, so of course we dropped everything and came."

"Pauline doesn't think much of him."

She snorted. "Look at this place. There's no such thing as a fairytale prince who looks like that and buys you a million-dollar villa. I'm not as stupid as Dot is." Her eyes widened for dramatic effect. "Beth is into something bad, and I don't think she gets it."

"Did you ask her to go home with you?"

"I did. Several times. But she's got freakin' stars in her eyes. She'll come when she's ready. Or not. I mean, maybe he really is everything she thinks he is. Maybe he's the heir to a coffee conglomerate or something. But I doubt it."

We sat quietly, watching the crowd. Armando Gonzalez had moved to Guadeloupe just before Engel's murder. And he was a drug dealer—a *suspected* drug dealer.

In Miami, I might consider it a coincidence that I'd ended up at this party, but this wasn't Miami. This was a tiny island. There were no coincidences in a place like this. The world shrank until there were only three degrees of separation between every person on the island.

We stayed on the bench, sipping champagne. Mandy seemed subdued. I was grateful for her silence. I'd accomplished my goal. I'd found Engel's replacement. But I didn't know what to do next.

Mandy finally stirred. "Do you think Federico will still be around?"

"Maybe," I answered. "Want to go find out?"

She smiled. "You're a good person, Anne. I invited you to this stupid party, and it's totally boring, and you're not even complaining."

"I guess I'm not really in the mood for a party. Let's go find Dot and Pauline and get you back to Federico. You need to say goodbye properly."

We wandered the grounds, searching for the other two women. They weren't on the pool deck, so we stepped onto the sprawling lawn. The grass was wet under my flats. We slowly moved through groups of people, listening for Dot's squeaky voice.

On the far side of the lawn, we followed a path along the cliff's edge. I heard a familiar voice speaking in rapid Spanish. I froze. She was close, with her back to me. Mandy noticed I'd stopped, and she called out, "Anne?"

Sidero whipped around. Her eyes flashed before she drew a shade across the anger and smiled. "Anne," she cooed. I suppressed a shiver.

"Sidero, how nice to see you," I said.

"Anne," Mandy called. She waved at me, and I made an apologetic shrug.

"Have a wonderful evening," I said to Sidero's group. A few of them smiled politely.

"C'mon," Mandy said. "I see them."

We hurried along the concrete path to catch up with Dot and Pauline. They argued about whether they should find Elizabeth and say goodbye. Mandy wanted to return to Federico, Pauline wanted to leave immediately. Dot was outnumbered. She looked at me as if wanting me to back her up.

"You could just call her tomorrow and apologize for leaving early," I said. "I'm sure she'll understand."

"I'm sure she won't care," said Pauline.

The cab ride was a new argument between Dot and Pauline about what Armando did for a living, but I didn't listen. I knew what he did. I knew who he was.

What I didn't know was why Sidero Romero Rojas was there.

#

The *Solitude* was stuffy. Every time I drifted to sleep, I saw Sidero's face. Had I misinterpreted surprise as anger? I didn't think so. But what made her angry?

Just after three a.m., I gave up trying to sleep and climbed to the top deck. The air was cooler. The marina was peaceful—no clanging, no squeaking, only muffled groans of dock lines straining against the tide.

A wisp of cigarette smoke curbed my loneliness for a moment. Someone was nearby—another sleepless person somewhere in the darkness. I sank into the chair, leaned against the wall of mesh netting, and peered below, searching for the smoker. I didn't expect to find anyone, but a tiny orange glow dropped in a short arc and disappeared. I thought I'd imagined it until a dark shape separated from a concrete pile and moved away.

I held my breath as he neared a lamp pole, but just before he stepped into the circle of light, his bald head gleamed. Then he swiveled and returned to his post near the *Solitude*, disappearing into the shadow.

I tiptoed down the steps, pulled the hatch closed, and checked the lock.

Sidero's security guard. Watching me. She *had* been angry that I was at the party. But why was she having me watched?

Chapter 22

The sky glowed pale yellow when I unlocked the hatch and climbed up to the top deck. The concrete pile rose from the water, sending a long shadow across the dock, but the bald man was gone. I used binoculars from the chart table and stared until my head hurt.

I dressed and jogged the length of the marina. When I reached the slip where *La Hormiga* was moored, I paused with my hands on my knees and stared through the sliding glass door. What was the connection between Sidero and Armando Gonzalez? And was the bald man there to watch me? Or protect me?

At nine-thirty, I packed and delivered my bags to the trunk of the Dacia before I walked to the marina office.

"Hi, Claire," I said.

"*Bonjour.* How was your stay?"

"Perfect. Any chance you have another one?"

"I will search, but it might be some time. I have an appointment arriving shortly."

"Can you message me when you find something?"

"*Bien sur*," she agreed.

I drove away and headed to Bertie's house.

#

"I know who took over for Engel. His name is Armando Gonzalez."

"How do you know?"

Bertie's tone surprised me. I expected excitement—perhaps a pat on the back for accomplishing my goal, but she sounded angry.

"It was an accident. I got invited to his house by someone I met in a bar. Everyone called him a drug dealer behind his back. And he lives in a mansion. The million-dollar kind. But the biggest clue was that he just arrived. Right before Engel died. It can't be a coincidence."

"What did you learn about him?"

"Not a lot. Once I figured it out, I got out of there. He met his girlfriend, Elizabeth, in Puerto Rico. She's weirdly obsessed with him. He's from Caracas."

She pursed her lips. "Venezuelan. The house doesn't prove anything. People buy houses here all the time. We need more than that."

"Venezuela? Maybe that's how Sidero knows him."

"What?"

"I ran into Senora Rojas at the party."

"If Armando Gonzalez is who you say he is, Senora Rojas is probably his attorney."

"Why?"

"She defends the worst of the worst. Murderers. Drug cartels. And sometimes, she wins because witnesses disappear. Or evidence disappears. That's why it didn't make any sense for her to take took Sandy's case. Maybe Gonzalez asked her to. To stay informed."

"And maybe she has no intention of winning the case? She wants Sandy in jail?"

"I'm not sure yet. I do know that Senora Rojas does not lose. So why would she take a case with the intention of losing? It's not as simple as wanting to ensure Sandy stays in prison. She wants something else. And I'm sure it's not good."

"What do I do now?"

"Stay away from Rojas. And this Gonzalez character. Don't do anything. I need to think."

I stood and watched her. She looked like she was about to say something, but she paced back and forth for a few minutes.

"One more thing," I said. She looked up at me. "One of Sidero's security men was watching me last night—outside the boat where I stayed."

"You can't stay there!" she shouted.

"I know. I moved out. I'll go to a hotel."

"Your detective. Have you told him any of this?"

I shook my head.

"Call him. And then go do something touristy in a public place. Be around lots of people for a while, okay? I don't want to sit around worrying about you. I need to think. I need to make some calls."

"Sorry I dragged you into this."

She ignored me and continued pacing like a caged tiger.

I walked out to my car and drove back to the marina.

Can you meet? I texted Ari.

Lunch? he answered. *An hour,* and he sent an address.

#

Ari arrived in white shorts and a burnt-orange, short-sleeved shirt that clung to his chest and biceps. As he approached, I gulped water too fast and coughed.

"Are you okay?"

I cleared my throat, took another drink, and then croaked, "I'm okay."

He hovered over me in a cloud of orange blossoms and bergamot until I waved him into the chair opposite me.

"What are you having?" he asked. I tried to ignore how the muscles in his forearms shifted as he picked up the menu. Tiny dark hairs lay neatly across the smooth skin of his arms. He glanced up to see me staring. "Anne?"

I cleared my throat again. "Yes. I mean, I don't know. What do you recommend?"

His tongue ran slowly along his bottom lip as he read silently.

Get a grip, Anne. Sandy was right. I had a type: tall and dark. Handsome. Cops. I hid behind my menu.

"I'm having the *Fricasse mouton*, but the chicken in coconut sauce is *magnifique.*"

"Chicken sounds great," I answered.

He signaled a waiter and ordered in French. Then he leaned back in his chair and asked, "What have you been up to?"

"Not much," I shrugged. "Do you have any updates? On the case?"

His hands tightened on the arms of his chair as he answered, "It's not normal procedure to update friends of my main suspect." His voice was stern, but he didn't sound angry. There was something else in his voice—an effort to maintain control—like he knew I could manipulate it.

I leaned over the table and spoke softly, "I hope I'm more than that."

Shameless. But it worked. His knuckles went white for a moment, and then his arms relaxed, and I heard him sigh. "Yes. I'm sorry. I wasn't trying to hurt your feelings. I'm trying to maintain a professional distance."

"I know you are, but you're my only hope to save Sandy."

He shook his head. "I don't have anything new to share."

"Do you know who killed Remy Castillon?"

"There are no leads." His grip tightened again. I opened my mouth, but I hesitated and bit my lip instead.

He noticed. "What is it?" he asked. "You didn't leave it alone, did you? And now you have new information." I retreated into my chair as he lunged forward. "Tell me."

"I can't."

"It's bad enough that you're investigating on your own. It's dangerous. But not sharing what you learn isn't an option. I can arrest you for withholding."

"You wouldn't, though, would you?"

His lips curled into a tiny smile, and he shook his head. "We'll never find out because you're going to tell me what you know."

If I told him, he could arrest Armando Gonzalez. Once they had another suspect, they'd have to release Sandy. But I still hesitated. Remy had died after I told two people about him: Milena and Ari. If Ari was a dirty cop, and I told him what I knew, I wouldn't just ruin my chance of saving Sandy, I'd never leave the island alive.

"Actually," I said, stalling. "I called you because I'm worried that I went too far. I didn't want to be alone today. I was going to visit someplace very public. You know, to be around a lot of people, but I'm not sure that's safe enough."

"What did you do?"

"Nothing yet. I just—"

"If you know something, you have to tell me. The last lead you found was killed."

My temper flared. "That wasn't my fault. And he was killed right after I talked to you, by the way. How do I know I can trust you? Maybe you're playing me. Maybe you're a dirty cop."

The hurt that spread across his face told me he wasn't. He flattened his palms against the table and stared at them. I took a few deep breaths to calm down.

He answered softly, still staring at the table, "I understand your instinct not to trust anyone. I've been investigating with the same mindset—not sharing anything. I don't know who's involved." He met my gaze before he continued, "I don't want to talk here. Let's eat, and then we'll go somewhere—"

"Not hiking," I interrupted.

He smiled. "Okay. Where?"

"Somewhere public. With lots of people." I snapped my fingers. "The zoo."

In the parking lot, Ari stopped next to his car. "You've been to the zoo?"

"I thought it sounded silly, too, but I really enjoyed it. Have you been?"

"Yes, several times with my nieces and nephews. And I worked a case there once. But I haven't gone in a while." While he spoke, he stared over my shoulder. I turned to look, but his arm went round my waist, and his other hand held my chin. "Don't look."

"What—"

"There are two men in a car across the street. Get in. We'll see if they follow."

He pulled his car onto the street and made several erratic turns. I gripped the door and tried to stare forward, but my neck tired from the strain. "Well?" I asked. "Are they following?"

"Yes. It's not the first time. For a few days, I felt I was being watched. I thought I was just being paranoid, but apparently not." He was quiet for a while as he focused on his mirrors. "We can't go straight to the zoo. I'll never lose them on that road. Okay if we detour a bit?"

"Sure," I answered. I stared out the window. Just beyond the road, the ever-present forest of ferns and palms was broken only by strip malls and crumbling parking lots. Occasionally, we passed ruins of a building that had lost a battle with the forest.

We approached a roundabout, and traffic moved slowly enough to watch passengers in the other cars—regular people going about their daily lives, running mundane errands. None of them were hiding from drug dealers and murderers. None of them had to decide whether to trust a handsome cop with their life.

Ari entered a three-lane, divided roadway and sped past green fields and forests of banana trees.

"Isn't this the road back to the marina?"

"Yes, but there's a turn-off that will take us north."

I pictured the map of the island. Guadeloupe was shaped like a butterfly—each of the two islands was a wing, separated by a river—the *Riviere Salee*. We'd eaten lunch across the bay from the marina, on the same part of the island as the zoo. But the zoo was directly west—not north.

"You think they were following you and not me?" I asked.

"Do you want to explain why they'd be following you?"

"Not really," I mumbled.

He exited the roadway and continued on a narrow, two-lane road. After a while, I could smell the ocean again, but the foliage obscured the view except on the steepest downhill sections. Several times, he reached up to adjust the rear-view mirror. When the beach peeked through the trees, and the road curved west, I knew we'd reached the northern end of the island.

After another twenty minutes of silence, my eyes were heavy. I yawned. "Are we almost there?" I asked. I shifted in my seat and stretched my neck. Ari adjusted the rear-view mirror again. "Are they still following you?"

"Yes."

Without warning, he wrenched the steering wheel. I slammed into his shoulder. He parked in a gravel lot and jumped from the car. I blinked and glanced around before I opened my door and stepped outside.

"Who do you think it is? Who's following you, I mean," I asked.

Cars whizzed by, and he stared for another minute before he rounded the car, took my elbow, and steered me to the edge of the gravel lot. "Let's admire the view."

We descended a steep concrete staircase onto an open grassy area bordered by banana trees. Through a gap in the trees, I saw two sailboats anchored in a small cove. A sandy path led away, and I imagined a beach below.

"I don't know who's following me," he finally answered. "Yesterday, I caught a man staring at me in the grocery store. I keep seeing the same car behind me. A gray Toyota, but the plates are always different. Am I seeing the same car or just noticing every gray Toyota that passes? Today, it's a new car. But the feeling is the same."

"You pulled off the road to let them pass?"

He nodded. "Along this stretch of road, there are a series of these turnouts for beach access. They probably took the next turnout, and they're waiting until we pass to fall back in behind us. But we're not going to pass them. There's a road into those hills." He pointed above the road.

"Are we still going to the zoo?"

He nodded. "Yes. Just taking the scenic route."

We climbed the steps to the parking lot, and he pulled back onto the road, driving in the opposite direction. After a mile, he turned right onto a narrow road. We passed an ornate iron gate with lines of palms leading up a driveway and a sign for a boutique hotel that appeared bright white against the green hillside.

The road climbed. There were no longer any driveways or power poles—just trees. I gripped the door handle. Could I trust Ari? Was his paranoia an act—an excuse to bring me into a secluded forest? I'd suggested going to the zoo because it was public, but we were on a remote road, and I hadn't seen another car in several minutes.

We passed a driveway and then another. When they appeared at regular intervals on both sides of the road, I relaxed. Ari remained quiet until he turned onto a larger road.

"We're clear," he said.

I yawned again. "I need coffee," I said. "I didn't sleep last night."

Chapter 23

Inside the zoo, Ari ordered coffee in to-go cups. We meandered the one-way path like tourists, but we didn't stop to look at the animals. He steered me to the treehouse entrance and up the stairs to the first sky-bridge. He walked to the middle and waited for me to join him. I shuffled in halting movements, one-handed along the guide wire, pausing to sip coffee.

When I reached him, he turned to face me. His eyes were hidden behind sunglasses, but his posture was rigid. "You think I could be responsible for Remy's death, but have you considered that someone else was there in the marina—that someone saw you talking to him?"

I shook my head. "Nobody else was there, and we weren't talking loudly." A tiny muscle in his cheek twitched. "If it wasn't you, it had to be Sidero. I called her assistant, Milena, before I called you."

He tapped his fingers on the wire. I felt the vibrations in my tight grip.

"I tried to drop the case against Sandy," he said. "I pushed hard, and my boss agreed. But someone high up doesn't want that to happen. I was told to let it go. Or else. And now it feels like someone is watching me." He shifted his weight, and the bridge swayed. I closed my eyes against a wave of dizzying nausea. "The only way to get her out now is for her to win the trial."

"Can we walk across?" I asked. "I'm a little dizzy."

The bridge was too narrow to walk side by side. I waited for him to reach the other side and followed him to the next wooden platform.

"I thought I was the leak at first—that I'd gotten him killed," he said. "But the timing doesn't work out. He was killed before I told anyone. Rojas makes more sense." I sipped my coffee and stared into the trees. "You have more to tell me," he said.

A group of teenagers gathered on the other side of the bridge. We listened to them chatter and giggle for a moment, and then they burst across the bridge in a trot.

The three leaders shouted, "*A gauche!*" as they stomped in unison. Their footsteps created a wave that slammed the final wooden plank against the tower with a *thwack*. There were four others—two boys and two girls at the far end of the bridge, standing in a line. They whooped as the bridge bucked beneath them.

When the bridge stopped moving, the four at the back took a turn bouncing the other three. I pressed against Ari as they ran past us and onto the next bridge.

We were quiet while the kids bounced the next bridge and the one after that. I finished my coffee, and Ari took both cups, descended the stairs, and returned empty-handed.

On the stairs, he paused two steps below the platform and removed his sunglasses. I bit my lower lip and stared back at him. "I think Armando Gonzalez killed Engel and took over the drug scene in Guadeloupe."

I was close enough to hear all the air escape from his lungs.

"You've only been here a couple of days," he said. "What proof do you have?"

"I don't have any proof. That's your job, isn't it?"

"What do you know about him?"

"You first."

"You'd make a good cop. If I didn't already know you weren't one, I'd assume you were. But I checked on you. Your Detective Inspector in Saint Martin thinks very highly of you, by the way."

I smiled. "He's being generous."

It had been difficult to trust Moreau when I'd been in trouble in Saint Martin, but my instinct about him had been correct. Now, I was betting my life on the same instinct. Was I right to trust Ari?

He nodded toward the next bridge. "Keep walking." Once again, he waited for me in the middle before he whispered, "I'm only telling you this because I think you have more to tell me. And it's important you know how dangerous Gonzalez is."

"What do you know about him?"

He sighed. "Moreau told me that trouble seems to find you." He stared at me for a moment. "I think he's wrong. It's the other way around." He sighed again and then continued, "Gonzales was arrested in Puerto Rico a year ago on murder charges, but the case fell apart. Guess who his attorney was?"

"Sidero Rojas?" He nodded, and I continued, "And the reason the case fell apart? Witnesses were killed?"

He nodded again. "Exactly. He's been on and off the island for several months. We've been watching him. How did you find him?"

"Dumb luck. I ended up at a party at his house."

His face shifted from curiosity to concern. "His house? How?"

I shrugged. "I got an invite. From friends of his girlfriend. Like I said, lucky."

"That's a hell of a coincidence."

"Not really. How many people live on this island?"

"About four hundred thousand."

"There are over six million people in the Miami area. The odds of going to the right party there aren't very good. But here?" I shrugged. "How many parties were going on that night? But yeah. It was lucky."

His eyebrows raised. "How did you—No, that doesn't matter. You were smart to call me. If Gonzalez finds out you're poking around… Does he suspect you?"

"I don't think so. I was there as a random friend-of-a-friend. I only met him briefly."

He walked away from me, and I followed him across two more bridges before he stopped and waited for me to join him on the tower.

"Sidero saw me last night," I said. "At Armando's party."

"Did she ask why you were there?"

"No. I think she was too surprised to see me. But if she's working for Armando…" I let the words hang in mid-air before I finished. "Remy was dead within hours of my phone call to Milena. And before I moved out of Sidero's villa, she increased her security. One of them was watching the boat where I spent the night."

"You can't go back there."

"I know. I packed this morning. My suitcase is in the car. I don't know where to go tonight, though." He nodded and crossed another bridge. When I met him on the other side, I said, "That's everything I know."

He didn't look at me. He leaned over the railing—processing my news or maybe thinking of a way to get me to leave the island. He wasn't wrong. I wanted to leave—to climb aboard Sandy's boat and drive away—to Saint Martin. To return to Luke. I wasn't confident in my skill at navigating the open ocean, but speeding away from the island seemed like a good idea.

"It's not enough," Ari said.

"What else do you need?"

"Proof."

"I can go back to Sidero's. That's where all the answers are. I'll explain I went to that party by accident with someone who *was* invited. It's the truth."

"You can't go back there. It's not safe."

"I didn't come here to feel safe. I came here to help Sandy." I felt my temper rise again, accompanied by another wave of dizziness, and I leaned against the trunk of a palm tree. The tree shifted under my weight, and I lost my balance. Ari grabbed me, pulling me against him. I stayed in his arms for a moment, breathing his scent, and then I pulled away and sank to the wooden platform.

He crouched beside me. "Are you feeling okay?"

"Just tired. Sidero might be suspicious, but I haven't done anything other than show up to that party. You said you needed proof."

"Maybe," he said. "But I'll arrest you if you go back there."

He helped me up, and we crossed the next bridge. Our feet slapped the wooden planks in a regular rhythm. I stopped in the middle and lifted my backpack to let the breeze cool my back. The backpack was heavy. I hadn't wanted to leave the money, my notebook, or my laptop in the trunk of my car.

At the next platform, Ari's hand gripped my forearm, and he pulled me behind a wide tree that supported the tower.

"What is it?" I whispered.

"Someone is following us."

"Of course they are. It's a one-way path. Everyone has to go the same way."

"No. Two men are following us. They don't look like tourists."

"The men from the car? How did they find us?"

I glanced back and saw a man duck out of sight.

"C'mon. Keep up," he said.

We ran. Heavy footsteps behind us slammed the wooden planks—moving fast.

"Can't we climb down?" I asked.

He stopped. "I have an idea."

"What?"

He pointed up to the tallest bridge. "Go up there. I'll lead them away."

"You want to split up?"

He nodded. "I want to see who they follow. Follow the bridges to the end and then climb down. I'll meet you on the far end." I heard footsteps again. "Go," he shoved me and sprinted away.

I hurried along the next bridge and crouched behind the palm fronds at the edge of the tower. Below me, Ari's orange shirt was easy to follow as he ran along the path. Both men followed him. He slowed, and the men gained on him. *Hurry*, I silently urged. He was fit. Why was he slowing? But then he stopped and turned to face them.

I couldn't hear their conversation, but Ari's hand gestures were aggressive. One of the men walked past him, slapping the ferns. Searching. Ari said something, and they halted their search and stood directly in front of him.

A family approached, a man and woman with two kids. They walked on the far side of the path, and as they passed Ari, the father must have sensed the tension. He sped up with a hand on the backs of both kids. They disappeared around a corner.

Something glinted in the sunlight, and one of the men—the shorter one, lunged. Ari met the man's arm in mid-air, and they struggled. I clamped my hand over my mouth to stifle a scream. They went to the ground, wrestling until the shorter man rolled away and stood. The two men ran—in the opposite direction the family had gone.

Ari lay still in the middle of the path. A dark stain grew across his white shorts and puddled on the concrete. I emerged from my hiding place but stopped at the top of the stairs when the father returned. He shouted, and the women appeared from around the corner. She held a phone to her ear while the two kids huddled around her legs.

The man kneeled and pressed his hands against Ari's abdomen. I searched for the two men. They weren't on the path. I crossed a bridge and climbed a set of steps. Then I spotted them. They were climbing the stairs— three bridges behind me. I turned and ran.

I crossed the next bridge at a sprint—not caring about hand holds. And another. On the next tower, I found another cluster of palm fronds and ducked behind them to watch. One man had reached the point where they'd seen me. The other man was back on the ground, running ahead, trying to cut me off.

I stood and sprinted again, and I heard his footsteps below me. He left the path and crashed into the ferns—on a direct path to the next tower. The man behind me stopped to wait. The man on the ground had disappeared, but I saw movement in the bushes near the stairs. If he climbed before I crossed, I'd be cut off.

I sprinted onto the bridge, gripping the guide wire, expecting the wood planks to buck beneath me when the man followed. But he didn't. He paused on the tower.

I'd misjudged the distance. The span was too long, and I wasn't moving fast enough. The other man appeared on the far side. The bridge shifted as both men stepped onto it.

I was more than halfway across, and I backed toward the middle and peered down. I was about three stories high—too high to jump. The two men approached slowly. The wire shook violently in my hands, and I struggled to maintain my hold. The man at the far side of the bridge sneered and shook it harder. I lost my grip and grasped a coconut palm trunk for support. Hanging alongside the palm tree were several thick vines. "Tarzan escape," I whispered.

I hesitated. But I remembered the sight of blood pooling around Ari. I grabbed the nearest vine and swung my legs up and over the wire. I slid. My hands and thighs burned on the rough surface. I tried to grip tighter to hold myself in place—to control my fall, but my skin felt as if it was tearing. I cried out as I lost my hold and fell.

I crashed into a cluster of cannas, landing on my back with my legs in the air. I crawled out of the canna stalks and ran—away from the bridge. Fern fronds crunched underfoot. The smaller leaves snapped, but the larger ones pushed back. I raised my hand and used my forearms to protect my face. I'd traveled only thirty yards when I hit a wall of banana trees. I dropped to my knees and crawled, weaving around the trunks. My backpack snagged on the leaves, trapping me repeatedly. My hips got stuck, and I clawed the ground and rotated until I slid free. Soil caked under my fingernails and in the cuts on my hands and knees.

I escaped the banana trees and ran again. I reached a clearing and felt the sun on my back before re-entering the tree line. Roots, hidden beneath the thick shrubs, tripped me. I crashed into a pineapple bush and stifled a scream. For the next ten yards, I slowed, choosing my footing more carefully and rubbing my right arm. It stung from the pineapple spines. A giant elephant ear plant forced me into a crouch, and I crawled again until I crested a small hill. I paused to listen for footsteps behind me, but the only sound was my own ragged breathing.

Behind me, I noticed drag marks made by my knees. I smoothed them with my hands and walked again, giving the larger trees a wide berth. I searched for a hiding place—somewhere to stop and catch my breath. I neared a wide circle of thick philodendron. The massive leaves grew in layers, folding over one another in a waist-high dome. I climbed through the fragile leaves gingerly. One snapped off, and I ducked underneath and crawled, carrying the leaf and using it to smooth my trail. Ensconced within the grove, I removed my backpack and leaned against a tree trunk.

Under the giant leaves, I was invisible, but I was also blind. I closed my eyes and listened for footsteps. At first, the only sound was my own heartbeat, but as it slowed and shrank back into my chest, the forest revealed itself layer by layer—like a Vivaldi concert. Flutes echoed against the canopy above—trills, whistles and chirps in a symphony of birdsong. Wings fluttered. A woodpecker drummed.

There were no voices. No footsteps. I waited ten minutes. My knees throbbed, but I stayed cross-legged, unmoving.

After twenty minutes, I shifted into a fetal position—moving only when the breeze rustled the leafy roof. I rested my head on my backpack. Buzzing near my ear drowned out everything else. I waited.

CHAPTER 24

I woke to darkness. The forest had quieted. I listened for footsteps or voices, but there were none. Even the breeze had stilled sometime during the night.

My watch read just after nine. The zoo was closed. And I was trapped—not inside exactly, on the outskirts, but on the wrong side. I reached into my pocket for my phone, but it wasn't there. I searched the ground around me. Nothing. In a panic, I stood and pushed my way out of the philodendron. I stomped a small fern, flatting it against the mossy ground.

I turned in place. The trees were black against the gray sky. I didn't know which direction I'd come from. Something brushed against my leg, and I reached down to find a fern that had bravely curled back up. I stomped the ground again, crushing the leaves.

"There are no snakes, Anne," I whispered. "Only in cages." I shuddered as I thought of the bright green anaconda Milena and I had seen in the reptile house. "No snakes in the forest," I reassured myself.

The moon wouldn't be up for an hour. Once it arrived, I could navigate. I knew I'd traveled north into the forest. To return, I had to keep the rising moon on my left. I sank to the soft ground and sat cross-legged.

I wondered if Ari had survived. If an ambulance had come…but I pushed away what-ifs. I needed a plan. If I made it back to the zoo, what then?

I had to get off the island. Sandy's boat had fuel—she'd told me she always filled it. Luke had taught me how to use the navigation and the radio on his boat. But I had to get to the boat first. The keys were in the bag inside my trunk. And my car was still at the restaurant—probably being watched.

I yanked a fern frond and plucked each individual leaf, one at a time. How could I get to my car? I could call a taxi. There would be a public phone at the zoo entrance.

I checked my watch again. Only six minutes had passed.

I waited for the moon by plucking fern leaves. I cursed Sandy for needing my help and then silently apologized for deciding to ditch her. Did leaving mean I was giving up on her?

I worked on a plan. The zoo probably had security cameras. If I was seen on camera and someone called the police, I'd risk getting caught and arrested. Or worse. Ari had implied I couldn't trust the police. I couldn't walk through the zoo at night. That meant waiting for daylight, or longer—opening time was probably three or four hours after sunrise. I reached for my phone and remembered it was missing.

Opening my trunk was the biggest unknown. I had to visit the restaurant when it was busiest: lunchtime. I made a simple plan: wait for the moon, find the zoo, wait until I heard voices, find a restroom to clean up, walk to the entrance and call a taxi, and retrieve the keys from my trunk.

My eyes adjusted, and the dark shapes around me became recognizable plants. I paced, peering upwards, but the horizon was hidden by the tree line. I thought of climbing higher, but my hands were cut from sliding on the vine. I wiped them gently on my shorts.

Another hour passed before the moon peeked through the trees. The philodendron glistened in the silvery light. I reconsidered my justification for keeping the moon over my left shoulder, and then I began to walk.

Running into the forest, I'd stayed mostly upright, crashing through the leaves, uncaring about what I'd find on the other side. In the moonlight, I chose a path more carefully, pushing aside the fronds and leaves. The light reflected off the leaves, blinding me to what lay below. I tripped constantly. Tree roots and smaller plants underfoot caught my sandals. The low light affected my depth perception. Several times, I reached for a tree for support to find it was farther than I'd judged. Each time I fell, I rose and dusted my hands and shorts—a useless gesture.

My progress was slow. After I'd walked thirty minutes, the foliage thinned, and I moved faster until I stepped past a banana tree about the same height as me and found a gulley.

I sat on a boulder at the edge. I hadn't crossed a gulley on my run into the forest. I was traveling in a different direction. I imagined the zoo map again. If I miscalculated, I could miss the zoo entirely, but if I traveled directly south or west, I'd reach a road. If I went north or east, I would walk into miles of forest.

The gulley traveled east-west. I wanted to continue south, so I had to cross to continue in the same direction. The drop was only about five feet. Boulders lined both sides, and small puddles reflected the moonlight in places. Most of the surface was rocky.

I dropped onto the stones below and stepped across smooth river rock that sank into the sand under my weight. I crossed to the other side and searched for a place to climb. I found an opening between two large boulders and hauled myself up by clutching handfuls of ferns. I climbed a hill on my hands and knees. At the top, I panted for a long minute before I pushed myself into a seated position and looked up. The moon was still there—hovering over my left shoulder.

I descended the slope on the other side, but after a few feet, it leveled off, and I walked through a field of tall grass. In the middle, I turned and saw my path—the trodden blades were already springing back into place.

I entered the forest again. I'd only walked a few feet when the hair on the back of my neck tingled. The canopy blocked the moon. I stood and stared. Ahead of me, glowing in the dark, were two yellow eyes. Wide-set eyes—not a raccoon. Something much bigger.

I held my breath until my eyes adjusted to the darkness and saw the chain-link.

"Hey, big guy," I whispered. "You scared me."

The cat answered with a strange noise between a snort and a cough. I let out a long breath.

"Which one are you?" I moved closer, up against the chain link, and the cat moved, stepping into the moonlight to show off his sleek, black coat. "Jaguar," I said. "You *are* the big guy. What's your name? TiMal?" I remembered the nameplate on the front of the cage that housed two jaguars—a male and a female, "Or Keezer. No, Keeza."

There were two fences about a foot apart. I gripped the chain link on my side, and TiMal paced on his side.

"I can't tell you how happy I am to see you, buddy. I made it back. There was a chance I was going to be stuck in the jungle all night. Or maybe forever."

TiMal snorted, and I giggled with a mixture of relief and fatigue. I walked along the fence, and TiMal followed. A wall blocked my path.

"You don't happen to know if there are any security cameras in there, do you?"

He snorted again.

"That's what I thought. And I can't call a taxi at…" I looked at my watch. "Almost three in the morning. So, you're stuck with me for several hours. Do you know what time the zoo opens?"

He paced a few feet away, rubbing against the chain link and snorting.

"I feel the same way. It's nice to have someone to talk to. I can't walk through the zoo like this. I need to find somewhere to clean up. You don't have a shower, do you?"

I retraced my steps, walking along the fence. The grassy field I'd crossed appeared silvery white in the moonlight. TiMal followed me, keeping pace until he met the wall of a shed at the back of his cage.

"I'll be back, buddy."

The chain link made a ninety-degree turn, and I rounded the corner to find another zoo wall. In front of it was a paved road, and on the far side, I heard the drip-drip of a faucet.

There was no hose—just a hose bib tall enough to fill a filthy bucket. I kneeled, rubbed the dirt from my hands, and then cleaned my face and arms. I removed my tank top and shorts, scrubbed the fabric, and wrung them out. I tried to wash my hair, but the faucet was too low.

When I was as clean as possible, I dressed in my wet clothes and returned to TiMal. He followed me back to the wall, and we sat in a circle of light under a lamppost.

"Do I smell better?"

He snorted. I giggled.

For the next six hours, I told TiMal how I'd arrived in Guadeloupe. If I stopped talking, he'd snort a few times, and I'd giggle and continue. Every half hour, I'd stand and pace to stretch my legs. The cat followed me the first time, but after that, he stayed still, pressed against the chain link, his fur sticking through the gaps. I talked about Luke, and I told him Sandy's story. And eventually, when I couldn't avoid it any longer, and the sky began to glow orange, I told him about James.

"In all those years, I never considered anyone getting out of the car. In my mind, they all died in the car accident—not by drowning. Because that's what I was told—that they'd died in a car accident. But James got out of the car. When Sandy told me, it opened a new door—the possibility that he'd survived. If I'm honest, I was never as angry at Sandy as I was with myself. For not being there to help him and for not trying to find him. If I'd been there, maybe I could have saved him."

TiMal snorted again. I looked up to find him staring at me.

"I know. You're right. I need to move on." I sighed. "I wish this fence wasn't in the way. I really want to hug you. But that's probably not a great idea. Especially if you're as hungry as I am."

I ran out of topics. TiMal didn't complain when I was silent.

At about eight in the morning, he stirred and walked away silently. I assumed he'd heard something or he knew his feeding schedule.

I waited for him to return while I listened to the zoo wake up. I shifted closer to the wall to stay hidden and heard the drone of a small engine pass on the other side. I wrinkled my nose as exhaust wafted through the gaps in the fence. My watch ticked off the seconds too slowly. My legs ached. In the sunlight, the skin across my knees was angry pink and already scabbed over in places.

Five minutes after nine, I stood, stretched my legs, and looked for a doorway through the wall. TiMal still hadn't returned. I hesitated when the wall curved, and I lost sight of his cage.

"Thanks, buddy," I whispered.

After ten yards, the wooden fence ended, and I rounded it, climbed through the ferns, and stepped onto the concrete path. I fought the instinct to run.

"Follow the plan, Anne," I repeated a few times under my breath. When I reached a restroom, I ducked inside. I found a hair tie in my backpack and pulled the tangled mess into a bun at the nape of my neck. I used paper towels to scrub dirt from my face. Rubbing it pinked up the skin but opened several tiny cuts. My tank top was ruined. I put it on inside out.

Arrows on the path directed me back to the entrance, and I found the gift shop. I yanked an orange T-shirt from a hangar and pulled it on. The shirt was too large and hung mid-thigh, covering the worst of my arms and my dirt-stained shorts. Across the front, a friendly raccoon sat astride the zoo logo—cartoonish letters with animals inside.

At the counter, I ripped the tag off and paid with cash. "Sorry, all I have is US dollars," I said.

The girl at the register shrugged and said, "*C'est bon.*"

"You don't have prepaid cell phones for sale here, do you?"

"*Non.*" She gave me a quizzical look.

"I lost my phone," I explained. "I need to call a taxi."

She shook her head and pointed. "Taxis. Out front."

"*Merci!*" I shouted over my shoulder as I sprinted to the parking lot. Two taxis stood waiting. I raised my hand, and the grumble of the engine was the best sound I'd ever heard.

Chapter 25

"Do you know the restaurant in Petit-Bourg named Chez-something?"

The driver turned to me with a confused look. "It's not open yet. Too early."

"I know. But it's where I parked my car."

He nodded and pulled out onto the street. The engine whined as we climbed higher and higher. I recognized the view from the drive back from the zoo with Milena. In only a few minutes, the road would drop down into *Petit-Bourg,* and the taxi would drop me at the restaurant. And then what? I couldn't risk being followed back to the marina.

I wanted to call Bertie for advice, but I didn't know her number. And I didn't have a phone.

"Do you know if there's a shop near the restaurant that sells phones? I lost my phone at the zoo." The taxi driver nodded. "Can you drop me there instead?"

His eyes caught mine in the rear-view mirror with a flash of annoyance before he nodded. In another fifteen minutes, he stopped on a street that dead-ended at the waterfront. He pointed across the street.

"Can I walk to the restaurant from here?"

He nodded and kept pointing. "Straight down there. Three blocks."

I peeled off a hundred-dollar bill and handed it to him. "*Merci.*"

The wireless store didn't have prepaid cell phones, but a young man directed me down the block to a market that had a little of everything. I bought a phone, a straw hat and a bottle of water.

My stomach growled with the smell of bacon and frying oil. Next to the market was a restaurant, and I ordered an American breakfast of scrambled eggs, hash browns, and bacon. The waitress brought coffee and a glass of juice—a mixture of so many tropical fruits it was impossible to distinguish one flavor from another, but the sugar was welcome. So was the caffeine.

I removed my laptop from my backpack and watched the screen load my wallpaper—a shirtless photo of Luke on the deck of his boat. He held a yellow mahi-mahi—not a large catch, but it had been one of my good days—one of the days when I thought I could make it work. His teeth gleamed bright white against his bronzed skin. He wore a baseball cap backward to contain his mop of curly hair. I saw my reflection in his mirrored glasses. I closed my eyes and remembered the way he smelled like coconuts.

The waitress interrupted my memory and shared the Wi-Fi code. I used my laptop to translate the instructions for the phone and powered it up before my food arrived. I googled Bertie's bar and saved the number. I dialed it, but there was no answer.

I dialed Luke's cell—the only number I knew by heart.

He answered after only one ring. "*Bonjour.*"

"It's me," I said.

"Hey, I was getting worried about you."

"I lost my phone," I said. "I'm okay. Just having breakfast."

I wanted to ask him to come get me, but I couldn't wait. I needed to get off the island immediately.

"You sound tired."

I smiled. "I haven't slept well the last few nights. Things got a little complicated, but I'm coming home."

"Today? When does your plane land?"

"Not on a plane. I'm taking Sandy's boat."

He paused and then asked, "By yourself?"

"I can do it. You taught me everything, and if I get into trouble, I can call you."

"You can't count on it—unless you bought a satellite phone. Have you checked the weather?" He paused again. "Wait for me. I'll catch the next flight out."

"I can make it."

"When are you leaving?"

I could hear the concern in his voice, and I knew if I spent another minute on the phone with him, I'd change my mind.

"I'm not sure yet. Hey, my food's here. I'll call you before I leave. I promise. You can do a pre-flight checklist over the phone. Okay?"

"Okay. Talk soon."

Breakfast was hot and greasy. When I finished eating, I packed up my laptop and walked to the end of the block. Four buildings away, I spotted a sign for *Chez Cha-Cha*. And stopped. It wasn't the restaurant I'd visited with Ari. This wasn't where I'd left my car.

Panicked, I closed my eyes and pictured the menu, trying to remember what the logo had looked like. I remembered the parking lot in front of the building and the carwash across the street. And something else—a large, faded-purple J. But I had no idea what the name of the restaurant was.

I returned to the place where I'd eaten breakfast and waved the waitress over.

"Is there a place called Chez-something? Not the one just there. Not Chez Cha-Cha. Another one?"

"Are you hungry again?" she teased. "Yes. Two blocks that way, go right. Chez Rennes."

"*Merci,*" I answered.

I walked two blocks and turned the corner. The J sign hovered overhead. It was a sign for a tire company. My relief at finding the restaurant evaporated when I realized how close I was. Anyone watching the restaurant could see me. I looked at my watch. Just after ten-thirty. Too early for the restaurant to be open. The street was deserted.

I sauntered at a snail's pace, peeking into each car from underneath the wide brim of my hat. I planned to walk past the restaurant—past my car. If someone were watching the car, they'd have to be within the block or in the parking lot. My car wasn't visible from farther down the street.

My steps were loud on the pavement, and my heart hammered in my chest. I passed one empty car and then another. They were all empty.

I reached the parking lot and scanned the four cars—including the blue Dacia. Nobody was there. I broke into a run, unlocked the car door, and dove inside. I drove away and headed to the marina.

#

In the marina lot, I parked and grabbed the boat keys and a change of clothes and headed to the bar.

"Where have you been?" Bertie shouted before the door closed behind me. The two regulars weren't on their usual stools. I wanted to hug her. "When I couldn't reach you, I called Detective Fournier to ask what happened. He's in the hospital. He was attacked!"

"I know. I was there. Is he okay?"

"I don't know. They wouldn't tell me anything. What happened?"

"Two men followed us. They stabbed him and chased me. I spent the night in the zoo and escaped this morning."

"You escaped from the zoo?"

I dropped my head into my hands. My shoulders shook until Bertie rounded the bar and held them in a bear hug.

"Are you laughing or crying?" she asked.

"Both," I mumbled between my fingers.

"You look like you fought a war and lost."

I sniffed. "I need to change."

"Agreed. That orange shirt is all wrong for you." I lifted the oversized zoo T-shirt over my head, and Bertie whistled. "Girl. You definitely lost."

"Everything hurts."

"Do you have a change of clothes?" I nodded. "Go change and then meet me in the kitchen. I'll set up a triage station."

I went to the restroom and peeled off my clothes. I dressed in denim shorts and a worn gray T-shirt. I dropped my dirty clothes in the trash can and pushed through the swinging door into the kitchen.

Bertie had a white towel laid out with first aid supplies. "You're in over your head, girlie. I've been talking to my old contacts. Armando Gonzalez is bad news. You've stirred a hornet's nest. Something is happening, and I don't want you to be anywhere near it."

"I know. I'm going to get on Sandy's boat and go home."

"Good. Did you tell the detective about Gonzalez?"

"Yes."

"I checked him out. Fournier is a straight arrow. Let him handle it from here. You should be proud of yourself. But it's time to walk away."

"I know. It feels like giving up, but I'm leaving."

She poured rubbing alcohol onto a clean white rag. "This is going to hurt. By the looks of things, you need a bath in this stuff." She wiped the rag across the back of my arm, and I winced. "I reached out to someone I used to work with—someone still in the game. I asked for a contact he trusted."

"Someone from the States?"

She laughed. "Spoken like a true ex-pat. Yes. Someone from home. He's been tracking Gonzales for years but says he's a little fish. He doesn't want you stumbling into the middle of it—not because he's worried about you. He's worried if you get any closer, the little fish will clean house and swim away. Understand?"

"He's after someone else. Someone higher up," I said.

"Exactly. I want you off this island right away."

I nodded. "Can you return my car?"

She taped a bandage across my bicep and pulled my sleeve down. "You did good, girlie. Jump up on the table so I see the rest of you."

She dampened a new rag and wiped alcohol across my knees. It stung, but briefly, and her words minimized the pain.

"I told my contact about Sandy. He said he'd do everything he can."

"Thanks, Bertie."

She patted my knee. "Come back and visit, okay? After all this is over."

"Like an actual vacation?"

I stayed in Bertie's kitchen for an hour. She finished cleaning my cuts and scrapes and packed a bag with sandwiches, chips, cookies, and bottles of water.

"Take care of yourself," she said as I opened the door to the bar and stepped outside. I turned and flashed her a wide smile.

"Thanks, Bertie."

I removed the rest of my belongings from the rental car and left the keys on the back tire. And then I walked to *The Second Chance.*

Inside the cabin, I stowed the food in the fridge. The engine rumbled to life. The hull vibrated, anxious to leave the slip after so many days in harbor. The fuel gauge showed full.

The boat was stern-tied, moored on anchor. Untying the stern ropes was easy enough, but then I had to ease the boat out and pull anchor. Sandy's boat was set up to be operated by one person. The controls for the anchor were in the cockpit with everything else. I'd practiced the maneuver a few times but was still nervous about doing it unassisted.

As I moved around the boat, it shifted and bounced between the two neighboring sailboats.

"C'mon, Anne. You can do this," I coached myself.

I stepped off the boat to untie the stern lines and saw my next problem: someone had run a shiny metal chain through the cleat. It was padlocked.

"Seriously," I said under my breath.

I stepped back onto the boat, turned off the engine and peeled four hundred dollars from the bundle in my bag and walked to the marina office.

"Hi, Claire," I greeted the perky blonde. "Sandy's boat—the one in slip three-one-six. It's been here too long, and I guess I owe you fees."

I'd seen it happen in the marina before. Boats that were late on monthly slip fees were chained to the dock until the owners paid up. Sandy had docked with the intention of staying only a night or two. She'd been here two and a half weeks.

"Let me look it up," she said. "Are you leaving the slip?"

I nodded, and she picked up her phone and typed with her thumbs. Then she moved to the computer and tapped the keyboard.

"Yes. You owe two weeks' rent. Two hundred and eighty Euro."

"Would four hundred US work instead?"

"Close enough," she smiled. "I'll send someone to the slip to unlock it."

In the doorway, I asked, "Any chance they can help me move the boat out? I'm not great at it."

She hesitated for a second, and then her face brightened again, and she answered, "Of course."

I walked back to the boat. While I waited, I opened the windows to let in the breeze and took my shopping bags down the stairs and dropped them on one of the beds.

The boat rocked. I climbed the steps and called out, "Be right there."

I'd assumed Claire had arrived to help me leave the slip. But it wasn't her.

At the top of the stairs stood the two men from the zoo.

The shorter one—the one who had stabbed Ari, reached out and caught my arm. I yowled, and he covered my mouth. He hauled me up the remaining two steps and slapped my cheek with a gloved hand. Small metal rivets sewn into the glove scratched the skin. I reached up to my face and held my cheek.

"*Callate*," he said. "We are going to walk out of here. Nice and easy. Don't run away." He lifted his shirt to show the butt of a gun tucked into his pants.

I nodded. "Where are we going?"

"No questions. Just walk."

Chapter 26

We marched through the marina. The man in gloves pushed me onto the back seat of a dark SUV and slammed the door. They climbed into the front seat. The man without gloves dialed a number on his phone.

"*Sí,*" I heard someone say.

"*Tenemos la puta.*"

My Spanish wasn't very good, but I understood enough. Someone wanted me. I hoped they wanted me alive.

Each time the car turned, I slid on the slippery leather. I held the door handle with my left hand and braced against the seat with my right. I stayed silent. My face throbbed, and my hand smeared pink bloodstains on the white leather. I reached up to touch my face gingerly and regretted it as the bearded man turned another corner, and I slammed against the door.

The door was unlocked. When we stopped behind a line of other cars waiting for their turn at a roundabout, I considered jumping out of the car. But the oncoming traffic moved too fast to risk darting in front. And if I exited the other side—the side where the gloved man was, he could follow me.

I stayed put, holding on, waiting for my chance.

"Don't think about running," the driver said. I watched his eyes in the rear-view mirror.

I pushed farther back into the seat and tried to appear small.

He turned the car onto a familiar road and careened around a turn. He parked in the circular driveway in front of Sidero's villa.

She stood at the top of the stairs in a white pantsuit, arms crossed, one hip jutted forward like a runway model. Silky fabric fluttered in the breeze. One of the spaghetti straps slipped from her shoulder, and she pushed it back into place.

"Anne," she said as I was hauled out of the car and walked across the gravel. Her voice carried anger and frustration, but there was something else—a hint of amusement. Perhaps I'd surprised her—a mousy American with a slow, southern drawl had figured out her role.

She led our parade down the steps, and then she held the door open and followed me into the white room. Men with guns stood in the doorways: one in the kitchen, one at the back patio, and the third guarded the hallway that led to Sidero's bedroom.

On the couch sat Milena. Her left eye was swollen and purple, and her lip was bleeding.

"I should congratulate you," Sidero said. "I knew there was a leak. I never suspected sweet Milena." She gestured to the man near the kitchen. "Move them downstairs. Make sure she doesn't bleed on anything. It's a rental."

The man in the kitchen doorway stepped toward me. He wore a black button-down shirt with sleeves rolled up to his elbows. Over his sweat-stained shirt, he wore a gun holster. He lifted an arm to wave me past him, but a door slammed, and we both turned toward the entryway.

Armando Gonzalez walked into the living room. I swallowed loudly.

"*Patrona*," he said.

My knees wobbled. I knew enough Spanish to know what the word meant. Patrona. Boss. Sidero wasn't working for Armando. He worked for her.

Sidero laughed when she saw the astonished look on my face. "Downstairs. We'll move them when it's dark."

The man in the black shirt grabbed my arm and pulled me into the kitchen. Milena walked ahead of me. Downstairs, he pushed us into a bedroom. "Sit," he said, motioning to the bed with a quick nod. He fastened my wrists with plastic zip ties and then did the same to Milena.

Then he left the room and shut the door.

"Are you okay?" Milena asked.

"Me? You're the one who's bleeding. Are you okay?"

She smiled, and the cut on her lip began to bleed again.

"She said they'll move us when it's dark. Where are they taking us?" I asked.

"They'll take us out into the ocean and shoot us in the head."

"How do you know that?"

"It's what they do," she said.

I stood and walked across the room. "We have to get out of here."

She held up her bound hands. "How?"

I looked around the room. Bed. Nightstand. Closet. I slid the closet door along its track, cringing when it squeaked. But the door didn't open. I pushed it a little farther. A single blanket was folded on the floor. No hangers. The nightstand was an open cube. No drawers.

"Get up," I hissed.

I reached under the mattress and lifted it, grunting with the effort. The bed frame was cheap wood—laminated particle board. Wood slats across the width were only held in place by the weight of the mattress. There were no visible screws.

I crouched on the ground, reached underneath, and ran my hand along the underside of the frame. No screws. But when I reached up into the corner, between the footboard and the support that ran to the headboard, I found one: a single bolt.

Milena watched me from the other side of the room. "Even if we get our hands free, what would we do then? He has a gun! They all have guns!"

I grunted again as I lifted the mattress and held it aloft with my back. I crouched over the corner and ran the zip tie across the metal bolt.

I slumped against the bed frame. "I was so close," I said. "I was on the boat. They must have been waiting."

"Someone called—or texted. They ran out of here and returned with you."

"Claire?"

Milena nodded. "She works for them. Everybody works for Sidero here. Whether they know it or not."

"You knew. This whole time. You knew she set up Sandy. I don't get it. Why did she take on the case if she never intended to win?"

"I didn't know. I swear, I didn't." She looked up at me with huge, wet eyes. "Sidero was shocked when Engel was killed. She didn't know who did it. She took the case to figure it out."

"Did she figure it out?"

"No. Sidero thought you might have. She was really mad that you got away."

"I was at the zoo. All night."

She smiled. "I wish we could go back there. I'd rather die there than in the water. I've never liked boats, and I don't want to be eaten by a shark."

"We're not going to die. We're going to get out of here."

"How?"

"Not sure yet. She said they weren't going to move us until dark, so we have a few hours to figure it out."

It took an hour of sawing against the bolt on the bed frame to break the zip tie. I made Milena do the same. Once our hands were free, I stepped onto the bed and grabbed the latch on the window. I froze when it squeaked. Nothing happened, and I slowly slid the window open.

"Turn off the light," I whispered. "Someone's coming. As soon as he's past the window, I'll help you out. Keep your legs soft. I'll follow you."

My eyes adjusted to the darkness while we waited. When the guard passed the window and rounded the house, I mouthed, "Okay, go." Milena dropped through the window. I pulled my knee up onto the windowsill and jumped.

The ground came faster than I expected. My ankles buckled, and I fell face-first onto the concrete. Milena limped over and helped me up. We hopped down the stairs in a three-legged race. When we reached the first terrace, I turned to look at the house above. The patio was lit, but nobody appeared. We continued down the rest of the stairs, speeding up as Milena mastered the short hops.

"We have to climb below the gazebo. We have to keep moving."

"Okay. You go first," Milena whispered.

I closed my eyes and thought about what I'd seen below the gazebo. The hill was steep. The best approach was to climb over the back side and use the wooden framework as support to descend the slope.

I jumped into the ferns that lined the gazebo but kept one hand on the framework as I slipped. I rounded the gazebo, climbed between two posts, and whispered, "Milena!"

I heard the ferns rustle as she followed me. When her hand grasped my shoulder, I helped her into the space below the gazebo. I fought the urge to stay there, hidden. Milena moved first. She let go of the wooden framework, and I heard a scuffle and a crash. I followed, sliding down the hard-packed soil. "I just put on clean shorts," I said as I landed.

The hillside leveled out for a while, and we grasped ferns as we descended. We didn't speak, but I began to understand Milena's moans. I moved with my hand around her waist and hers on my shoulder. A soft moan meant she'd put too much weight on her ankle, a high-pitched one meant acute pain—after one of those, I'd stop for a moment and let her rest.

It began to rain. Milena's arm tapped mine to ask for a rest, and she hugged the trunk of a small tree. I raised my face to the rain and closed my eyes. The huge wet drops rinsed the salt and dirt. The rain hid our trail and covered the noise we made, but it also made everything slippery. We kept going, but Milena slipped and cried out, and as I bent to find her, I slipped and slid past her into a tree. Just ahead, concrete glowed in the light from a house. I stepped out into the road and let the rain wash away the dirt.

I whispered, "We made it."

Milena limped toward me.

"They could already be looking for us. We need to get to that house and call the police."

There were no cars. The road was slick with rain, but we walked arm-in-arm, steady in the pouring rain.

I rang the doorbell. Before the door opened, a light flipped on, and I saw what a mess we were. Milena's black eye, my clothes caked with mud. A man stood in the doorway, his mouth agape.

"*Bonjour,*" Milena said in a squeaky voice. I almost laughed.

The man recovered and waved us inside. He disappeared and returned with a stack of towels. We stayed in the entryway, toweling ourselves, smiling at each other, and dripping.

When we'd dried ourselves off, he motioned us to follow him into the house. The dry breeze from the air conditioner lifted goosebumps along my arms. The three of us stood in the middle of the room while the man watched us. He smiled. And pulled out a gun.

"There's nowhere to run, my friends. Everyone here knows Senora Rojas. No one will hide you."

He pulled a phone out of his pocket and dialed a number. He kept smiling while he spoke into the phone in Spanish.

I felt Milena's hand on my arm and reached for her. I squeezed her hand.

#

We were herded back out into the storm. The rain had lightened to a drizzle. A dark van pulled into the driveway, and we were pushed into the back. And then we were moving. We hugged each other with one arm and used the other to brace ourselves as the van turned.

When the van stopped moving, the two men exited and stood outside, talking quietly in Spanish.

"They're waiting for something," Milena whispered. "No—wait. One of them doesn't want to go. He hates boats. He wants to do it here." She paused. "The other one is making fun of him. Calling him…Oh. He can't swim."

The shorter man opened the back of the van and waved his gun, motioning us to follow the taller one down a dock. Milena and I followed in a three-legged trot. Halfway down the dock, I felt the gun in the small of my back.

"Faster," the man said.

At the end was a small, inflatable dinghy. The tall man motioned us to get inside. Milena climbed onto the narrow bench seat. I joined her.

"Hey!" someone shouted from another dock. Both men turned to look. The taller man seemed to spot the source of the voice. He ran along the dock—back the way we'd come. The shorter man climbed into the dinghy. He struggled into an orange life vest but couldn't fasten it one-handed. The engine coughed to life.

"Untie us," he barked.

I stood to climb back onto the dock, but the man shouted, "No. From here."

The dinghy was tied at both stern and bow. I leaned forward and yanked the rope. The rubber side of the dinghy squeaked against the dock, and the rope loosened. I unhooked it and let it drop into the water.

The stern line was out of my reach. I shifted my weight, leaned against the dinghy's side wall, and yanked to provide slack, but the rope was too short. I struggled, grunting with the effort of holding myself up.

There was a loud splash, and a voice called, "Annie!"

I stopped working on the rope and looked up at the dock. A dark shape approached. Running.

"Hurry up," the man in the dinghy said.

Milena whispered, "Who is that?"

I kept yanking on the rope, wanting to stall, but the man waved the gun in my face. I yanked on the rope again, and it finally came free.

As the man gunned the engine, the dark shape on the dock ran into the light, and I recognized him. Jimmy. He launched himself from the dock and landed at the stern.

The two men were one large shape in the darkness, fumbling and grunting until a gunshot sounded. The shape dissolved into two distinct, smaller shapes. The shorter man resumed his seat in the corner, his wide chin unmistakable against the starlight. Jimmy was a heap on the bottom of the boat. Not moving.

The short man maneuvered the boat through the marina.

As the dinghy passed the *Solitude*, I thought of jumping into the black water, but I couldn't leave Milena. Or Jimmy.

The dinghy sped up. We bounced in the waves. Water sprayed my face. Milena clutched my hand. When I looked at her, the starlight showed the fear in her eyes. Tiny droplets ran down her face. I turned to look at the man with the gun.

He perched on the back corner, steering left-handed. The orange vest was too small for his wide shoulders. The left side flapped in the wind.

The harbor lights grew smaller. And then Jimmy stirred.

"Annie," he said.

Nobody had called me that in a long, long time. My father called me Annie. And James. He always called me Annie.

"Are you okay?" I asked, grasping his outstretched arms. I helped him sit up against the wall of the dinghy. "Why did you call me that?"

"I've always called you that." He didn't whisper this time. His voice was so familiar in the darkness.

"What? What are you talking about?"

"Annie," he repeated. "There may not be another time to tell you."

"Tell me what? What are you saying? Were you shot? Are you okay?"

"I wanted to tell you so many times," he said.

"What are you talking about?" I asked.

"I don't have time to explain it. I tried to get you to leave—to go back home."

"What?" I asked.

"Annie," Jimmy whispered. "I know you're really freaked right now. Set that aside. We have to get out of here."

"Quiet," the man said.

"You two have a lot to work out," Milena finally spoke. "Too bad you won't have time." She leaned against me. Her hand squeezed mine, and then she let go. "We have to jump," she said. "Now. Before it's too late. He's going to shoot us. If we jump, we have a chance."

She launched herself over the side.

"Milena!" I screamed. I looked at the lights in the distance. We were too far away.

The man with the gun slowed the engine. He peered behind the dinghy, unsure if he should turn back to search for her.

I launched from the bench and hit him with my shoulder as a wave hit the bow. The boat tipped, and then I was weightless until I slammed into the water.

CHAPTER 27

The man landed next to me and surfaced, sputtering and grabbing at me. The vest was splayed to each side of him, holding his arms afloat. I yanked on it, trying to pull it away from him. His hands slapped the water—he'd lost the gun.

The vest slipped from one of his arms, and he held tight and shouted as I kept yanking. He was frantic, flailing, and the vest slipped from the other side. I wrenched it away and tossed it out of his reach. His body was a weight, clutching me, pulling me underwater. I kicked and punched, trying to free myself. He flailed with spasms. His right hand caught the side of my head. I instinctively bent my legs, forcing my body back into a fetal pose. He propelled himself from me, pushing me farther underwater. I kicked away and swam to the surface.

My lungs burned as I broke the surface and gasped for air.

"Annie!" Jimmy shouted.

The dinghy's motor was far away. James sounded closer.

"James!" I shouted. "James!"

There was no answer, just splashing and coughing. I treaded water and scanned the surface.

"James," I called softly. "Where are you?"

Another splash, this one quieter, controlled. "Annie." Barely a gasp.

"Keep talking so I can find you."

"Here." The word was lost in a gurgle, and I followed the sound, pulling myself easily through the water.

I paused, not wanting to overtake him. "Say something, James."

I kicked as something grazed my leg and felt him just beneath the surface. I somersaulted and dove underwater, reaching for him, searching with my fingertips. But he wasn't there any longer. I swam in circles, searching deeper and deeper until my lungs burned.

When I surfaced, he was there, just out of my reach.

"You kicked me," he complained.

I reached for him and wrapped my arms around his shoulders. I wanted to hold him and never let go.

"He shot you?"

"In the leg."

"Is it really you?" I asked.

His hands flitted at his sides. The moon appeared from behind a cloud and lit his face. He grinned, but his face was pale.

"I'm bleeding. We can't stay in the water."

He floated, and I treaded water next to him, holding his back, keeping him above water.

"My leg… I can't swim," he said.

"I can swim for both of us," I answered.

"You have to leave me here. Go get the dinghy."

I heard the persistent whine of the engine.

"It's going in circles," I said.

"Yeah. Until it runs out of fuel."

"Okay, I think I know what direction to go."

"I'll wait here."

"No!" I shouted. "I'm not letting go of you. I'm not leaving you."

"Annie, you have to let go. We need that dinghy." His voice was quiet. Calm. My father's voice. "Annie," he said again.

"I can't, James." Sobs racked my body, violent convulsions that interrupted my scissor kicks, and I bobbed in the water.

"Annie, take a breath." His voice was farther away now. "Go. You can do it. You can find me again."

"I'll be right back," I said. "Keep floating."

He nodded. His body dipped below the surface for a moment, and when he resurfaced, I turned and swam away.

I pulled myself through the water for several minutes before I paused and listened. The whine of the dinghy sounded farther away, but as I listened, it seemed to turn, and the sound grew louder. I swam again, and the sound grew and receded.

It seemed to be traveling in a circle with a radius of maybe twenty feet, but as I swam, the path of the dinghy seemed to recede. I changed direction, watching the horizon. I didn't want it to run over me.

Then I saw it. It was moving fast, too fast for me to catch. I watched it complete half a rotation, and then I swam into the middle of what I estimated was its circle.

I'd have to grip one of the handholds at the front or along the sides—preferably one on the front. If I held a grip too far to the rear, the boat would pull me along, and my legs or feet could get caught in the propeller.

I swam into the path just as the dinghy passed me. I reached for the front, but it was moving too fast, and I cried out as the hard plastic connected with my hand in a sickening crunch.

I pulled my hand back, using only my legs to keep me upright. Pain surged in a nauseating wave, and I waited for it to recede. The dinghy circled me, speeding around me, oblivious. The pain increased into an acute throb. I suspected my fingers were broken.

James! My brain screamed. Ignore your hand. You *have* to get on that dinghy.

The boat approached again. This time, I forced myself farther out of the water and reached with my other hand, palm flattened. I caught the handhold and gripped as the boat pulled me along.

Adding my weight threw it off-balance, and I struggled to keep my head above the water. I reached my right arm—my injured hand into the dinghy and then hooked my right foot inside. I tried to wedge my foot into the edge, and then I heaved myself into a roll, pulling with my foot, pushing against the wall of the dinghy with my good hand.

And then I lay on the floor, shivering in the breeze and gasping for air.

The circles were disorienting. I sat up, grabbed the rudder, and slowed the motor to a crawl, scanning the horizon, searching for the island.

It was there—brilliant lights like huge stars on the horizon, and I aimed directly for it.

"I'm coming, James," I whispered. The waves slapped the boat. "I'm coming," I repeated.

The boat engine whined as I crawled along. I watched the horizon with my head low against the dinghy—as low as I could manage while still steering.

I tried to slow my breathing, slow my heart rate. But the pain in my hand was a distraction. When I'd gone far enough, I cut the engine and sat quietly, searching and listening. But the only sounds were the waves against the boat and my own heartbeat.

"James," I called out softly. "Make noise so I can find you."

I pictured him underwater, sinking farther and farther. I stayed quiet, listening until I was sure he wasn't close enough, and then I started the engine and aimed the boat toward the island lights.

I repeated the process, cutting the engine. Listening. Searching until the light on the horizon became a blur. I called and called. But still nothing.

The moon played a game of peek-a-boo on the horizon. When the clouds parted, the moonlight reflected off the waves in a compact silvery channel, but everything beyond was blackness.

"James," I called out. "Please answer me," I pleaded.

"Annie." Just my name. A whisper. I closed my eyes and listened for another sound—something to help me pinpoint a direction. I wondered if I'd imagined it, but the whisper repeated, "Annie." Gurgling this time. He was sinking.

"Keep talking, James," I called out to the darkness. "I don't know where you are."

The moon burst out from behind a cloud. Ten feet away, James floated within the path of light.

"I see you! Hang on. I'm coming."

I navigated the boat alongside him and cut the engine. I grabbed a handful of his shirt with my left hand.

"What took you so long?" His voice was faint. He was slipping away.

I kneeled against the side of the dinghy and hooked my arms under his and dragged him over the side. He landed on top of me, and we both cried out in pain as I struggled from underneath him.

I left him on his side and aimed the boat for the island.

"Milena!" I shouted. "Hang on, James. We have to find Milena."

I cut the engine again and listened, but James was panting. He coughed several times and moaned.

"Milena!" I shouted.

I started the engine again and moved closer to shore. If she was a strong swimmer, she could have crossed more distance.

The moon disappeared again, and I cut the engine and listened. I could only hear James. His breathing had quieted, and he'd stopped coughing.

I drove again, moving at the slowest speed the dinghy could manage. I pressed my cheek against the rubber of the dinghy and searched the horizon.

"James. How are you doing?"

He didn't answer.

"James?"

I shook his shoulder, but he didn't respond. He didn't even moan in pain.

"Milena!" I screamed. "I'm coming back! I'll bring the entire coast guard."

I cut the engine again and listened—one last chance to find her. Nothing.

"I'll come back, Milena. I promise," I whispered.

I started the engine and sped toward the island. We bounced across the waves as the harbor lights grew larger and brighter. The moon rose above the clouds, and I slowed the dinghy to navigate around moored boats at the harbor entrance.

"Where's the coast guard?" I asked.

James didn't answer. I aimed the boat at the brightest lights in the harbor. When I neared the dock, I started shouting.

"Help! Somebody help! I need an ambulance."

I misjudged the distance and slowed the dinghy too late. We crashed against the dock. Men were already there, running toward the boat, reaching to tie us off.

"He's been shot," I said. Arms lifted me from the dinghy. A blanket appeared around my shoulders.

"What's his name?" someone asked.

"James—No. Jimmy. He's my—" I hesitated. "His name is Jimmy."

A man's face appeared in front of me, startling me. "Are you hurt?"

"No. There's someone else out there," I said. "A woman."

"Where?" he asked.

"In the water," I said. He held a plastic bottle to my lips, and I drank. "Straight out of the harbor." I shook off the blanket and stood. "I'll go with you. I'll show you."

The man turned to shout in French. He took me by the elbow, and I flinched as my fingers bent.

"I think my hand is broken," I said.

"I'll call another ambulance," the man said.

"No, we need to find Milena. I'll go to the hospital later." He frowned, but before he could argue, I said, "We need to find her. She's in the water."

He nodded. Men rushed around us, boarding a large boat. Jimmy was lifted onto a gurney and hurried away.

The man guided me into a building. "Sit there," he said. "Let me see."

I lay my hand in his palm and grimaced. My two first fingers were bent at an awkward angle. Seeing them brought a fresh wave of pain.

"What's your name?" he asked.

"Anne," I answered.

The man held my hand in both of his, gingerly moving it back and forth. Then he looked me in the eye and grinned as he said, "Anne, this will hurt you more than me."

In a flash, he grabbed both fingers and yanked. A popping sound was followed by new, searing pain, and I screamed and pulled my hand back into my body, cradling it within my other arm. The pain subsided to a dull ache, and when I looked at my fingers again, they were straighter. Swollen and red, but normal.

"Just dislocated, I think," he said. He offered his open palm again. This time, with a gentle smile. "I'll wrap your hand. It will be enough until we get you to the hospital."

He wrapped it in a bandage, helped me into a sling that pinned my arm against my body, and then led me up to the bridge.

I answered questions while a man in a white hat directed the boat speed and direction according to my answers. Lights shone across the front deck. And the moon helped.

The man who had wrapped my hand directed me back down a set of stairs and into a large room. I sank into a cushioned booth. He handed me a bottle of water and a candy bar. "Stay here," he said. I couldn't open the water bottle with one hand, so I dropped it into a plastic cup holder on the table.

Why had I thought Jimmy was James? Because he'd called me Annie? I replayed his words in my head. "I wanted to tell you so many times," he'd said. Tell me what? That he was James?

He had my father's voice. And his freckles.

James had died that night. He was alive when Sandy found him. But she couldn't save him. James drowned. So why did Jimmy seem so familiar? Why had he called me Annie?

CHAPTER 28

I woke to someone shaking my shoulder and opened my eyes to find the same man who fixed my fingers.

"Your ambulance is here, Anne."

"Did you find her?"

He shook his head. "Not yet."

"How is James?" I asked.

"I don't have any news about your friend," he said.

He helped me climb into the back of an ambulance. The man in the back arranged the gurney into a seated position.

"Can you climb up there?" he asked.

"Of course," I said. "My fingers were dislocated. That's all. I probably could have taken a taxi."

He laughed. "You look terrible. Did you get in a fight with a cat?"

I smiled. "I did spend the night with a big cat. He was a great listener."

He laughed again. "You might have to explain that, or I'm going to admit you for more than your fingers."

"It's a long story. I spent the night in the zoo. The cat was a jaguar."

"How did you get here?"

"I was kidnapped and taken to sea. To get shot in the head."

He didn't laugh. "Sounds like you've had an exciting few days."

"Are you the same ambulance that picked up the man from here a few hours ago?"

"No. I just started my shift. Was he on the boat with you?"

I nodded. "He was shot in the leg."

"We can find out his status when we arrive. Are you safe now?"

I didn't answer. Two men had taken Milena and me to the marina. Only one was lost at sea—likely drowned. The other man—the taller one, would have returned to the villa. Sidero would know something went wrong. And she'd send someone for us when the shorter man didn't return.

"Let's get you to the hospital and find your friend."

"I need to find Detective Fournier. He was stabbed yesterday. He's probably in the hospital."

"You are not a safe person to be around."

"I need to get off this island."

"And we need to call the—"

"No!" I shouted. "Don't call anyone. I can't trust anyone except Detective Fournier. Can you find out if he's there? And if he's…okay?" He nodded. "Promise you won't call anyone."

"Okay," he said. "I have to bring you inside. While they get started, I'll find the detective for you. Just stay put for now."

The driver opened the back door, and they wheeled me into the bright whiteness of the Emergency Department. I hopped from the gurney and climbed onto a hospital bed. A nurse took my vitals and asked questions. I gave her brief details. A doctor arrived and asked the same questions. He unwrapped my hand, wiggled my fingers, and ordered an x-ray.

When I was alone, I climbed from the bed and paced. Could I trust the paramedic? Why had I told him about the zoo? About Ari? I poked my head through the curtain. Nurses in baby-blue scrubs stood around a desk in the middle of the large room. The doctor I'd seen emerged from another room. As he passed, I ducked behind the curtain.

I sat in a plastic chair next to the bed. The paramedic returned.

"I found him. Your detective," he whispered. He pulled the curtain closed and squatted in front of me. He leaned forward and spoke quietly. "He had surgery, but he's okay. He's upstairs. Room two-two-three."

"And my friend?"

"Jimmy, right? They removed the bullet and stitched him up. He lost a lot of blood, but he'll be fine. The police were notified already. If you're going to go, you should hurry."

"Why are you helping me?" I asked.

"You can't hide fear on a heart monitor. They ordered an x-ray for your hand, but the machine is always backed up. They won't come looking for you for at least an hour. C'mon. I'll take you upstairs."

I followed him through the Emergency Department, tiptoeing on my bare feet.

"What's your name?" I asked. My voice echoed in the stairwell.

"Teo."

"I'm Anne."

He nodded and held the door open. He led me down a corridor, past a nurse's station, and stopped at room two-two-three.

"Good luck," he said. "Jimmy is downstairs. Go down the same stairwell and turn right. Second door."

"Thanks, Teo."

He walked away, and I opened the door to Ari's room. He was awake.

"Anne!" He sat forward and grunted with the effort. "I was worried."

"I'm fine, but I don't have much time. Sidero tried to have me killed." He shifted again, and I moved close to him and rested my hand on his shoulder. "I just wanted you to know we had it wrong. Sidero is the boss. Armando Gonzalez works for her. Everybody works for her."

He stared.

"I'm going home. I'm taking Sandy's boat."

"Okay. I'll make sure Sandy is released. It might take some time, but I'll get her out of there. I promise," he said.

"Thanks, Ari," I said.

"Take care of yourself."

I hurried back down the stairs and found Jimmy's room. He sat in a chair, struggling to tie a soggy tennis shoe. The other sat on the ground beside his bare foot.

"We gotta go, Annie."

"Are they releasing you?" I asked.

"No. Doesn't matter. They can find you here, so we gotta get you out of here."

"They don't know who you are. You should stay. I'll go."

"I'm going with you." He grimaced as I shoved his foot into the shoe and tied the laces. "Grab that bag. Your friend Teo gave me that."

A small, brown paper bag sat on the bed. I picked it up and pulled Jimmy out of the chair. "Can you walk?"

"No choice. Cops are on the way. Teo said he'd give us a ride if we hurry."

He put his arm around my shoulder and limped alongside me as we walked straight through the Emergency Department and out of the ambulance bay. Nobody stopped us.

Teo stood next to the back door of his ambulance.

"We'll have to kick you out if we get a call," he said.

I nodded, pushed Jimmy onto the bench seat, and climbed up next to him. Teo slammed the doors, and then we were moving. Away from the hospital.

"Where are we going?" Teo shouted from the front seat.

"The marina," I said.

I held Jimmy in place when the ambulance turned. He was silent during the drive. I wanted to tell him my plan—the same plan that failed the first time. If Claire had unlocked *The Second Chance,* we could leave. But if it was still chained to the dock, I'd need a backup plan.

"Do you have a boat?" I asked.

"No," Jimmy answered.

"But you're always in the marina!" I shouted.

"I'm always in the marina because that's where you were."

The ambulance stopped. Teo opened the back doors and helped us out. He shook my unhurt hand tenderly. "Good luck," he said.

"Thank you." I helped Jimmy onto the sidewalk and said, "See those little palm trees. Go sit behind them. I'm going to check out the boat, see if anyone's watching it. If anyone sees me, I can run faster without you. Okay?"

He grinned. "I forgot how bossy you were."

I sprinted down the dock and slowed as I neared *The Second Chance*. The deck was clear, and the back door was wide open, but the chain was still in place. I stepped aboard and moved quickly through the cabin and downstairs. The boat was empty. The keys were still in the ignition. Everything was exactly as I'd left it. But I was stuck.

I sprinted to Goti's boat. The hatch was open, and light shone below.

"Goti," I called. I crossed the deck and peered below.

He was seated at the table, eating.

"Bonjour," he said.

"Goti, I need help. Do you have bolt cutters?" He smiled. "You want to break Sandy out of jail?"

"No, her boat is chained. I need to go."

His grin widened. "I can do better than bolt cutters," he said. "I know the combo."

Goti followed me back to *The Second Chance*. While he removed the padlock and untied the stern, I ran back up the dock and returned with Jimmy.

"Can you drive a boat?" I asked.

He laughed. "Of course. Go secure the anchor."

Goti helped me pull anchor. He shook my hand before he hopped from the boat.

"Good luck," he called.

Jimmy steered the boat out of the marina entrance and into the bay.

"Where are we headed?" he asked.

"North."

He nodded. We sat in silence for a few minutes.

"Are you really James? How are you alive?"

He grinned. "You sound mad. Like I stole a candy bar."

"Are you really James?" I repeated.

He nodded.

"How could you not tell me you're alive? Where have you been?"

"It's a long story," he said.

"Start at the beginning."

#

"Most of what I know about that night was told third hand. Tia told me what Tio Rey told her. He refused to talk about it, and she wanted me to know the truth before she died."

"Who?"

"My adopted parents. I called them Aunt and Uncle—Tia and Tio. She got sick a few years ago. Cancer. She fought it for a while, and then…she was tired. She gave up. A couple weeks before she died, she sent Rey away and told me the story."

"They never told you?"

"I always knew I was adopted. I'm white. They weren't. But I told the story enough times I *became* Tia's nephew. And they became my parents."

He shifted in his seat and winced with pain. "Do you need something?" I asked. "Painkillers?"

"No," he answered. He reached down and moved his leg with both of his hands. And then continued, "Tio

Rey was there the night Mom and Dad and Mia died. He heard the crash and saw the car go over the bridge. He saved me. Pulled me out of the water. But nobody else got out. And nobody showed up right away. He didn't know what to do with me."

"Why didn't he tell anybody?"

He smiled. His cheeks creased into dimples on either side of his face. "He couldn't. He wasn't supposed to be there."

"Why?"

"Because he was running drugs." His voice was just above a whisper.

"Surely that doesn't matter anymore. Not after all this time."

"Probably. But they weren't legal. They'd taken me—kidnapped me. They couldn't tell anyone. After the accident, they watched the news all night and all the next day. The news reported that the whole family died—including me. Everyone thought I'd drowned. They searched for my body, but nobody was hopeful. They assumed a croc got me."

"Your whole family wasn't in the car," I said.

"The news reported that we were survived by an older sister who tried to kill herself. Tia was never going to return me to a big sister who would do that."

I nodded. I deserved Tia's judgment.

"Rey had a cousin in Panama City, and we stayed there for a few weeks. Tia worried about how they'd register me in school, so Rey returned to Homestead and broke into our house. He found my birth certificate and some clothes. We kept moving west until Tia felt safe. We settled in Biloxi. I went to school. I became a normal kid. I forgot everything else. It was easier that way."

"But didn't you remember me?"

He swallowed loudly. "For the first couple weeks, I cried for you every day. I don't remember that part—Tia told me. She said after a while, I only cried out in my sleep."

My tongue caught a single tear as it slid past my mouth.

"They told me you died. I don't remember when they told me—I only remember that you died too. But I wasn't allowed to talk about it. They repeated our cover story over and over until it became my story. It wasn't until she got sick that she told me the truth. I swear I didn't—" His voice cracked. "I didn't know, Annie."

"It's okay. You were just a kid."

When he spoke again, his voice was stronger. "They were good parents. They worked hard, and they were kind. They were cautious and overprotective, but they really cared for me. It was a good life, Annie."

"How did you end up here? How did you get from Biloxi to Guadeloupe?"

"Well," he smiled again. "That's your fault."

"How? I didn't even—"

"Over the first few years, Tia kept track of you. She meant to give me back—those were her words. But she couldn't. On her deathbed, she apologized for being selfish. She made me promise to find you and tell you. She knew where you lived. She always knew."

"But if you knew where I was, why didn't you find me?"

"I did. Right after I buried Tia, I got in my truck and drove to your house. I drove straight through. Twelve hours. I got a hotel room and crashed. Got up the next morning. It was a Sunday. I drove to your house. You were outside, on the front lawn. I couldn't believe it. I couldn't believe I'd gotten you back after so long. And you looked exactly the same." Tears flowed down my cheeks, and I wiped them away. "My big sister. Alive."

"But why didn't you tell me?"

"I almost did. I was out of the truck and crossing the street. And then a yellow car pulled up in front of your house."

"Sandy," I said.

He nodded.

"You knew who she was?" I asked.

"She was in my nightmares for years. Just her face. And there she was. At your house." He paused. "And you were friends with her."

"I didn't know who she was then."

"But you know now." His face was quiet. Filled with anger. "How? How can you be friends with her?"

"It's complicated," I answered.

"It's not complicated. She killed Mom and Dad. And Mia. She almost killed me."

"She went into the water. She tried to save you."

"Is that what she told you? She didn't need to save me. I was a strong swimmer."

"I know. I taught you."

"I tried to get away from her, to swim away. She kept pushing me underwater. She was shouting and splashing, and she almost drowned both of us. I finally got away. I tried to follow the streetlights. But then Rey was there. He pulled me into his boat. And we stayed quiet while she climbed out of the water. She climbed back up to the road, and she drove away. She drove away, Annie! She didn't call anyone to help. She just left me."

For several moments, we listened to the rumble of the engine.

"I didn't know who she was back then. How could you just walk away from me without any explanation?" I asked.

"My mother—my adopted mother, had just died, and I was flooded with bad memories. Then I found out my long-lost sister was friends with a monster. It was a lot to handle."

"I get that."

"I followed you guys that day. I could tell you were close. I didn't understand it, and I needed to. It became an obsession—to figure out why you were friends with her. I stayed in town. I was supposed to start college, but I never went. I stayed in Miami."

"How did you get here? How did you get from Homestead to Guadeloupe?"

"I followed you."

CHAPTER 29

"Where are we?" I asked. "I need a shower. And food."

"There's a marina ahead."

"Let's stop," I said.

I went below and searched for my backpack. It had slid off the bed, and the contents had spilled across the floor. The prepaid phone lay in the middle of a pile of cash.

I had twenty-seven missed calls from Luke. And twenty-three messages. The last call had been seven minutes ago.

"Oh my God, Anne," he answered the phone. "Where have you been?"

"I was busy."

"When I didn't hear from you…" he sighed.

"There were complications," I said.

"Where are you?"

"Still here in Guadeloupe. In another marina. We're stopping to get food. And then we're headed out."

"Tell me where. I'll come."

"You're here?"

"I flew in last night when I didn't hear from you."

"Hang on," I said. I climbed the stairs and shouted to Jimmy, "What marina are we in?"

"No idea," he answered. "There's a sign across the street. Antilles Yachting."

"Did you hear that?" I asked.

"Yeah," Luke said. "Who is that with you?"

"It's my…It's Jimmy. I'll explain when you get here."

"I'm at the hotel by the airport. I'll catch a taxi. Jesus. It's like an hour's drive."

"We'll wait for you."

Jimmy maneuvered the boat into a slip at the marina entrance. I tied off the lines.

"Was that Luke?" he asked.

"How do you—"

"I know everything about your life, remember?" He settled on the couch. "Can you find a store? Buy some water. Food."

I nodded and went back down the stairs to get the backpack.

"I have sandwiches," I called from the galley.

"How long have they been in there?" he asked.

"Less than a day."

I helped him to the sofa and sat across from him to unwrap two of Bertie's sandwiches. I hadn't realized I was hungry. I tossed him a bottle of water.

We ate in silence. I finished the sandwich and a cookie before I said, "I'll be back. Don't leave without me."

I visited the pharmacy, bought supplies for Jimmy's wound, and filled my backpack with water bottles. I returned to the boat to drop off the supplies and then crossed the street again to shop for food. On my third trip, I went to a fishing store and found a pair of cargo shorts and a Hawaiian shirt. Jimmy scowled at my choices.

"At least they're clean. You'll live for the day."

He rolled his eyes and limped down the steps. He couldn't shower because of the dressing on his leg, so I found a washcloth and left him alone in the bathroom.

I was stowing food when he reappeared. I covered my mouth with my hand to keep from laughing.

"You picked this out on purpose," he said.

"No. I swear. It was the only one."

The shirt was turquoise with a repeating pattern of yellow pineapples and navy blue palm trees. It was too large and over-starched. The sleeves maintained stiff peaks even as Jimmy raised and lowered his arms. It looked like he was still wearing the hangar.

"It's fine," I laughed.

"It's itchy."

I laughed harder as he flapped his arms up and down again. And kept laughing. Tears formed in the corners of my eyes, and I wiped them away.

The phone rang.

"Almost there," Luke said.

"I can't wait to see you." I stepped outside and climbed onto the dock. "I'll walk out to the street."

The other side of the phone was quiet for a minute, and then he said, "Who's Jimmy?"

"It's a long story. I'll tell you when you get here."

"Where is Sandy?" he asked.

Sandy. I hadn't thought about her in hours. "She's still in jail," I said.

As I walked up the dock to the road, my heart was in my throat. A taxi stopped in front of the pharmacy across the street, and he stepped into the sunshine. He crossed the street in a sprint and opened his arms. I leaped and crashed against his wide shoulders and let him hold me off the ground. I couldn't stop the tears.

He kissed me. My neck, my tear-streaked cheeks, and my lips. By the time he pulled away, I was breathless. "I missed you."

"Explain. What's going on?" he asked.

"On the boat. We need to go."

He eased me back to the sidewalk. "No. Right now. Who is Jimmy?"

"James. He's alive."

He stared at me.

"My brother," I said. "My brother is alive."

He scratched his head, eyes wide. "How?"

I shrugged. "He survived the crash. He was rescued and adopted."

"Why didn't he ever try to find you?"

"I promise we'll get all the answers. But Sidero tried to have me killed last night, and I really want to get off this island."

"Who is Sidero?" he asked.

"I'll tell you everything while you drive."

I took his hand and pulled him down the dock. We climbed aboard *The Second Chance*, untied the lines, and Jimmy steered us back out of the marina.

Jimmy and I took turns telling the story. Luke got lost several times as the two stories merged—what had happened on Guadeloupe and what had happened to James. We repeated ourselves and interrupted each other. Luke sat next to Jimmy in the cockpit, and I kneeled on the couch behind them. Luke's head swiveled between us.

After an hour, Jimmy slowed the engine and stood up. "Can you take over?"

"You okay?" I asked.

"I'm going to go below and lay down."

Luke kept the boat steady while I helped Jimmy down the steps and onto the bed.

"He doesn't believe me," Jimmy said.

"It's a lot to handle."

He nodded, but his eyes were already closed.

"Get some sleep," I said. I climbed the stairs and settled into the seat next to Luke.

"Do you believe him?" Luke asked.

I shrugged. "He knows things. Things that only James would know."

"Don't you think it's a little too convenient?"

"He risked his life to save me. When he saw I was in trouble, he came running. He got shot. Why would he do that if he wasn't James?"

Luke didn't answer.

"When was the last time you slept?" he asked. "You look terrible."

I sat up straighter and stretched my neck. "I'll sleep when you sleep. How soon until we can anchor?"

"Couple hours. Montserrat is close. We'll anchor in Little Bay. If we leave early, we can make the long run to St. Kitts. Home the day after." He glanced at me and said, "Open my bag. I bought you a present."

I unzipped the bag. "A phone!"

"I bought it yesterday when I canceled your old one." He paused. "Who's Bertie?"

"She owns a bar in Guadeloupe. She helped me. How did you know about her?"

"I read your recent texts. I hadn't heard from you and couldn't reach you on the burner."

"Bertie's a friend."

"And the other number? Someone else was asking about you."

"Detective Fournier, probably."

"He seems to really care about you." He didn't look at me this time. "Not the way a regular cop cares about regular citizens, though?"

"Jealous?" I chuckled. "Ari was kind. We spent some time together. I think he realized that I was in over my head, and he tried to help. Nearly got himself killed."

"Remind me to thank him for keeping you safe."

I leaned against him and closed my eyes. "I don't want to talk about Guadeloupe anymore. Tell me what's happening at work."

He talked about plumbing fixtures with the wrong finish and cabinets too short for kitchen islands. He described every setback he'd experienced in the past two weeks. His problems were normal and mundane.

In another hour, Montserrat came into view.

"There's a volcano," Luke said. "Want to hike it?"

I laughed. "No thanks. I have no desire to climb another volcano. Ever."

"Can't climb this one anyway. Most of the island is off limits."

"Why do people live so close to a volcano?"

The top of the mountain was lost in the clouds. A wide gray scar sliced the island. In its path, the ruins of a town were still visible. Luke slowed and steered closer, and we passed in a reverent silence.

"Pompeii," I whispered as the blanket of ash disappeared behind a green peninsula. Luke resumed his speed, and we passed towering walls of scraggy rock rising above black sand beaches. Orange tiled roofs dotted the hillsides.

A dozen other boats were moored in Little Bay. Luke set the anchor and dropped the dinghy. I woke Jimmy and told him we were stopping for dinner.

"I'll stay on the boat," he said.

Luke steered the dinghy to the beach, and we walked to the closest restaurant and ordered lobster bisque and linguini. After we ate, we wandered the town. Luke handled the paperwork for our visit and bought ice cream. But I couldn't stop yawning, so we returned to the boat.

I found a package of pain medication in the brown bag Teo had provided. I changed the dressing on Jimmy's leg, gave him a pill, and tucked him into bed.

"Sleep well. We leave early tomorrow."

Luke checked the weather before he climbed into bed next to me. I rolled into his arms and smelled coconuts.

#

The next day, we pulled anchor before sunrise. The sea was calm, and Luke set a faster pace.

"We could make it in a day, but there's no need to beat ourselves up. We'll stop and refuel in St. Kitts and anchor as far north as we can get. Tomorrow will be an easy day."

By the time we pulled into port, I was happy to climb out of the boat and walk on solid ground. I bought Jimmy some clothes and a toothbrush, and we ate cheeseburgers from a diner near the fuel dock. Then we were back on the boat, enduring the constant rumble of the engine until Luke found a cove and anchored.

I made peanut butter sandwiches for dinner, and Jimmy ate in bed. He seemed intent on avoiding Luke. I changed his dressing and gave him another pain pill. Then, I joined Luke on the couch.

"I'm worried about Milena," I said. "I wonder if they found her."

"How can you find out?"

"I can call Ari," I said. "I should let him know I'm safe. And I should call Bertie." I picked up my phone and stepped outside.

"It's Anne," I said when Ari answered. "How are you?" His voice was garbled on the other end, and I paced the deck, searching for a better signal. "Is there any news of Milena?"

I froze as his voice came through clearly, "They found her body this morning." He continued talking, but I didn't hear the rest.

I collapsed into the chair on the back deck. Luke stepped outside and wrapped his arms around me.

"Thanks for letting me know," I said. "I'm on my way home. To Saint Martin."

"Good," he said.

I ended the call without saying goodbye.

We watched a sailboat arrive and struggle to set their anchor in the waning light, and we stayed outside as the sun slipped below the horizon. Then Luke pulled me back inside, and I collapsed against him on the couch.

"I missed you," he murmured into my neck.

He kissed me. Tenderly at first, but as his lips moved down my neck, I responded, arching my back, and his kisses became more insistent and greedy.

He pulled away and asked, "What about Jimmy?"

I heard snoring and whispered, "He's fast asleep. I gave him pain meds."

Luke's hands gripped my hips. He kissed me again, and I pulled away, breathless, and shimmied out of my shorts. I wasn't wearing anything underneath. He pulled me onto his lap. His hands stayed on my hips, directing me, pacing me. I closed my eyes and rocked against him until his hands tightened around me, and he let out a long breath.

I stayed in his lap, my head against his bare chest, until his breathing changed.

"I missed you too," I said.

"Let's go to bed," he answered.

Chapter 30

The ocean was silvery glass in the early morning. *The Second Chance* skimmed across the surface.

"I need to see Moreau when we get back," I said.

Luke nodded.

"Who's Moreau?" Jimmy asked.

"He's the Detective Inspector here. I work for him. Kinda."

"You work for the police?" he asked.

"I thought you knew everything," I teased.

"They can't know about me, Annie," Jimmy said.

"Why not?" I asked.

"Because of Tio Rey," he answered.

Luke's eyebrows raised, but he didn't say anything.

"I don't want to be in the way here. I can stay on the boat," Jimmy said. I argued, but he said he wanted his own space.

"I'll come check on you after I see Moreau," I told him.

We arrived in Philipsburg before breakfast. Luke arranged a guest slip for a week, and we gathered our bags and took a taxi home. I stood in the shower for a long time. When I finally emerged in clean clothes, Luke served banana pancakes and fried eggs.

#

At the police department, Moreau greeted me with a hug.

"You got into trouble again," he said.

I nodded. "Where do I start?"

"Special Agent Fox is on his way. Let's wait."

We walked to the conference room, and someone I didn't recognize brought two mugs of coffee.

"What happened to your hand?" Moreau asked. He settled into the chair at the head of the table, and I sat beside him.

"I dislocated my fingers, but it feels okay now." I wiggled my fingers.

Special Agent Fox arrived and shook my hand. "Good to have you back, Anne," he said. "What happened?" He opened a notebook.

"I went to Guadeloupe because Sandy called. She's—"

"I know who Sandy Brown is," Fox interrupted. "Why did she ask you to come?"

"She didn't say, but when I arrived, I met Detective Fournier. Ari. You spoke with him, I believe." Moreau nodded, and I continued, "Sandy was arrested for murder. They claimed she killed a man named Engel."

"Johan Engel." Fox nodded. "Go on."

"I hired an attorney for Sandy. And I stayed to help prove her innocence. The attorney was Sidero Romero Rojas." Moreau and Fox exchanged a look. "She tried to kill me. Well, she tried to have me killed."

Fox nodded again. I continued, telling them about visiting Gonzalez at his party and about going to the zoo with Ari. About the kidnap and the escape with Milena.

"Gonzalez works for Sidero," I said.

"Do you have any proof?" Fox asked.

I shook my head. "Not really. Not anything other than hearing her telling him what to do. He called her *Patrona*."

Moreau said, "A few months ago, you delivered a money laundering ring. Now you've uncovered the head of the drug network in the Caribbean."

I chewed my lip.

"Miss Wilson," he began. I held my breath, waiting for the chastisement I deserved. "If you're going to continue to put yourself in harm's way, it might be nice for you to have some training."

I smiled. "Like real police?"

"We needed you," Fox said. "There's a new stack of bank ledgers on your desk. If that's not too dull." He smiled.

"I prefer to be at my desk," I said. "Much safer."

"We'll make sure you're safe," Moreau said.

"Do you think Sidero will come after me?"

Fox nodded. "Yes."

"And Luke?" I asked. "And my—" I paused. Jimmy told me not to mention him. "My boyfriend," I finished. "Luke?

Moreau answered, "Yes. Of course. We'll keep you both safe."

I answered questions for another hour.

"Can you start tomorrow?" Fox asked.

I nodded. "Yes. I'll be here in the morning."

I drove to the marina. Jimmy was on the couch with his leg propped on a pillow.

"How are you feeling?" I asked.

"Did you tell them about me?"

"No," I answered. "Why?"

"Because—" he sighed. "Not everything I've done has been legal."

"Like what?" I asked.

"Look, I get it. You work for the cops. You don't want me around. I can go. I'll catch a fishing boat off the island." He tried to stand.

"No," I sighed. "Stay. You're injured. Sandy doesn't need her boat right now. Stay here until you get better."

"Then what?" he asked.

"I don't know. We'll figure it out. Just focus on getting better."

I changed the dressing on his leg and checked the cupboards. "I'll bring more supplies tomorrow. Okay?"

He was slumped against the couch, eyes closed.

"I'm going to leave you my prepaid phone, and I'll save my number and Luke's. Call me if you need anything."

He nodded.

I left, but I turned back to look at the boat as I reached the parking lot. Sidero knew I lived in Saint Martin. She knew Sandy's boat, and she must already know I'd taken it. If I couldn't tell Moreau about Jimmy, how would I keep him safe?

I climbed into my car and started the engine. I'd discuss it with Luke. We'd find him another place to live—or convince him to stay with us.

#

I waved at two uniformed officers sitting in a police car

in my driveway and entered the house. In the kitchen, I slipped off my shoes and walked out to the patio. I curled my toes around the concrete and leaned forward to peer down at the sandy beach.

I descended the warm sandstone steps to the tiny cove beneath our house. The late afternoon shadows had already crossed the beach, but the sand was still hot. I sat on the wet rocks at the water's edge and dialed Bertie's number. She answered on the first ring.

"Girlie! Where you been?"

"It took a few days to get home. Did you miss me?"

From her end of the phone, I heard running water and the clink of glasses.

"I don't miss you," she grumbled. "My life was quiet before you arrived."

"I'm gone now. You can go back to your quiet life."

She snorted. "They dragged me back. Someone named Fox is flying here tomorrow."

"Special Agent Fox?" I asked. "I just met with him."

"I don't know why he wants to talk to me. Everything I know fits on a postage stamp."

"Sorry," I said.

"Glad you're home safe. Goti's been asking about you. I'll let him know you're home. Cops have been in here several times. Looking for you."

"I called Ari from the boat. Told him where I was heading."

"Rojas got away," she said.

"Do you think she'll come after me?"

"Maybe."

I dug my toes in the wet sand. "Maybe they'll catch her before she gets the chance."

"They will. But until they do, stay safe."

"I will. Thanks, Bertie. For everything."

"Anytime, girlie."

I hung up the phone, but I stayed in the shadows, watching the waves until the sky darkened, and then I climbed the steps. Garlic wafted through the open kitchen door. A trail of candles led from the patio to my gazebo.

Luke was inside the gazebo, in my chair. Next to him was a matching chair. He handed me a glass of white wine.

"You bought another chair," I said.

He nodded.

I'd missed the view. The gazebo sat on the edge of the rocky point. The water reflected the orange sky, blurred by imperceptible waves. I turned away from the water and climbed into Luke's lap. He grunted under my weight and said, "We have two chairs now."

I laughed. He kissed me.

"Let's eat," he said. I slid to the floor and dangled my legs over the edge. "Does it feel good to be home?"

I nodded. "Sandy's still in jail, though."

"You don't have to fix everything," he said. "Sandy can take care of herself."

I nodded. "I know. I just—" I sipped wine before I continued. "I had this idea that if I got her out of jail, everything would go back to the way it was."

"You can't go backward."

"Yeah." I paused. "I know. But now James is here."

"If that is James," he said. "There's an easy way to find out."

"What? Like a DNA test? You want to test him?"

He nodded. "Don't you?" he asked.

I didn't say anything. Jimmy seemed so familiar. Because he *was* my brother? Or because I wanted James to be alive?

"For now, can we focus on keeping him safe? And letting his leg heal. Even if he's not James, I owe him that much. He saved my life."

"Why isn't he safe? Did Sidero know who Jimmy was?"

"The guy in the marina saw him."

"In the dark?"

Luke was right. Sidero didn't know who Jimmy was. She had no reason to track him down. He was safe. Probably.

"How was Moreau?"

"I start work again in the morning," I said.

"Good. You need to stay busy. And I like the idea of you stuck in a room with a bunch of cops."

My phone rang from an unknown number.

"Hello?"

"You did it!" Sandy's voice. High pitched. Excited.

"I did what?" I asked.

"I'm out! They just let me out. I can't leave the island, but I'm out!"

I pulled the phone away from my head as she shrieked again. Luke mouthed, "Who is it?" and I hit the speakerphone button.

She continued, "I can't believe you did it! I mean, I can believe it because you're amazing. Thank you! Seriously. Thank you."

"That happened faster than I thought."

"The detective told me you went home," she said. "You took the boat?"

"Yeah."

"I'm glad you left. How's Luke?"

"He's fine. He's right here. Where will you stay?"

"They have a plan. I have to stay in Guadeloupe for a while, but I'm just happy to be free."

"Me too," I said.

"I love you, Anne."

A sob choked me. Luke scooted closer and took the phone. "She loves you too, Sandy," he said. I nodded and wiped away tears. "She's too happy to talk. I'll have her call you back, okay?"

He hung up the phone and pulled me into his arms.

"I don't know why I'm crying," I said.

He stroked my back. "Because your friend is finally out of jail. Because you've been through a lot in the last few weeks. And because you're home. Safe. In my arms."

I nodded.

"Never leave me again. Okay?"

He lifted my chin. I smiled. "Or what?"

"Or I get out the duct tape."

I laughed.

We ate dinner in the gazebo. When the sky went from violet to gray, Luke returned to the house with the dishes. I stayed in my chair, staring at the waves until the horizon was lost. Then I turned my back on the darkness and tiptoed to the kitchen.

Luke was bent over the dishwasher. He rose and asked, "All done out there?"

I nodded. "Yes," I answered. "I don't want to be alone anymore."

ACKNOWLEDGEMENTS

Getting this book out into the world was more difficult than the first one. Life kept throwing curveballs; publication was an obstacle course. I want to thank everyone that nudged me, boosted me, and supported me along the way.

Thanks to you guys, the readers. Your reviews warm my heart and give me confidence to keep writing. So many of you have enjoyed this journey with Anne. I hope you keep reading.

Thanks to my beta readers. I know one of you wants me to refer to you as a beta-bitch, but I'm not sure everyone agrees. Thanks for running endless scenarios. Thanks for stopping me from killing off Luke. That would have been a mistake. But…there's still another book. And thanks to my reading group who inspire me to meet my writing goals.

Without Marie Guinto's calm, subtle direction I wouldn't have any books. She's my person. Steve Parolini is the voice inside my head. When I don't listen to that voice, he slashes my pages with his decisive red pen. He makes me a stronger writer. Every time. Cherie Fox brings my stories to life with her brilliant cover design.

A special thanks to my family. My two boys provide constant inspiration. They support my writing time and endure hours of me reading aloud to myself. Colt and

Grayson, thanks for your patience. And hugs. Mike, I couldn't do any of this without your immeasurable support. You are the Unicorn. I love you.